Different is Nice

Different is Nice

Randi Toler Sachs

iUniverse, Inc.
New York   Bloomington

This is a work of fiction. All of the characters, names, incidents,
organizations, and dialogue in this novel are either the products
of the author's imagination or are used fictitiously.

iUniverse books may be ordered through booksellers or by contacting:

iUniverse
1663 Liberty Drive
Bloomington, IN 47403
www.iuniverse.com
1-800-Authors (1-800-288-4677)

ISBN: 978-1-4401-8615-8 (sc)
ISBN: 978-1-4401-8616-5 (ebook)

Printed in the United States of America

iUniverse rev. date: 10/23/2009

Dedicated to my four wonderful men, Danny, Matthew, Evan, and Jeffrey And in loving memory of Zelda and Irving

ONE

"DIFFERENT IS NICE, BUT it sure isn't pretty. Pretty is what it's about. I never met anyone who was different, who couldn't figure that out." Roxanne was fourteen when she first heard those lyrics sung in the Broadway musical, "A Chorus Line," and she felt as if the actress on stage was singing her song. Now, at 42, she would have thought she'd have gotten over feeling that she wasn't pretty enough. But then again, the character in the show was no longer a kid either.

"I just wish I could experience what it feels like to be beautiful," she complained to her therapist, Ann.

"Why?"

"If you were me you'd know why," she said.

"Okay, but I'm not you. Do you know why you feel so strongly about that?"

"Because all my life I've felt ugly, or at my very best, average looking. Even at my wedding, no one said I was a beautiful bride. Oh, they said, 'You look great, fantastic, amazing, but not beautiful.' I can only imagine how the beautiful people feel. It's got to be a completely different self-image than I have, and it's got to be a hell of a lot better than this," explained Roxanne.

"You'd think I'd have gotten over feeling this way after all these years," she said. "I mean, I've managed to get married, have children, have a fairly successful career, and still I'm plagued inside by the same feelings I had as a child and adolescent. Why?"

"Because what happens to us when we're young, very rarely leaves us," said Ann. "But now that you've seen how you've 'overcome' what you consider your shortcoming as a youth, would you really want to go back and change your life?"

"Damn straight I would. If I had three wishes from a genie, one of them would be to experience life as a beautiful person. I'd even settle for just pretty—just looking in the mirror and never hating what I saw there—actually liking what I saw there. I wonder what life is like for those people, and I know that they have no clue as to how fortunate they are, just because of a twist of fate. Of course, I'd use the other two wishes for world peace and a cure for cancer, I'm not completely selfish."

"You seem especially worked up over this today. Did something happen to upset you?"

"No, I guess I'm just in a bad mood and feeling sorry for myself for no particular reason. That's okay to do here, isn't it?"

"Of course. Does it help to express it?"

"I don't know. It's really the same old problem. I just feel like I'm treated different than other people because I'm not pretty. I mean, I honestly believe if I looked different that cop would have let me slide yesterday when I missed that stop sign."

"I know that's how you feel, but I have to ask you, in reality, you *do* know that you are an attractive woman, don't you?"

"I know that I look good at times, and that no one would point me out as ugly, but there's a huge gap between that and feeling good about my appearance. Like I said, I just wish I could somehow experience how the other half lives."

"Well, our time is up, we'll talk more about this next week, okay Roxanne?"

"Fine, see you next week."

Roxanne left Ann's office once again wondering if she was wasting her time in therapy. In the grand scheme of things her problems seemed so insignificant. Every morning the newspaper told of people who had real tragedies in their lives. *But knowing that doesn't change how I feel. If this can help me feel better, I should allow myself to keep at it.*

As she turned the key in the ignition, Roxanne had already switched out of what she considered to be her "self-indulgent" mode and was focusing on the business of the Saturday that lie ahead. Her middle child, Justin, had an allergist's appointment, her youngest son, Gabe, had a soccer game she was expected to attend, and she needed to get to the supermarket to replenish food basics for the family. Ben was taking their eldest, Allison, to the main library branch for research on her economics paper. As lopsided as that distribution of parental tasks was, Roxanne knew that she could only blame herself if the scales were tipped too heavily on her shoulders.

Ben could take Justin to the allergist, but he won't ask the right questions, and he won't remember the answers even if I give him the questions to ask, she thought.

I really need to go to Gabe's soccer game so I can see for myself if the coach is treating all the kids fairly. Ben wouldn't know one kid from another if I paid him.

She also concluded that sending Ben to the supermarket was more stressful than it would be to go herself. She'd have to write down everything she wanted, and even if he came back with the whole list filled, there would still be items left off. No, the only way to get what she needed was to combine list shopping with seeing what was on sale and available. She let Ben go shopping when there were just one or two specific items she needed, otherwise, she owned the job.

As soon as she pulled into the driveway, Gabe came running out of the house.

"Mom, the coach called and they moved the game up an hour. We have to go now!"

Ah, the glamorous life of a soccer mom, thought Roxanne. "Well, come on then. Do you have your shin guards and your water bottle? Do you have a jacket?"

"Mom, I don't need a jacket."

"Never mind, there's one in the back, let's go."

Roxanne and Gabe arrived at the field in plenty of time and as Roxanne set up her lawn chair alongside the other parents, Gabe joined his team for some warm-up drills.

"Oh Roxanne, did you get the message I left you this morning?" called Marge Karp.

Roxanne looked up reluctantly. Whatever Marge had wanted to tell her could not be something she wanted to hear. Marge was one of the mothers Roxanne had to make nice to because the boys were in school together and on the same team. But if she had any other choice, she would have avoided all contact with the woman.

"Umm, no. I was out all morning, and Gabe hopped in the car to come here before I could even go inside the house."

"Oh. I guess that leaves us without a team snack. Carmella was scheduled for today but Sal came down with strep last night. You're next on the list."

Of course, because I don't have enough to do, Roxanne thought. "Don't worry about it Marge. There's still time. I'll just run out and get something for the kids now."

"Would you? That's great." Settling that crisis, Marge went back to yelling at her younger kids for splashing in a dirty puddle.

TWO

Roxanne never saw the bus.

A quick trip to the nearest Stop and Shop and she returned to the field with three bags of cookies (no peanuts because of Joel F.'s allergy) and fifteen juice boxes (no juice *drink*, only 100 percent juice was approved by the code of snacks). She evenly distributed the grocery bags between her two arms, secured her handbag on her shoulder, and then leaned back into the car to retrieve Gabe's unwanted jacket, which was just beyond her reach. Snatching it by the zipper pull, she jerked back her arm and lost her balance on one of the many potholes in the field parking lot. That was the last thing she recalled.

The next thing she saw was her family holding up the Sunday issue of the paper.

SCHOOL BUS SMACKS DOWN SOCCER MOM

So, I finally made the paper, Roxanne thought. *And I wasn't even trying.*

Ben, Justin, Gabe, and Allison stared at her as she lay immobilized in the hospital bed.

Can this really be happening? she wondered. *Maybe I'm dreaming*, and she closed her eyes again hoping that this would make it so.

"Roxie, Roxanne," Ben called to her. "Hey, we've been waiting for you to wake up. Don't go back to sleep now."

Roxanne forced her eyes back open.

"How do you feel?" asked Ben.

"Like I was run over by a truck," she said almost choking on the bandages that covered most of her face.

"No Mom, it was a bus, see," said Gabe. "You're famous. You made the front page."

"Great. I'm just going to sleep for a while now." Roxanne closed her eyes and tried to shut out some of the pain that was getting worse as she regained consciousness.

"So, how's she doing?" Dr. Vogel burst into the room followed by a cluster of medical students.

"Damnit," Ben whispered to Allison. "We broke that long-time rule. Never go to the hospital in September. That's when the new medical students are just starting and they don't know anything."

"Well, not too good," he said to the doctor. "She opened her eyes for a minute there, but then she went right back to sleep."

"Let's just take a look," said Dr. Vogel. He very gently lifted one edge of the bandage covering Roxanne's chin.

"YEEOWW!" Roxanne would have bolted upright if she could.

"Still has a lot of tenderness, I see. I'm sorry Mrs. Thornton, I'll have the nurse bring you some more medication for the pain. Mr. Thornton, can I talk to you a moment?"

"Sure. Kids just stay here with Mom. And don't touch her," said Ben.

Roxanne wanted to close her eyes and shut out the pain, but her children were too excited. She let them talk to her, not really listening as she tried to comprehend exactly what had happened to her.

Dr. Vogel led Ben into an empty visitors lounge where they could speak without Roxanne listening.

"The good news is that her vital signs are stable. With the exception of the fractured ankle, it seems she suffered most of the injuries to her face. She has multiple facial fractures and her skin was badly abraded."

"So you're telling me she has a broken face," said Ben. "Just give me a minute here. I'm feeling a little broken myself."

"Sure, have a seat. I know it sounds bad, but we have a wonderful team of plastic surgeons who can do phenomenal reconstruction. She'll look the same as she always did when they get through with her."

Ben's head was spinning. Reconstruction...plastic surgery...how were they going to get through all this? How long would it take? Would he actually have to take time off from work?

"I will need some recent pictures of her though, do you happen to have one?" the doctor asked.

"Yes, I do," said Ben, quite surprised at his own answer. "We just got these photos back from my daughter's Sweet 16 party and there are a few really good ones of Roxanne. I have them in my bag. I brought them to show her."

The doctor took the photos and looked at them long and hard.

"Mr. Thornton, has your wife ever expressed an interest in cosmetic surgery? Under the circumstances, all the surgical repairs would be covered by your medical insurance. So if she ever wanted to have, say, a nose job or a chin lift, now's her chance."

"Doctor, are you saying that you can not only fix her face, you can change it?" asked Ben.

"Well, yes. Not to make any less of the suffering your wife is having, but this is one accident that may very well have a happy ending."

"Doctor, let me explain something. I love my wife and I've always thought she looked great. But she has *never* been happy with her looks. Do you think the surgery could change that?"

"Oh, absolutely. When your wife is feeling better, talk to her about what she would like done."

"Actually, I think nothing would make her feel better than to discuss this right now"

"What do you mean?"

"This could be just the thing to cheer her up and help her forget some of the pain she's in. Let's talk to her now."

"Well...if you really think she is ready to handle this."

"Doctor, she's been ready her whole life."

THREE

"MR. AND MRS. THORNTON, this is Dr. Moscowitz," said Dr. Vogel. "I've asked him to consult on your surgery. He's very skilled in creating new looks. I thought you would like to see some of his work."

"You mean like a fashion show?" asked Ben.

"No, no. But we have a Power Point on this laptop with some before and after shots that might be able to give you a good idea of the kind of work that can be done. Ready, let's just take a look."

Dr. Moscowitz clicked on the computer presentation and Ben and Roxanne watched as plain faces morphed into glam shots. Roxanne wondered if what she was seeing was really too good to be true. *Could these doctors really give her the "high school cheerleader" good looks she had always envied?*

"Wow, you really can do extreme makeovers," said Roxanne. "Are you sure you can do that with me?"

"Certainly, Mrs. Thornton. Tell me, whom do you think of as attractive? Can you name any actresses you think are pretty?"

"Jennifer Aniston, Cameron Diaz, Debra Messing is really pretty," Roxanne began. "Oh, and Reese Witherspoon is adorable. I always liked Valerie Bertinelli when she was on

'One Day at a Time, and now that's she's lost all that weight she looks great again.'"

"That's pretty interesting. Do you realize you've mentioned all women much younger than you?"

"Oh." Roxanne hadn't realized that.

"Can you name any more mature women whose looks you admire?" asked Dr. Moscowitz.

"Well, let's see, there's Candace Bergen—I mean not now, but when she was my age, and Nicole Kidman, but I suppose that's being too extreme. Doctor, I just want to look pretty. I want a small, straight nose, great eyebrows, cheekbones, a cute little chin, and can you do anything about these wrinkles I'm starting to get?"

"Fine, we'll give you style number 16A," said Dr. Moscowitz.

"Are you kidding? Do you really have style numbers for faces?" Ben asked in amazement.

"Of course not. I'm just joking with you."

"Mrs. Thornton, may I be frank?"

Roxanne nodded.

"When I saw the photograph of you I knew immediately that I could make a big difference in your appearance. You're really what I call an easy fix."

"Oh? Why?"

"You just need some reshaping. Your fractures already have in a way, prepped you for this type of reconstruction. Where you've had plain, undistinguished features, with the exception of that unfortunate nose of course—that's going to be beautiful, by the way—I can give you cheekbones, a lovely chin, with a dimple perhaps, and shape your brow so that your eyes not only see, but are seen. The windows to the soul and all that, you know."

"Doctor, just how much change are you thinking of?" Ben asked, his voice going up an octave.

"Shh, Ben, the doctor knows what he's talking about," said Roxanne.

"You don't have a thing to worry about. When we're all done Mrs. Thornton will be ready for a modeling career."

All of a sudden, Roxanne's painkillers started to kick in again and a huge wave of drowsiness hit her.

"Okay, do your magic. See you later…" and she was back in dreamland.

"Hi Sweetie, how are you feeling today?" Ben asked Roxanne the next morning. "Is there anything I can do for you?"

"Lunch money," said Roxanne, straining to get the words out without moving her face.

"Oh, don't worry, the meals are all included here," said Ben.

"Not ME! The kids!" Roxanne tried to voice her frustration without moving.

"Oh, sure, I'm taking care of it. I sat down with the kids last night and made lists of what they need each morning, what time they go to school, and what activities they need to be driven to. I put it all on Excel. I don't know how you do it your way. I'll show you when you get out of here, which I'm afraid will not be for a few weeks according to the doctor."

"Carpools?" Roxanne asked.

"Oh, the women have been great. All your carpools called and with the exception of Religious School on Sundays they have basically taken me off the hook. They're going to fill in your place on the schedule and they told me not to worry about anything."

Roxanne could hardly believe her ears. After all the disputes, heated arguments, and heavy negotiations that she had to go through with each one of the carpool mothers, now they were saying that they actually had flexibility to CHANGE

THEIR SCHEDULES. When she had wanted to switch Tuesday afternoons with Wednesday evenings with Andrea the woman had reacted as if any switch in her schedule would require an Act of God. *I don't know if they just don't trust Ben to actually take his turn on the right day and time or they really want to make things easier for him because they care about me. Who would believe that,* she asked herself. As astonished as she was by Ben's news, she didn't have the energy to show her true reaction.

"Great. It's good to know I won't be missed," said Roxanne summoning up a bit of sarcasm.

"Now, don't start thinking anything like that," said Ben. "We want you back home as soon as possible. But you don't have to worry about the kids and me. We're going to take care of ourselves. You just concentrate on getting better."

Roxanne's eyes closed and she drifted off again as the most recent dose of painkiller kicked in again.

The next time she opened her eyes it was because the smell of flowers was so strong it actually woke her up. An enormous vase of flowers was perched a little too close to her, on the pull-up tray for her bed. The card told Roxanne it was from the office.

"Oy, I suppose I have to call them. I don't know what to tell them," she said to Ben. Her words were cut short by the phone ringing.

"Hello"

"Roxanne, how are you? We're all so sorry to hear about your accident what does the doctor say how do you feel how long will you be in the hospital when are you coming back to work?"

Miriam's words all ran together into one sentence. Roxanne knew it didn't really matter. The one answer that Miriam really wanted to know was to the last question.

"I …really…don't…know…yet," said Roxanne. "It looks

like I'll be out for a while. Do you want to go over my calendar and we can figure out what to do about my appointments?"

Ben took the phone from her hand.

"Hello Miriam, this is Ben. She's had a very bad accident and is going to be out for some time. She's really not up to dealing with the office right now. But I promise she will call you when she has had some more time to recover. I'll give her everyone's good wishes. No, she's not ready for visitors, I'll have to let you know when. Oh, and thanks for the flowers. Very nice. Goodbye."

Dr. Vogel entered the room just as Ben hung up the phone. Again, his group of medical students trailed him. Just like on TV, he looked at her chart before saying anything to her.

"You're doing much better. How do you feel?" he asked.

"Terrible."

"I wish I could tell you differently, but it's going to get a little worse before it gets better. You're stabilized and we'd like to begin the surgery. Is that okay with you?"

"Sure, I think I can clear my calendar."

"Great, we're going to make you so beautiful you won't ever recognize yourself."

"Doctor, will I be able to play the piano?"

"I'm not falling for that old one, but I'm glad to see you won't need any sense of humor transplant."

"Because of the extent of your injuries, it's going to require a series of procedures over the next three weeks. We'll keep you as comfortable as we can with medication, which means that you may have to be somewhat out of it for a while."

"Fine with me, doctor. I am no hero. As long as Ben can handle the kids, you can keep me as stoned as you'd like."

The doctor and his entourage left and for the first time since the accident, Roxanne felt very frightened. Her first surgery was scheduled for that afternoon. *Was she told old to make these changes? What would she look like, and would she like the new face?*

"Ben, are you sure this doctor knows what he's doing? I'm getting scared."

"Honey, I've checked him out and we got lucky. He's usually very hard to get, but he read about you in the paper and offered to treat you. All the movie stars wait months to get appointments with him. You should see how many hits he has on Google."

"Well, if you're sure. I'm going to just let you take care of this. Ben, I love you."

"I love you right back. I promise everything will work out well. You've got a few rough weeks ahead of you, but I'll be right here with you. I'm taking off the rest of this month from work."

"You're kidding?" Now Roxanne didn't know whether to be angry or pleased.

"Is this what it takes to get you out of the office?"

Before he could come up with an answer, Ben was interrupted by a nurse wheeling a little cart around to the other side of the bed.

"Here's your medication Mrs. Thornton, she said cheerfully. "Just take this little pill, and I'm going to put something in your IV that will make you very relaxed."

"Honey, I'm just going outside to make a phone call," said Ben. "I can't use the cell in here."

"I'm not done with you yet," said Roxanne.

FOUR

"Mom, Mom are you awake?" said Justin. At 13, Justin had little patience for sitting around watching his mother sleep. He was what Roxanne called "reluctantly turning teenage," still more interested in video games than girls and at present going through the awkward adolescent stage where his hands and feet looked as if they belonged to someone else—a much bigger person, while his chest was still concave and his voice continually jumping between high and low.

The third surgical procedure in a week had been this morning, and as Roxanne awakened she tried to determine if there were any new pains or sensations she could distinguish. Her face remained bandaged, but she was aware of the feeling that things were happening.

"Oh, hi Justin. Where's Dad?"

"He dropped me off while he went to Gabe's soccer game. They're playing this one just for you. I wanted to ask you something."

"What honey?"

"Can you call my guidance counselor on Monday and see if I can switch band with lunch? There's no one in my lunch, and there's another percussion group in fourth period that I could join if I take band then."

"Justin, darling, sweetheart. Do I look like I'm in any shape to call your guidance counselor? Did you ask Dad?"

"He's afraid of teachers."

"No, he's not."

"Well, I think he saves all his good arguments for his business meetings. I just know if he called it wouldn't get done. But you're real good at getting teachers to make changes. Please, Mom, please just call."

"Justin, even if I tried, I doubt I would get through. As far as I can tell the guidance office is permanently on voice mail. What if you wrote a note and I signed it?"

"Well, could we play the accident card?"

"What?"

"Just mention how I was so traumatized by your accident that I really need to be with my good friends at lunch, you know, for support."

"Okay, we wouldn't want a perfectly good accident to me to be wasted without using it as a bargaining chip for you, now would we?"

"That's true. Okay, we're on the same page. Here, help me write it and you can sign it."

Justin took out a spiral notebook and began to write:

> *Dear Mrs. Kresge:*
>
> *I am unable to call you from my hospital bed, so Justin is writing this letter for me. I have a small request to make. Could Justin please switch his fourth period lunch with his sixth period band lesson? He is quite unhappy with the way it is now, and I would appreciate your helping him out with this, as under my current circumstances I am not able to help him as much as I would like to.*
>
> *Sincerely,*
> *Roxanne Thornton*

"Are you sure you don't want to sign it Justin's mother?" asked Roxanne.

"Huh, what do you mean?"

"Never mind. Don't you think we're laying it on a bit thick with that?"

"Don't worry, it's fine, Mom. How can she say no to this letter? Here, just sign it. It's okay if your signature is shaky. That makes it more convincing. Mom, please. You can't imagine what it's like for me having lunch without any of my friends there."

"Oh, I think I can," said Roxanne, who was beginning to feel the pain medication kick in again. "Here, I need to sleep again. Love you."

Justin folded the note and placed it in the outside pocket of his backpack. He then took out his English book, settled in the chair comfortably, and within a few minutes his eyes were shut as well.

FIVE

ROXANNE COULD IMAGINE EXACTLY what it was like for Justin to have lunch without his friends in junior high (even though now they called it middle school). Her own memories of lunch at junior high were among the most harrowing of her adolescence, and she hadn't even been alone. She knew if she hadn't had any friends to sit with things would have been immeasurably worse.

In seventh grade Roxanne had been at her peak of awkwardness. Skin constantly breaking out, braces on her teeth, and hair that insisted on frizzing up no matter how carefully she dried it or how tightly she wrapped it around her head when she went to sleep. Why couldn't she have hair like Liza Schwartzberg? Liza's hair was straight and shiny, and never looked out of place. Even when they had gym (another time of torture for Roxanne), Liza would just pull her hair back with a big barrette. After scoring three goals in field hockey, Liza would just unsnap the barrette, give her head a big toss, and every long blonde hair would fall neatly into place.

But the lunchroom was a place for bullies to strut their stuff. The day Roxanne crossed the Belasco twins was one she could never forget.

The Belasco twins were tough girls who had their own unique sense of style at a time when schools were just giving in on the dress code to allow girls to wear "slacks, no jeans" in recognition that Connecticut winters were just too cold to insist the girls wear skirts and dresses.

The Belasco's were ninth graders (for at least the second time) when Roxanne was in seventh grade. Identical twins, they had long, straight dyed red hair, and tall, well-developed bodies that made them look like a different species altogether from Roxanne and her friends who had just started wearing training bras, whether they needed them or not.

Roxanne could only imagine that they had no parents at all, because no parent that she knew would have allowed their kids to dress that way. Always in exactly matching outfits, the Belasco's wore high-heeled black or white patent leather boots, micro-mini skirts with nude pantyhose, and low-cut blouses with ruffles on the collar and cuffs. Their make-up was applied with quite a heavy hand, and included enormous false eyelashes and purple-white lipstick to give that deathly pallor look to complete the outfit.

One day, Roxanne was hurrying into lunch with a stack of books she'd just checked out of the library for her research paper on Greek mythology. She spotted her friends at a table on the other side of the cafeteria from their regular spot, and tried making her way through the crowd. In a most unfortunate turn of events, the book at the top of her stack slipped off and fell onto the tray of one of the Belasco's. (It never mattered which one was which; they were basically interchangeable.)

"Hey, what the hell are you doing throwing your book into my lunch?" roared the twin.

"I...I...I'm sorry, it slipped," said Roxanne.

"Well, it talks," said the other twin.

Everyone in the cafeteria had stopped what they were doing and were now staring at Roxanne and the twins.

"Well your little slip has ruined my lunch. How am I going to eat with this in my spaghetti?" The twin took the book, opened it and poured the remains of her spaghetti with meat sauce onto the open pages."

Roxanne looked around for a lunch monitor, but they all seemed to have taken their break at that time. They didn't want to mess with the Belasco twins either.

"I…I…I'm sorry. I'll pay for your lunch. Here," said Roxanne holding out three dollars.

"If you pay for it then it's yours," said the twin. She grabbed the money with one hand and with the other hand she slammed the spaghetti-filled book on Roxanne's head.

"Hey, don't forget dessert," said the other twin, smashing her red jello with whipped cream into Roxanne's chest.

As the Belasco twins and what seemed like everyone else in the entire school had a great laugh at Roxanne's expense, Roxanne stood paralyzed, actually waiting to see what would be poured upon her next.

But she got a little lucky. Mr. Cowen, the assistant principal, came into the cafeteria upon hearing the laughter, and the Belasco twins darted out the back door.

"What's going on here?" he asked looking at Roxanne and trying to hold back his own laughter at the sight of her.

"Um, nothing, just a little accident Mr. Cowen," said Roxanne. There was no way she was going to tell on the Belasco twins. Not if she wanted to live to see eighth grade.

Her best friends, Ricki and Jenny, came forward with a big bunch of paper towels.

"Well, will you girls help your friend get cleaned up?" asked Mr. Cowen.

"Sure. C'mon Roxanne let's go to the girls room," said Ricki, picking up the books that had fallen from Roxanne's arms.

From that day on, Roxanne made sure to enter the cafeteria with her small group of girlfriends close by. The Belasco twins continued to taunt their new target, and Roxanne prayed that at the end of the year the twins would be allowed to graduate to the high school.

SIX

BEING TORMENTED BY THE Belasco twins was the more dramatic story of her youth that Roxanne could describe, but it wasn't what caused the most harm to her self-esteem. Roxanne was smart enough to know that the twins were not girls she would ever want to be friends with. It was the more frequent, everyday little snubs that she felt from just about everyone but her close friends.

When Roxanne wanted to audition for the drama club play the director had her read for three different roles: the mother, the grandmother, and the judge. When Roxanne said that she wanted to read for the part of the teenage daughter, the director said she wasn't exactly right for the part.

"What does that mean?" Roxanne had raged to Ricki and Jenny. "How can I not be right to play a teenage girl? I AM A TEENAGE GIRL!! What that creep means is that I'm not pretty enough for the part."

Jenny let out a big sigh. "It just isn't fair. This isn't Hollywood, it's junior high in suburbia."

"What really kills me is there is nothing in this play that requires the girl to be pretty," Roxanne had said. "It's just discrimination. It's the story of my life."

Her friends nodded sympathetically. They knew just what it felt like to be judged by the way they looked.

SEVEN

"YOU KNOW HONEY, YOU'VE lost some weight." Roxanne's mother was always adept at stating the obvious. "See, every cloud has a silver lining."

"Well, I wouldn't recommend this as a diet method, but you're right," said Roxanne. "After all the times I've tried to lose weight, who'd think that actually not eating anything would work?"

"You know, you'll have to make sure you don't gain it back once you go home," Sheila, Roxanne's mom, continued.

"Now that's good advice," said Roxanne. But all sarcasm was lost on Sheila, who had flown up from Florida almost as soon as she learned about the accident. She would have come sooner, she explained, but her tennis tournament was just two days away, and she wouldn't want to disappoint "the girls."

"Actually, Estelle's daughter had something very similar happen to her. She was in the hospital with pneumonia and lost 16 and a half pounds. But as soon as she got home, she went straight to the cookie jar and gained it all back, plus a little more."

"Really, what kind of cookies were they?"

"Gee, I don't know, they might have been chocolate chip, but then, let me think, Estelle might have said that she had a weakness for shortbread. I'm really not sure."

"Never mind, mom. Did Ben and the kids get you settled in all right? Did he give you the comforter with the pink flowers?"

"Don't worry about me, honey. I can find my way around that mess you call a linen closet. I don't like to complain, but isn't there some way to keep the cat from jumping on my bed?"

"Well, it's usually her bed, mom. She thinks she's being quite the hostess by sharing it with you. But if she bothers you, just push her away."

"I try, but then she starts meowing at me, and Gabe and Justin look at me as if I'm some sort of cat abuser. I don't understand why you want to be bothered with having a cat. No matter where I sit down in your house, my clothes are always covered in cat hair."

Roxanne mercifully felt the pain killer kicking in, and let her eyes close.

"It looks like you're ready for a nap, honey. I'll check in with you later." Sheila picked up her sweater, tried brushing off some cat hair, and headed down the hall.

Nice seeing you mom, thought Roxanne, as she drifted off to sleep.

EIGHT

"I'VE GOT GOOD NEWS for you, Mrs. Thornton," said Dr. Vogel. "Your first round of surgeries went very well and you are healing beautifully."

"How can you tell anything with all these bandages on?" asked Roxanne.

"We have our ways, but you're right, we do need to take a look under the bandages. Are you ready for an unveiling?"

"Wait, I don't know," Roxanne felt the fear clutch her chest.

"Don't worry, honey, it won't hurt. I'll be very gentle," said the nurse waiting patiently beside Dr. Vogel and Dr. Moscowitz.

So ready or not, Roxanne sat up and held her breath while the nurse—as gently as she had promised—slowly removed the bandages that had completely covered her face. Except when she was under anesthesia during the surgeries, Roxanne had been fully bandaged since the accident.

"Now, you have to understand that your face is still swollen, and there is still healing going on," said Dr. Vogel.

"Can I look?" said Roxanne.

The nurse pulled over the bed tray and opened the drawer, revealing a pop-up mirror.

Roxanne looked in the mirror and stared hard at her

reflection. It was true that her face was puffy and there were still bruises of varying colors, but the structure of her face looked like no one she knew.

"Wow, you look fantastic," said Ben, who burst in from the hall where he had been waiting. "What do you think, Roxanne? Do you like the new you?"

"I don't know yet. My nose…"

"Remember it's still a little swollen but it's much smaller and straighter now. No more bumps," said Dr. Moscowitz.

"My chin…"

"That's one of my best styles," said Dr. Moscowitz with a grin. "We just shortened it a bit, made it round instead of pointed, and look, we even gave you a dimple."

"My cheeks…"

"You complained that you had no cheekbones, so we gave you some, the magic of implants. Mrs. Thornton, I think you look great if I do say so myself. What do you think?"

"I…I…I think I'm going to pass out."

When she woke again, Roxanne's bandages had been replaced with smaller versions of the mummy face she had before. But with the new bandages she could see that she did look a lot different. And not just different, she was sure she was going to look better. She couldn't really believe it. *After a lifetime of unhappiness with what she saw in the mirror, would she really be…pretty?*

NINE

ROXANNE LOOKED AT THE clock beside her bed and couldn't believe she had slept through the night. Seven a.m. It was Sunday, and everyone was enjoying sleeping late. Ben had assured her on the way home from the hospital yesterday that there was nothing planned for Sunday. No games, no parties, no last-minute homework assignments that required a trip to the library. Even Sunday School was closed, due to a teacher's conference.

Ben was snoring softly next to her, and Clarissa was curled at their feet. After five weeks, it felt good to be home. Nothing seemed to have changed. Nothing but her own face.

She eased herself quietly out of bed. Her ankle was in a walking cast, and there was only slight discomfort now. She slipped on one slipper, put on her robe, and made it out of the room without waking either husband or cat.

Peeking in on the kids, and seeing them all sound asleep, Roxanne congratulated herself on her decision to get out of bed first and start the day off with a nice cup of hot tea. She knew she had to start her life up again and was not quite sure how to go about it. For the past 20 years she had been responsible for setting the pace of her own life and Ben's, and then with each child's birth she had expanded that role and managed to keep five very busy lives operating in sync with one another as well as any family reasonably can.

The accident had brought that all to a crashing halt, literally, and Roxanne was worried that she would have trouble getting back in the driver's seat, so to speak. For five weeks she had been completely relieved of all duties. She was thrilled to be home now, but was she really ready to resume her life and all that it entailed?

All it entailed…all it entailed… The first order of business Roxanne needed to deal with was just that, business. Her office had been calling and calling and she knew that now that she was home her boss would expect to be given an exact date that she would return, and she'd expect it to be soon. The thought actually made her ill, and her head began to throb as she imagined what it would like to go back to the job she had been doing for the last seven years. She'd never been away from it for so long before. It gave her the pause for perspective she had never dared to take.

It was the kind of job that sounded very good when you described it to other people, "Creative Director for a Management Consultant Firm." In reality it was often boring; she was usually annoyed at or by the people in her office; and there was precious little "creative" about it. On the plus side, the pay was good, the boss was reasonably satisfied with whatever she produced, and the pay was good.

The phone ringing interrupted Roxanne's reverie.

"Sorry to bother you on a Sunday, but I wanted to add my welcome home and best wishes," said a voice she didn't recognize.

"Thanks, who is this?"

"It's Dave Cohen, your lawyer."

"Oh, Dave, how nice of you to call. Do you have any news for me?"

"As a matter of fact, that's why I'm calling. We don't have a final figure yet, but the bus company is not trying to place any co-negligence on you."

"In other words…"

"In other words, they'd like to settle this quickly without going to court and they're willing to pay one hundred percent of all medical bills and loss of wages and add a very reasonable sum for pain and suffering. After all, your pain and suffering was widely reported. They want this to be forgotten as soon as possible."

"Dave, that's great. When will you have an offer from them?"

"I've got a meeting scheduled for tomorrow morning. With any luck, I'll only need a few back and forth haggles and we'll be done. We'll demand immediate payment as a condition of settling so you may have a check to deposit by the end of next week."

"You know, Dave, I was thinking that maybe I wouldn't rush back to work so fast. Do you think the settlement will allow me to take a few months off?"

Dave's laugh boomed through the receiver. "No Roxanne, I think you'll be able to take a few years off, and then a few years after that. Take your time and decide what will make you happy. Then go for it. You'll be getting at least two million— and that's after our fee."

Roxanne hung up the phone and stared at it, as if it was something she had never seen before.

"What did Dave Cohen have to say?" asked Ben.

"Well, it was good news. Come, sit down."

"So what did he say, tell me?"

"He didn't know exactly how much we were going to get, but he said it would all be settled very soon, in a few weeks, and that they were going to pay all medical bills and loss of wages and also…." Roxanne stopped. She wasn't sure how Ben was going to react to the rest of the news.

"Yeah, what else?"

"He said we're going to get a large settlement for pain and suffering, somewhere around two million dollars."

"TWO MILLION DOLLARS?" Ben's eyes were wider than Roxanne had ever seen them.

"Yes. I guess we're going to have some decisions to make," said Roxanne. "And I was thinking that this might be my chance to quit my job and make a career change. Would you mind?"

Ben took a deep breath and then exhaled very slowly. *He's using my Lamaze breathing,* thought Roxanne, *I hope he doesn't have a heart attack.* After a few more breaths he was able to answer her.

"Honey, you've been dissatisfied in this job for too long. We're going to have to sit down with our accountant and figure out what we need to do so that we don't blow this money. But you have my full support to hand in your resignation. I'm going to keep working at my job, though, I really do like it."

"Oh my God, Ben, is this really happening? You know, the whole time I was in the hospital it felt like I was in a dream. Between the pain and the medication I felt like I had complete loss of control. Now I feel like I'm in another dream."

"But this one we're going to control, Roxie. You'll see. We just have to take it slow."

Dreams had always been a way for Roxanne to escape from the stresses and disappointments she had in her life. When she was in her teens and early twenties she would often fall asleep by saying something to herself like, okay, dream you've won the lottery, or dream you're cast as the star in a Broadway show. Her imagination would take her places she'd never been. After she was married and had children her dreams included her family. Ben gets a great new job…Gabe scores three goals in a soccer game…they go on Nickelodeon's Double Dare and win the grand prize.

It had been a long time since she had indulged herself in a "Roxcentric" dream. She was so wrapped up in her family and the individual and collective needs of the five of them that she couldn't separate her own desires from the rest of them. But she knew that would have to change. After all, it was Roxanne who had her face rearranged and it was Roxanne who was deciding to quit her job and make a career change. Ben and the kids had carried on quite well without her while she'd been in the hospital.

Wow, all those times I ranted to Ben that he needed to pay more attention to what was going on with the kids because I could drop dead tomorrow and I actually lived to see it happen, Roxanne thought. *How depressing. They would have been fine if I had died.*

TEN

THERE HAD BEEN PLENTY of times Roxanne had fantasized about quitting her job. The fantasy she had the most often had been a simple, straightforward, just telling her boss to "Take this job and shove it."

"Oh, well I'm sorry you feel that way," she'd tell her boss after letting her rant on about some little thing that had set her off. "In that case, why don't you just do it yourself? I quit. See ya."

Roxanne grinned at the thought of her boss getting enraged at her complete loss of power. She had swallowed a lot of abuse from a boss who thought that a superior position in business meant that she was indeed a superior being. As she had told herself so often, the job paid well, and if it meant putting up with an overly egotistical boss she would do it for the sake of Justin, Gabe, and Allison. They were the beneficiaries of her sacrifice. Along with the basics, like a home and food, they had their summer camps, piano lessons, and the easy way they went through life, taking it for granted that there would always be money for the movies, eating out, and upgrading their computers to stay on top of the current technology advances.

Still, as delightful as it sounded, Roxanne was scared. After all, if she wasn't "Creative Director for a Management

Consultant Firm," what was she then? Stay at home mom? No. She'd been there done that and it was bumpy enough the first time around. *Besides, I'm obsessed enough with these kids. I can just imagine how obsessed I'd be if I had nothing else to occupy my brain.*

ELEVEN

"Roxanne? Is it really you?" Ann gave her a big hug, something she'd never done as her therapist before.

"Yes, it's me. You know the old saying, careful what you wish for, well it looks like I actually got it."

"That's right, one of the last things you said to me was that you wish you could have a different face…"

"And just a few hours later I was lying underneath a bus. Now, I think I finally have the face I wanted."

"That is wild." Ann looked at Roxanne incredulously. "This is one for the books. Well, so tell me, how do you feel?"

"You mean about the face, or in general?"

"Both."

"Actually I'm still taking painkillers, so as far as that goes, I feel okay."

"And you look like you lost weight. You do look great."

"Yeah, well not eating for four weeks is a guaranteed weight loss plan."

"So what's next? What are you planning to do with your new face?"

Roxanne laughed. "That's a funny question."

"Well, I did mean it seriously. After all, you always

thought that your life would be different if your appearance was different. Have you noticed any changes in your life yet?"

"There have been a lot of changes, but they haven't actually been facially driven—not in the way you mean, anyway. But I have decided to leave my job and explore what else I want to do with my career. The insurance settlement has given me the freedom to do that. I really haven't gotten past the decision not to return to my job. That much I'm sure of."

"So what did your boss, the Evil Queen, say when you told her."

"I didn't exactly tell her yet."

"What are you waiting for?"

"Courage."

"As your therapist, and as someone who cares about you, I have to advise you not to let this opportunity pass. You've told me some wild things about the way your boss treats people. I'd really like to see you stand up for yourself and leave her with a piece of your mind."

"But, what about that old rule that you shouldn't *burn your bridges?*" Roxanne asked.

"You know, that is a very valid point, but I think in this case it might not matter. Let me ask you, regardless of how you choose to leave, do you think your boss would ever be so kind as to help you with employment in the future."

Roxanne laughed. "Actually, one thing I've noticed is that once people leave, she acts as if they never existed. She bitches for a few days, then she hires someone else and never looks back. In her mind, everyone is replaceable, except for herself."

"So tell me, what would you really like to say to her?"

Leaving Ann's office, Roxanne felt as if she had been injected with the courage she needed to pull off one of her all-time fantasies. Before she could lose her nerve, she called her boss's secretary.

"Oh, hello Miriam, it's Roxanne. Does the boss have some free time this afternoon? I'd like to come by."

"Let me check. How's 2:00?"

"Great, see you then."

At 2:20, after being kept the minimum twenty minutes her boss used to intimidate people, Roxanne walked into the office she knew so well. How many times had she been summoned here? Sometimes it was just to ask a question, other times it was to go over an assignment, and less frequently but ever possible, she was summoned here to listen to a harangue over the latest imperfection or oversight that had been deemed to be her fault. Even when things were going very well, Roxanne's boss had a talent for finding things to complain about.

"Well Roxanne, I don't think I would have recognized you," she said. "You've had a lot of work done haven't you?"

"I had extensive reconstructive surgery."

"So, when can you come back to work?"

"I'm not planning to, at least not here."

"What? You're leaving, after all I've done for you? Well, we'll need four weeks notice from when you come back. That should be enough time for you to finish up what you left hanging."

"No, I don't think so." Roxanne could hardly believe she was actually contradicting the boss. No one had the nerve to do that.

"I know how annoyed you get whenever a new hire insists on giving their employer any notice at all, so I've decided not to give you any."

"But, but…"

"And I really have no desire to come back here and be subjected to any more abuse by you. So good luck. I'm going to collect my personal things and I'll be out of here."

Roxanne turned around and without waiting for a

response, headed out the door. Her boss was already on the phone calling personnel to tell them to hire a replacement for Roxanne. It took her about 45 minutes to collect her personal belongings. She really didn't feel like any big goodbyes; so she slipped out the back way and closed that chapter of her life with a big sigh of relief.

Pulling out of the parking lot for what she hoped would be the very last time, Roxanne blasted The Who's "Tommy," track 21, and sang along, "I'm free, I'm free and freedom tastes of reality. I'm free, I'm free and I'm waiting for you to follow meeeeeeeeee."

TWELVE

"Honey, are you sure? Have you really thought this through?" Sheila questioned her daughter.

"Well no, I just did it without thinking at all," said Roxanne. "Mom, I'm forty-two years old, I have a husband and three kids—all of whom appear to be normal I might add—(Roxanne was not so subtly alluding to her own sister) I do know what I'm doing." *Well at least that's what I'm saying to you,* Roxanne thought.

"It's just that I know two million dollars *sounds* like a lot of money, but you know, the girls were just talking at mah jongg yesterday about Heddy's niece whose husband lost all their money in the stock market. You know, the stock market can wipe you out just like that," Sheila said.

"Mom, that may be true. But I'm not planning on putting all my money in the stock market. Therefore, it can't wipe me out. Doesn't that make sense?"

"I suppose. So what are you planning to do with all your time now? Once your ankle is healed I hope you're planning to join a gym or take an exercise class. You don't want to put back that weight you lost so nicely in the hospital."

"Don't worry Mom, I've got it all under control."

"So…what *is* your plan?"

"Actually, I've registered for some acting classes in the city. The next semester starts right after the new year."

"You're kidding," Sheila said, laughing at her daughter.

"What makes you think that?" Roxanne said, trying very hard to control the anger that was turning her ears hot and creating a knot in her stomach.

"I just can't believe you're going to fritter away your time and money like that. I can just imagine what your father would think."

"Mom, Dad died sitting at his desk at the office. He was the absolute definition of a workaholic and that's what made him happy. I think he would understand that this is what makes *me* happy."

"Oh, I thought your husband and children made you happy." Sheila said with the cutting edge she gets when her daughter "talks back" to her.

"Yes, of course they do. But the truth is, the place that I am most happy is on the stage. Why do you think I've done community theater for all these years?"

"Yes, but no offense dear, you've never had a really good role? What makes you think it will be different now?"

Roxanne stifled her impulse to shout at her mother, "Because I'm pretty now, so fuck you!" She still hadn't told her mother about the extent of her reconstructive surgery. She wanted to let her mother see it for herself when all the swelling was down and all the stitches gone. Instead, she thanked God for the millionth time that Sheila had made the move to Florida and was so happy there.

"Mom, I've decided to give it a try. I'm not expecting to win a Tony on Broadway, so don't worry. Besides, I haven't said that I'll be doing this the rest of my life. Can you just accept that I'm going to go ahead with this for now?"

"Of course, Roxie. Oh, that's my call waiting. It could be Gladys about the golf lessons. Talk to you later, love you, Bye."

Roxanne hung up the phone, took a deep breath and starting humming the song from *Avenue Q*, "For Now." "Everything in life is only for now," she sang to herself. Yes, this is what I'm going to do "for now."

"Mom, do you think you could take me to the mall after school?" Allison jolted Roxanne back into reality. "Can you walk around okay with that new cast?"

"Sure, that's why it's called a walking cast. What do you need at the mall?"

"I need new boots, there's a sale at BOOTIQUE, and I was hoping I could get some new sweaters. Okay?"

"Okay, do you want me to pick you up at school?"

"No thanks. I'll come home first. Thanks mom, you're the best." Allison gave her a quick hug, grabbed her backpack, and ran out the door.

THIRTEEN

ROXANNE STARTED STRAIGHTENING UP the kitchen. She'd now been home for six weeks and her face was pretty much healed. They'd kept Thanksgiving to just the family, but Chanukah/Christmas vacation was coming and Sheila would be flying in to spend the holiday. Ben had been back at work for four weeks and she'd been home getting her life back together. Next week, after her cast was removed, she would officially be through with her recuperation. Ready or not, she was taking her rightful place back in the carpools.

The settlement check had been deposited and Ben and Roxanne were meeting with a financial planner soon to discuss the best way to make investments and manage spending.

She had registered at the Actor's Studio for three classes: Voice and Speech, Improvisation, and Physical Acting. She'd be taking classes four days a week, commuting to the city, but still be home in time for the kids when they needed her. The schedule would be great!

But now she was preparing for the first really big test of what the new Roxanne was made of. She was taking her daughter to the mall.

Until today, Roxanne had been in a quiet kind of hiding. She didn't want to venture out in public until the bruising and swelling went down. And even though that had come to pass about ten days ago, she continued to use her ankle injury to turn down invitations and offers for visits. The truth was, Roxanne didn't have any good close friends in her community. Her life revolved around Ben and the kids. When Allison and Justin were very young, she had been close to a group of four women, but two had moved away and she and the others had let their friendships all but lapse completely when they returned to work full time. She still felt some guilt that Gabe had been so much younger when she'd gone back to work, but that was now history. Since she no longer picked up the kids at school, her daily contact with other women in the community was minimal. She had plenty of people to exchange pleasantries with at Stop and Shop, but for the past several years it hadn't gone much beyond that. She did keep in touch with some long-time friends, but that was mostly through email and long-distance phone calls. Now, her daughter, through her simple assumption that things could just go back to normal, had gotten her to commit to making her first foray in public without even thinking about it.

Roxanne stood before the mirror. She did that a lot these days, and was still surprised at who she saw looking back at her there. *Who is this woman with the small, narrow nose, high cheekbones, smooth skin, great eyebrows* (she always got excited about her eyebrows, Dr. Moscowitz had done a fantastic job there) *and a mouth that actually smiled at her own reflection? Could she really go to the mall like those other people she'd watched so many times in her life? Those people who could go into a store, try on something that looked good on the hanger and have it look good on her?* Roxanne never liked the way new clothes looked on her. It was the same when she got her hair cut or took greater care applying makeup than usual. The people in her office might say, "Oh, that looks great on you, don't you love it?" and invariably Roxanne would shrug and think, *It's still me in these clothes...makeup...hair, so how could I love it?* Of course she'd smile and say "thanks," but compliments generally bounced off of Roxanne like a pink Spalding off a brick wall.

Despite her apprehension, Roxanne smiled at the thought of taking Allison to the mall. Miraculously, Allison did not look like Roxanne, a fear that had almost kept Roxanne from ever having children. Every time she looked at her kids, Roxanne would wonder to herself, are they really that adorable or is it just that I love them so much? She knew that Sheila had never asked herself that question. "I call it like I see it," she'd say, never blinded by maternal love.

The truth was that Allison looked a lot like Roxanne's older sister, Grace. Allison had the same clear, olive complexion and straight, shiny honey-colored hair as her aunt. She was even the same height as Grace. At five-foot seven, Allison was the same height as Ben, and she towered over the sixty-one inch Roxanne. Grace had gotten the looks in the family, while Roxanne was "blessed" with the brains. So aptly named, Grace floated through childhood and adolescence with the ease that pretty little girls with lovely smiles and good manners enjoyed. Her teachers never seemed to hassle her, and by the time she turned thirteen, there were always plenty of boys calling and wanting to spend time with Grace. Roxanne, on the other hand, generally enjoyed the company of a tight group of girlfriends, although there were some very painful memories when even the girls who had been her friends rejected her because of her "difference."

Roxanne had hit adolescence on the early side. By the time she was eleven, she had the acne usually reserved for older teens. Her nose had gone through a growth spurt while the rest of her remained "petite," and braces and glasses completed the picture. Her good sense of humor and adventurous spirit made her well liked by the girls in her class, that is, until boys entered the picture as something other than a nuisance.

Roxanne decided never to have children of her own when she felt the sting of rejection as her friends made plans for the very first boy-girl party in sixth grade. Up until that time, Roxanne had been invited to every birthday party the girls in the class had. There were slumber parties where they stayed up all night, bowling parties with pizza, and skating parties at the roller rink. But when Stephanie decided to have a party with boys, it quickly became a "couples party," and Roxanne was left out, while all the rest of her friends were paired up and invited.

She tried not to think about it, but the hurt was too much to ignore. One afternoon while she was playing the piano and singing, appropriately, *Carousel*'s "You'll Never Walk Alone," the tears just came. She tried to keep singing and playing, but her voice cracked and her mother looked up from the sweater she was knitting.

"Roxie, what wrong?" she asked, "Why are you crying?"

"Stephanie didn't invite me to her party."

"That's not very nice, but I'm sure there's a reason. Did you and Stephanie have a fight? Maybe her mother made her limit the guests."

"That's not the reason. I know what the reason is."

"What?"

"They're having boys at this party, and they're keeping it couples only. Nobody wanted to be a couple with me," Roxanne choked out the words through her tears. "The boys don't like me because I'm ugly."

Sheila was quiet for a moment. She didn't know what she could say to ease the pain her daughter felt. Her own eyes welled up with tears and she sat next to Roxanne on the piano bench and put her arm around her.

"Those girls aren't the friends you thought they were. Maybe if I call Stephanie's mother?"

"No, mom, don't," Roxanne didn't want the girls to know how badly she felt.

"I'm sorry honey, I wish I could do something," Sheila

trailed off. "Hey, how about going into the city and seeing what we can get on the TKTS line this weekend?"

"Yeah sure," Roxanne went back to playing the piano. It was the look on Sheila's face that made her decide not to have children when she grew up. She didn't ever want to have to be where Sheila was now and have to look into her own daughter's eyes and try to console her because the pretty girls were snubbing her. She could also tell by the look on her face that Sheila was feeling embarrassed about having a daughter who was rejected by her classmates because of her appearance. *It'll be better not to have kids at all.*

But things do change. By junior year of high school, Roxanne's complexion cleared considerably, she developed a decent figure, and after many different combinations of perms, hair straightening, colors, and cuts, Roxanne came to terms with a hairstyle that flattered her. The braces came off and glasses were replaced with contact lenses. Still not pretty like her sister, she could no longer consider herself ugly. However, she noticed something that both pleased and hurt her at the same time.

When Roxanne would be at a party or a dance with boys she had never met before, it was not unusual for one of these boys to hit on her, ask her to dance, or to try and get her to make out. Roxanne figured it was because she looked more approachable than the pretty girls. Male attention was a whole new ballgame for Roxanne, and she was never quite sure how to respond. It never lasted though, as invariably the boy who had shown interest just wanted to have a good time for the evening. Meanwhile, the attitude of the boys she had known throughout school remained the same. While she watched many of her classmates turn to one another for romance as their teen hormones began to rage, the boys she had known for years never looked at her as "datable" or desirable. Roxanne believed that even if she were no longer an ugly duckling, the people who had known her all her life would never see any changes in the way she looked.

Roxanne met Ben Thornton in her first semester of college. He wandered into her class while she was taking her very first test. The class was The Contemporary American Novel. Ben came late and seemed very surprised the class was taking a test. He was short (but still taller than Roxanne), had long, messy hair, and seemed much too comfortable in class to be a freshman.

"Oh, that test is today?" he asked aloud.

"Just take an exam booklet and sit down," the professor said from the back of the room. "You've got plenty of time."

The class went back to the test and all was quiet for about 15 minutes. Then Ben spoke up, again addressing the class as a whole.

"What day is today? It's not Tuesday, is it? This isn't The Science Fiction Genre, is it?"

The entire class stopped working to stare at Ben. Who was this guy?

"Oh well, sorry, bye." Ben put the test and the booklet back on the desk up front and hurried out of the classroom, leaving everyone rocking with laughter.

Just a few days later, Roxanne met Ben at a dorm party. "You're that guy who came into my Literature test aren't you?" she said, with the courage to speak to guys that three screwdrivers tended to give her."

"Well, if I deny it, what would you say?" said Ben.

"I'd say you were lying."

"So how'd you do on the test?" Ben asked.

"Next question," Roxanne said.

"Do you want to go for a walk?"

"Okay."

Ben reached down and took her hand and Roxanne felt

herself blush with the warmth it brought her. She was relieved it was dark so that Ben wouldn't see her color. *Could this really be something?* She began to hope it was.

Later, Ben kissed her, and she felt herself enjoying the sensation more than she had ever before. When Ben mentioned he was a senior, she instinctively pulled away, immediately fearing that he was just using her as an easy "freshman target."

The next morning Roxanne's stomach did a somersault when she saw Ben waiting for her outside the cafeteria. "Going to breakfast?" he said, trying to sound casual.

And that was that. Roxanne and Ben just clicked right away, becoming best friends and lovers all at once. They quickly settled into a close, exclusive relationship and neither one of them ever looked back.

Roxanne was happier than she had ever been in her life. Feeling just like Nellie Forbush in "South Pacific" she would dance around her dorm room singing, "I'm as corny as Kansas in August, high as a flag on the Fourth of July! If you'll excuse an expression I use, I'm in love, I'm in love, I'm in love, I'm in love with a wonderful guy."

"Ben is nice, but how can you be sure he's the one you want forever?" her roommate, Jo, would ask.

"Listen Jo, I never expected to meet my life mate so young, but when you go panning for gold and hit it on the first strike, you just don't throw it back. I do know a good thing when I see it and Ben and I are just right for each other."

In the back of her mind, Roxanne wondered what was wrong with Ben that he loved her so much. It was the old Groucho Marx dilemma about not wanting to join any club that would have you for a member, but Roxanne forced herself to stifle that thought whenever it popped up. She had gotten unbelievably lucky meeting Ben, she felt, and it was about time for something good to happen to her. It almost made up for all her adolescent suffering.

Jo didn't believe in long-term relationships. She attracted college boys like a beer keg at a frat party, but she was never willing to commit to anyone. "How do I know there's not someone better out there?" she posed. "I like to keep my options open."

Jo kept her options open all through college. It was the days before anyone had ever heard of AIDS, and so two abortions and a few cases of gonorrhea later, Jo graduated with a B.A. in Art History, still searching for the one man who could make her forget all others. Roxanne clasped her Psychology degree in one hand, and waved an engagement ring on the other, and after an August wedding, she and Ben began their adult lives together. They didn't have a lot of plans for the future, but Roxanne did make sure that they were in agreement on one thing.

"Ben, I don't ever want to have children," she told him before accepting the diamond ring he offered.

"That's fine with me," said 23-year-old Ben. "I don't see what the appeal of babies is, personally. All that crying and mess. I can't imagine ever wanting to get into all that."

Then came life.

FOURTEEN

If Roxanne had managed to forget about the whole Chanukah-Christmas conundrum, a trip to the mall was enough to shock her back into reality. The Thorntons were Jewish, but Ben had grown up in a mixed marriage and even though he had been bar mitzvahed, he had always enjoyed celebrating Christmas with his paternal grandparents, now long gone. Christmas was just too good to give up, he had argued with Roxanne. So although they didn't put up a tree, they did stuff stockings and hang them over the fireplace, and when holidays would overlap, they'd have a big turkey dinner...with latkes on the side.

At the mall, there was no such holiday as Chanukah. Everything was Christmas, Christmas, Christmas. Christmas music blared from speakers throughout the mall. Santa had been at his North Pole picture-taking booth since the day after Thanksgiving. A long line of parents and children ranging from mewling infants to surly teenagers waited to get their pictures taken with the jolly old elf, steadily raising their sugar levels as they indulged themselves in candy canes and chocolate marshmallow treats handed out by Santa's helpers.

Roxanne walked through the crowds, occasionally making eye contact with another shopper. Were people smiling at her new face more than they had her old one, or was it just the holiday cheer she was experiencing? She'd always tried to be semi-invisible in public spaces, but today she was hesitatingly curious to look at others and see what they gave to her in return. Was it her imagination, or was there something different about the way the strangers returned her glance?

Meanwhile, Allison was in her element in the mall. She reveled in the gaudy trimmings around her, and she steered Roxanne over to The Gap to check out the sweater situation. She was inspecting a pretty periwinkle pullover when she looked up to see a somewhat familiar face break into a grin.

"Allison, how are you?" asked Marge Karp, the formidable soccer mom. "How's your mother doing?"

"Oh, she's great. She's right over there, looking at those coats. See her in the blue ski jacket?"

Roxanne was trying to look inconspicuous behind the rack. She did not feel ready to see Marge, of all people.

But Marge wasted no time in running over to see her. She gently took Roxanne's arm to greet her, and when Roxanne turned around, Marge gasped and took a step backward.

"OH MY GOD! Roxanne?? I can't believe it. You look so…"

"Different?" offered Roxanne.

"Right, you certainly look different."

"Yes." *It would be pointless to deny it.* "The accident did extensive damage to my face, so while the doctors were fixing me up, they made a few improvements," Roxanne gave Marge the response she had rehearsed over and over in her own head.

It's quite a dramatic change." She paused, then continued. "Well anyway, I'm so glad to see you're out and about again," she smiled and nodded her head woodenly.

"When this cast comes off I'll be good to go," said Roxanne. She looked up to see Allison (blessedly) waving to her from the cashier's line.

"Oh, it looks like she's found something to buy, gotta go," said Roxanne. "Have a good holiday."

Before Roxanne could reach the cashier, Marge was already on her cell phone, making the first call to PTA President Claire Goldrich.

"You won't believe it. She's had one of those extreme makeovers," Marge gushed the news to Claire. "Well, yes, she does look attractive, but in a very fake way, if you know what I mean….I imagine while she was having all that work done on her face she had some breast implants put in too…."

FIFTEEN

News of Roxanne's transformation traveled around town with astonishing speed. To Roxanne's dismay, the news traveled as far as Florida, and Sheila got the news from one of the "girls" lobbing balls on the tennis court.

"So Sheila, I hear your daughter had extensive work done. My daughter-in-law tells me she's completely changed. What did you think when you saw her?"

"Can you imagine how I felt when Gertie Bloomfield came out with that?" Sheila said on the phone, accusing Roxanne of trying to make her look bad.

"Um, Mom, this really isn't about you," Roxanne said, knowing that it would just add fuel to Sheila's fire.

"Of course not. You didn't think for a moment that it would affect anyone other than yourself. If I hadn't been so quick to cover my shock I would have looked like a complete idiot on the tennis court."

"Really, I just wanted to surprise you. I didn't think you'd hear gossip about me in Florida."

"I can't believe you didn't tell me about these plans when you decided on them. You know, I have that mitral valve prolapse condition. Did you ever consider that surprising a woman my age could have tragic results?"

"Mom, please, you're in better shape than all of us. Why would seeing my face changed give you a heart attack?"

Sheila couldn't quite think of a reasonable answer.

"I just don't like being the last one in the world to learn important news about my own daughter."

"Well, it's too bad that it happened that way. But you'll see for yourself what all the talk is about when you get here next week."

"You think I'm waiting until next week? No Roxie, I've changed my flight plans, even though they did charge me a ridiculous amount. I'm arriving tomorrow afternoon at 1:48 p.m. at JFK. You'll pick me up at the airport."

Roxanne knew that at this point she had no choice. There was no stopping the Sheilanator when she had her mind made up. She wrote down all the flight information she needed to know, and by the time she hung up she felt a splitting headache coming on.

SIXTEEN

"WE'RE ALL GOING TO the airport to pick up Grandma tomorrow," Roxanne announced at the dinner table.

"What time?" asked Justin. "I have plans with J.J."

"Her plane comes in at 1:45. Kids, please rearrange your plans. I need you all there with me when Grandma comes in. You too, Ben."

"I didn't say a word," said Ben.

"Why do we have to come? It's boring to just drive to the airport in traffic," said Gabe.

Roxanne couldn't say aloud what she was thinking. She didn't want to be alone with her mother when Sheila first saw her. Sheila was so critical, she worried that she would find fault with her new looks and start in on her. With Ben and the kids around, she'd have them to act as a buffer. The more buffers Roxanne had, the better she felt.

"We'll go early and have pizza in the waiting area," Roxanne offered. Gabe and Justin would agree to anything if pizza were involved.

"I have to study for my biology midterm," said Allison. "I'm meeting Shelby in the library at noon."

"Fine, you go study with Shelby, but the rest of you are coming to the airport with me."

The boys looked at each other and shrugged. Pizza was pizza, after all.

Later, in bed, Ben reached under the covers and drew Roxanne to him. They had not made love since before the accident.

"Ben please, I'm too tense to enjoy myself," Roxanne said, trying to push him away.

"Rox, that's exactly why you do need to enjoy yourself. C'mon, it's time. It's way past time. Besides, your mother will be here tomorrow, and then I won't have a chance in hell until she's gone. Look, I got you a present." Ben reached under the bed and pulled out a box from Victoria's Secret. It held a sexy lace short nightie. "Why don't you try wearing this instead of that extra-extra-large tee-shirt from Allison's sweet sixteen?"

Roxanne took the box and looked at Ben, her resistance weakening. They'd had their differences in the past, but sex was never a problem area, considering the unavoidable cramp that raising three children had put on their love life throughout their marriage.

She took the box and went into the bathroom to make the change. The tags were still on and as she snipped them with the nail clipper, she felt as if she was cutting the strings that connected her to her pre-accident self.

Ben knew exactly how to touch Roxanne to get her in the mood, if she didn't make up her mind to resist. He'd prepped for it, too, with a shower and application of a new body lotion that smelled of honey and jasmine. (The bottle said it was an aphrodisiac, and Roxanne had to admit she did like the scent.) His fingers found her nipples through the lace bodice and gently traced the circles around and around. He kissed her neck and then moved to her lips, all the while working on her breasts and pressing his body against hers. Despite her initial reluctance, it did feel good.

As always, Ben was rock hard in an instant. He could be satisfied quickly if he wanted, but he was in no rush.

Instead, he concentrated on Roxanne's pleasure, alternating his caresses with gentle and firm pressure, and delighting in how responsive she could be when she didn't fight it. Her nipples hardened and her breathing got heavier. As Roxanne succumbed to the experience, her soft moans let Ben know he was hitting the right buttons. He slipped his fingers into the crotchless silk panties that had come with the nightie and cupped her behind. Somewhat impatiently pulling the panties off completely and moving to the front, he pushed into her slippery, wet lips and tickled ever so lightly.

Roxanne grasped his wrist and pushed his hand higher up inside of her. She was beyond the tickle phase and wanted to feel the friction of his strong hands rubbing her g-spot, wherever that was. She just figured whatever brought her to orgasm was enough of a g-spot for her.

Fully aroused, with all thoughts of Sheila banished from her head, Roxanne suddenly pushed Ben off of her, quickly rolled him over, and mounted on top of him. "Oh, you want to take the lead?" Ben commented, quite pleased with the turn of events. Her breasts hung down and she thrust one in Ben's mouth for him to suck on. She guided his penis inside her and arched her back to get the best sensation. Ben switched breasts—"don't want to neglect anyone"—he whispered, and then after a few seconds of sucking hard, pulled away and lifted his head to kiss her mouth. Kissing deeply, Roxanne climaxed and Ben followed, releasing his load with a deep sigh of pleasure.

Uncoupled, but snuggled with Roxanne's head resting on Ben's chest, they took deep breaths until their bodies returned to a state of calm. Roxanne stroked the curly hairs on Ben's chest. Ben smiled that "just had good sex smile," and started to drift off to sleep.

"So how does it feel to make love to a pretty woman?" Roxanne asked.

"Rox, I've been making love to a beautiful woman for 24 years."

"Who is she? I'll scratch her eyes out."

"Very funny. But seriously, I think tonight you finally believed you deserved to enjoy it as much as I do."

As she always did following sex—no matter how much she enjoyed it—Roxanne headed for the bathroom to clean up and put on fresh panties (all cotton, with crotch) and a minipad to catch the "love juice" that would trickle from her during the night. She was glad she had given in to Ben's urges. That would have to hold them until after Sheila's visit, and at this point it looked like it was going to be for longer than they had planned.

The next morning, Roxanne awoke first, well, second if you count Clarissa, who nipped at her toes demanding some fresh food and water. After feeding the cat and taking in the newspaper, Roxanne put up water for tea and logged on to the computer to check her email. She was surprised to see an email from "harriedmom." She hadn't heard from Ricki in over a year. They hadn't actually seen one another in about ten years.

> *"Hey, what's new? I just got off the phone with Jenny and we're both coming in for New Year's to see the parents. Please say you'll make time to get together with us. We can do a "Thickhead Three" thing just like in high school. Only now we can legally drink! We were thinking that it would be great to leave the kids and husbands behind and take a hotel room in the city for a night, we'll be in town until January 4th, and Jenny and I can do it on January 2nd. We need you. Will you do it? Say yes! Love, Ricki."*

Roxanne read the email three times before she could think about replying. Jenny and Ricki were her closest friends throughout junior high and high school. They had shared their feelings on everything, and were always there for one another in times of trouble, disappointment, or just a bad hair day. Attending different colleges had moved the relationship from one of daily support to long-distance phone calls, and more recently to emails, but through college, marriage, Ricki's relocation to L.A., Jenny's move to Chicago, and motherhood (a total of nine children between them), their friendship had remained intact. Even though they had not been corresponding for the past year or so, Roxanne knew it was simply due to the overwhelming demands they each met in working and parenting.

She had often thought of how Ricki and Jenny would react to her new looks. But something had held her back from making the phone calls to her friends. At first, she was too incapacitated and in too much pain to think about calling them. Later, as they began the process of reshaping her looks she wanted to call, but couldn't quite get up the nerve. *Would her friends still feel the same way about her? Would they be happy for her or jealous of her new beauty and windfall wealth?* Now, in less than two weeks, she would find out.

SEVENTEEN

As ROXANNE POURED HERSELF a cup of tea she noticed her hand was shaking. She looked up at the clock. It was 7:42 a.m. and Sheila would be landing at JFK in just about five hours. The way she was feeling called for desperate measures. She got out her Filofax and looked up the phone number that Ann had given her "in case of emergency." She had never used it before. She went into the den, closed the door, and made the call.

"Ann, hi, it's Roxanne Thornton."

"Roxanne, what's wrong. Just a minute, let me take this call downstairs, my husband is still sleeping.

"Oh, I'm so sorry to wake you. Forget it, go back to sleep."

"No, no, tell me what's going on."

"Sheila is flying in today. She found out about my facial reconstruction from one of her tennis partners and she's changed her flight to today. I thought I'd be able to handle this when she came next week, but I'm actually feeling kind of sick. You know, faint, nauseous. Maybe I'm coming down with something."

"You are. It's called judgmental, critical, mother syndrome. Okay, Roxanne, let's go through it. What is your true fear?"

"I guess you could say I'm a textbook case of conflicted

emotions. I'm scared that she will react negatively to my surgery, but I'm also scared she'll react positively."

"Okay," said Ann. "Being scared of a negative reaction is understandable. What do you fear from a positive reaction?"

"We've talked about this a lot. My mother never hid her disappointment with my looks. She was always trying to change me, while my sister Grace was considered perfect just the way she was."

"So what will you feel if she likes your new looks?"

"I know that if she makes a big fuss I'm going to resent it. Growing up I got good grades, never got into trouble, followed her rules, and still she would look at me as if I were a stain on her blouse. It really didn't matter what I achieved. In her eyes, if a girl isn't pretty she's just a loser."

"Do you believe that you were a loser before the surgery?"

"Only in my own mother's eyes. Otherwise I think I've done pretty well."

"I would say so," Ann said emphatically. "You have a wonderful family, a great marriage, and you've been successful in your career. Now, you've gotten the courage to pursue the acting experience you've always wanted. You should be very proud of yourself."

"It sounds reasonable when you say it. But I still dread seeing her face when she sees me for the first time."

"Roxanne, do you think that your mother loves you?"

"Oh sure, she loves me."

"But she's always paid too much attention to your outward appearance and kind of taken your accomplishments for granted, right?"

"That's right."

"Then my professional advice as your therapist is to just say to yourself, 'Screw her.'"

"Screw her. That's it?" Roxanne wanted more.

"All your life you've felt that people have treated you

poorly because you haven't met society's standards of beauty, isn't that true?"

"Yes."

"Well, now you're meeting those standards and perhaps you will find that you are treated differently by strangers."

"Actually, I'm seeing a little of that already," Roxanne said, wanting to elaborate.

"Fine." Ann cut in. "But you should never have had to meet any standards of beauty to receive unconditional love from your own mother. As a mother of three children don't you agree?"

"Yes, but…"

"So, I say 'Screw her.' If she loves your new looks, that's great, if she finds fault, well, what else is new?"

"Thanks, I'll try to keep that in mind. I think that's what I needed to hear."

"Roxanne, I hope you enjoy your mother's visit. But if that doesn't happen, don't let it upset you too much. You really don't need her approval to be a success."

"Well, okay," Roxanne wasn't completely convinced. "Thanks very much Ann. I'll let you go back to sleep. Please tell your husband I'm sorry I woke him."

EIGHTEEN

For once, Sheila's plane was right on time. Roxanne, Ben, Gabe, and Justin finished the rather substandard pizza and went down to the baggage claim area to meet Sheila. It was always easy to tell when the flight from Florida came in at Christmastime. The travelers had that brown leather-like Florida skin (to go with their alligator shoes) and most of them were inadequately dressed for the cold. Many of them, like Sheila, relied on their families and friends to greet them with winter coats and snow boots.

Roxanne clutched the down parka she had brought for Sheila, holding it in front of her body like a shield. The hood's fake fur trim tickled her chin, providing further protection from Sheila's sharp eyes.

Roxanne saw her first. She had the same reaction she always did—surprise at how small Sheila looked. Although she had once been the same height as Roxanne—five-feet one inch—she had shrunk to the point that at 75, she was four-eleven if she stood perfectly straight. Now, she was walking through the airport as quickly as her legs could carry her. Her head turned back and forth searching for her family.

"Hi Grandma," Gabe ran up to greet her and give her a hug.

"Gabe, you're getting so big," she said. "Here, take

Grandma's suitcase," she said handing him her carry-on on with wheels that weighed as much as he did. Sheila packed the regulation size bag with all the essentials she would need for a week just in case the airline lost her luggage. She hated being left unprepared.

Roxanne pushed Justin forward. "Go ahead, go see Grandma," she urged him. Instead of going with him, Roxanne headed for the luggage carousel with Sheila's flight number and began searching for luggage, regardless of the fact that she had no idea what it looked like.

"ROXANNE, ROXANNE," Sheila called. "Where are you? Let me see you," she demanded.

"Hey Mom, how was your flight," she said, giving her a quick hug.

Sheila took a step back. "Let me see you."

"Oh my," she said, "Roxanne!"

"Mom, keep it down. People are beginning to stare at us."

"I'm sorry," Sheila was never one to make a scene. "I think I could have passed you right by if it weren't for Ben and the boys." She stared at Roxanne, taking in all the changes—the nose, the chin, the cheeks, and especially those great Dr. Moscowitz eyebrows. Finally, she smiled widely. It was clear that she liked what she saw. She looked at Roxanne, not as if she were seeing a stain on her good blouse. She looked at Roxanne as if she was seeing…Grace. "Wow, if your father could see you now."

"*He* wouldn't care," Roxanne said, without thinking.

"What are you talking about? Of course he'd care."

"Not the way you care."

"Well, no one loves you like a mother, dear." Sheila was clueless about Roxanne's intimations.

"Oh, there's my suitcase, the one with the pink ribbon attached," Sheila exclaimed. "Ben, can you grab it?"

Ben took both suitcases and lifted them onto a luggage

cart. Roxanne wrapped her mother in the down parka and rushed everyone out of the baggage area.

"C'mon mom, there's going to be traffic. Let's get home."

"Where's Allison?" Sheila asked after they were all settled in the minivan. "Is she too old to pick up Grandma at the airport?"

"She's studying for midterms. I'm sure she would have come with us if you'd taken your original flight. But next week she has to get through four tests before she can enjoy being on vacation."

"Well, don't worry, I won't get in her way," Sheila snipped.

"I wasn't saying you would…"

Roxanne leaned back in her seat and let Sheila's steady stream of conversation flow around her. It didn't require more than a few "reallys?" "oh, that's too bad," and "uh huhs" and "yeahs" to keep Sheila going without interruption. As always, she had a comment and opinion on everything and everyone that crossed her path. When the car turned onto their block, Sheila said, "Wow, the goyim have really gone all out this year. There must have been a sale on lights at Harrow's. Are you still the only Jews on your block?"

"There are a few other Jewish families, Mom," Roxanne replied.

"Well, I told you that before you bought the house. Check out the neighborhood in December if you want to know who your neighbors are."

"It's really not an issue Mom, we've been here for 15 years."

"Oh, Roxanne, I decided that since I came earlier, I would change my ticket going home, too. There's going to be a special New Year's party at the clubhouse and my canasta group was all very disappointed that I wasn't going. They're sharing a table with a men's poker group.

"Oh, so you mean you have a date?" Roxanne smiled.

"Ha, those men should be so lucky. No, no we're just all going together, but the girls really wanted me there with them, so I changed my ticket to go back on December 28."

"That's fine, mom. I actually have some interesting plans for after New Years. I'm getting together with my high school friends Ricki and Jenny."

"The one who married the doctor and the one who married the teacher?"

"Right, well Ricki's husband is actually a college dean, but yes, that's them."

"Wait until they see you," Sheila said. "They are going to flip."

"Yeah, or something," Roxanne mumbled.

Since Sheila was now visiting while the kids still had school (unlike Roxanne's original plan), they found themselves at home alone together Monday morning. Throughout the weekend, the kids had served to distract Sheila from concentrating heavily on Roxanne's transformation, but now, after the school buses left, Roxanne and Sheila were face to face sipping a second cup of tea and sharing a bagel.

"I just can't get over it," Sheila began. "It's absolutely amazing what doctors can do these days."

"Actually, every time I look in the mirror, I'm afraid that my old face will come back."

"Don't be silly, that's not going to happen. And that doctor did such a great job. Your skin looks lovely, not all pulled tight like you can't blink the way they did your father's cousin Selma."

"I know, Mom," Roxanne wanted to explain how she felt. She knew in her head that the changes would remain, but her heart still felt unsure of her new appearance, and her "inner child," the one that those pop psychologists said that no one could ever escape, still carried that same inferiority complex she always had.

"So tell me, what have people been saying when they first see you? I'll bet you're shocking a lot of people."

"Well, I really haven't been out that much. I guess the people who have seen me have been pretty complimentary."

"Well, wait until your sister sees you. Did I tell you she and Ira and the kids can come out for Chanukah?"

"What, they're coming here? We didn't discuss this, Mom."

"Well, I decided that I just don't have the strength to divide myself up between the two of you anymore. I asked Grace to bring her family for dinner and I promised to make my famous latkes—we'll have to get potatoes and matza meal. They're coming on the third night, that's next Sunday. I'm putting them up at the Holiday Inn, so you don't have to be inconvenienced. We'll have to get some gifts for you to give Emily and Carrie, but we have plenty of time."

Roxanne felt the beginnings of a panic attack and forced herself to breathe slowly before speaking. She had heard from Grace a few times after the accident, but her sister's questions were kept to a brief obligatory inquiry about her recovery, and Roxanne kept her answers to equally short updates on her physical condition. They really hadn't had a meaningful conversation since before Dad died. Grace had been out of the country on vacation when his fatal heart attack occurred and she had not made it home in time for the funeral. On the third day of shiva she finally showed up and, in Roxanne's opinion, had taken grieving to a whole new level, remonstrating so dramatically that the friends and family who had come to visit would all gather around her. Didn't they see that her tan was fresh, that she'd spent the past three days on the beach in Bermuda instead of with Sheila and Roxanne? But then, nobody ever thought badly of the beautiful Grace. She'd been able to get away with anything her entire life.

"So how's your ankle? Are you still getting the cast off tomorrow?" Sheila broke into Roxanne's thoughts in an attempt to change the subject.

"Umm, yes, that's what the doctor promised. But Mom, about Grace, I don't really think I'm up to having them. Maybe Passover…"

"Roxanne," Sheila took on her sternest tone. "Life is short. I would think that after that accident you would have realized that life is too short to hold grudges. I'm not going to be around forever and I hate to think that when I'm gone the only thing you and your sister will discuss is who's going to get the silver."

"But…"

"I'm here to do all the work. You can still relax and recover after they take off the cast tomorrow. I want to see my two beautiful daughters together. Is that too much to ask?"

Sheila's words felt like a prizefighter's punch to her stomach. *Now she had two beautiful daughters? What did she have before, Beauty and the Beast?* She forced herself to think of Ann's advice: *Screw her, screw her, screw her.*

"Fine, whatever you want."

Roxanne knew she couldn't prevent the inevitable. Now that Sheila had seen Roxanne's face for herself and was satisfied with her daughter's new looks, she began to devise plans for a "coming out" party for Roxanne.

"I was talking to my cousin Frieda and she and Arthur are going to be in town. They're staying with Lydia and Hal and they'd love to see me and you and the kids. Is it okay if they stop by on Sunday for dessert? That way they can see Grace's family too?" Sheila said trying to sound nonchalant.

The next day while Ben took Roxanne to the doctor to have her cast removed, Sheila added more names to the list. "Phyllis and Stu are in to see their grandchildren and they said they could make it for dessert on Sunday too. Oh, and your father's cousins Cyd and Sid said they would try to make it too, and they're going to bring Nana Sadie."

Nana Sadie? Roxanne could hardly believe it. *They were taking her late father's mother out of the home just so she could see Roxanne's new face before she died?*

"Mom, how many people are you inviting to my house?" Roxanne asked, her voice traveling up an octave.

"Don't worry yourself. I already called the bakery and put in an order for cakes, pies, cookies, and pastries. It's just dessert. You won't have to do a thing, just make coffee."

Ben stared at his mother-in-law with an expression on his face that was rarely used. Voicing an objection at this point was futile. Ben very rarely raised his voice, so when he did, he actually got the attention of his family.

"Now wait a minute," he said loudly. Roxanne and Sheila turned to see what he had to say.

"Can I ask one favor?" he said.

"What is it dear?" Sheila asked ever so sweetly.

"No more. What is it the kids say? Gates closed. Not one more person invited, okay?"

"Nothing like closing the barn door after the horse is gone," said Roxanne sarcastically.

"Rox, I'm sorry, but it's the best I can do at this point. Why don't you go upstairs and soak the ankle like the doctor suggested? Maybe it will be fun," he said with no conviction.

NINETEEN

Sᴜɴᴅᴀʏ ᴍᴏʀɴɪɴɢ Rᴏxᴀɴɴᴇ ᴘᴇᴇᴋᴇᴅ at the alarm clock. Seven a.m. She pulled the covers over her head and tried to block out the fact that in six hours or less her sister would be there, and then, a few hours later the house would begin to fill up with relatives and old friends of the family.

Think of something else, think of something else, she ordered herself, but it was no use, she couldn't think of anything else, and she couldn't fall back asleep. *Might as well get up and use the bathroom in peace while everyone is still asleep,* she decided.

Still groggy, she brushed her teeth and then threw some cool water on her face. She looked into the mirror and said aloud, "Well face, ready or not, they're coming for you." She was still getting used to having this pretty face look back at her each morning, and she wasn't quite fully connected to it being Roxanne. For her entire life, the reflection in the mirror had been something she had avoided. She'd check to see if her part was straight, smooth on her makeup, and then get away from the mirror as soon as possible. She had hated looking at uneven skin, a nose with not one, but two bumps, a long chin that was too pointed, and cheeks that seemed sunken even when she tried applying blush. This new face held her gaze. *It's so strange,* she thought. *I still have two green eyes, a nose, a mouth, a chin, and they're all still there together forming my face, but some reshaping, some removal of a little fatty tissue and cartilage, and the tightening of a few muscles have created a face that is so much more pleasing to the eye.*

There are an infinite number of different faces, she mused, *but everyone knows which ones are the good-looking ones. They say it's all about symmetry.* She took a closer look at her reflection in the mirror. *Am I more symmetrical now,* she wondered? *Shit, I'd better get my symmetrical self into the shower before Sheila gets up and wants to use the bathroom.*

Dressing for the day presented more than the usual challenges. Roxanne wanted to look good, but not so good that it looked like she was trying to look good. It was a holiday, but it was casual. Chanukah was a casual holiday. You didn't dress up like the Christians did for Christmas. Still, she was the hostess of this get-together, even though it was gotten together without her input. "Got it!" she said aloud, actually pleased with her choice. Black velvet pants and a royal blue ultra-soft sweater. Blue for Israel, even, she thought. Because it was at her house, she could wear her black velvet slippers with the blue and pink flowers—a perfect match to tie the two colors together.

She dressed to the sound of Ben's snores and wished she could let him sleep longer. However, she was no martyr. She needed him awake and useful. She anticipated having to send him out for a last-minute shopping trip. She also wanted him done with their bathroom so she could straighten it up for company.

"Ben," she said softly, caressing his hair. She was glad he still had a full head of hair. So many of their male friends were bald or balding. Ben's hair was mostly still dark, with gray on the sides. "Honey, time to get up. I can't do this without you."

Ben rolled over and stretched his arms over his head with a big yawn. "What time is it?"

"It's almost eight."

"And I really have to get up now?" he asked, already knowing the answer.

Roxanne sighed. "Please, Ben, I'm pretty freaked out now. If you love me you'll be as helpful as you possibly can."

"Okay, okay. I'm getting up." Ben rose and grabbed his bathrobe. "Is the bathroom free?"

"It's all yours."

A loud clatter came from the kitchen. Sheila was trying to rearrange all the pots and pans in logical, size-order.

"Good morning," she said. "I don't know how you find anything in this kitchen. Is that what you're wearing dear?"

"Good morning Mom," Roxanne decided to ignore all other remarks.

Yesterday, they had purchased all the ingredients for today's dinner. Sheila had made the pot roast last night. (It's better the next day, she explained, and this way we just have to heat it up and can make the latkes fresh.) Sheila had also peeled the potatoes the night before, keeping them covered with salted water so they wouldn't turn black. She had agreed to use the food processor to make the potato, egg, and matza meal mixture. Roxanne's dad had been the official potato grater when she and her sister were kids and ever since his death latkes made her a little sad. Her father had always used the hand grater. It was his once-a-year kitchen stint. "My fingernails are the secret ingredient," he would always joke.

"Everything is set for the latkes. I'm not going to fry them until everyone's here," said Sheila. "We can set the table, now, though."

Roxanne set the table with her good china. The centerpiece was the menorah Allison had made at a Jewish Youth Group camping weekend a few years before. She put the three candles plus the Shamos in their holders. There, that looks very cozy, she thought.

Presents for the nieces were wrapped and ready, stowed with the presents for Allison, Justin, and Gabe. Adults didn't exchange Chanukah gifts in Roxanne's family, just those Christmas stockings, which Sheila had made certain were thoroughly hidden from any visitor's prying eyes.

Actually, Ben had bought Roxanne one Chanukah gift. Not only did he know Roxanne would like it; he also knew that it would irk Sheila in just the right way to further please Roxanne. He pushed the button on it now to set it in motion.

The little Roomba vacuum robot happily beep-beeped and then set off on its course around the kitchen, dining room, and living room. Roxanne loved watching it pick up dust and dirt without her having to do anything but get the electric cords out of the way. Sheila sneered at the cute little machine with utter disdain.

"That thing doesn't really clean anything does it?" she asked in more of a challenge than a question.

"Sure it does," said Roxanne, catching Ben's eye, and sharing a smile with him.

By one o'clock the kids were all getting impatient.

"When is Aunt Grace getting here?" asked Gabe for the third time.

"Gabe, you know Aunt Grace is always late. She operates in her own private time zone," Roxanne said, making sure Sheila could hear her.

"Gabe, they probably hit traffic," said Sheila. "I'm sure they'll be here soon."

At 1:47 the doorbell rang. Emily and Ashley burst through the door first and Sheila was waiting for them with open arms.

"Sheyna maidelas," she said hugging them both to her. "Oh my, you're getting so big."

Six-year-old identical twins Emily and Ashley giggled. "Oh Grandma, you always say that," said one.

"We're still the smallest ones in the whole first grade," added the other.

"Well. You must have a first grade full of giants in your school," Sheila declared.

Allison was delighted to see her little cousins. "Hi sweeties," she squealed to them. "Want to come up to my room and play with my Beanie Babies?"

The girls were off in a flash, and Justin and Gabe followed shortly. Roxanne watched them run up the stairs, and when she turned around, Grace was walking in laden down with packages. She was quickly swallowed up in Sheila's arms.

"Hey Ira, good to see you," Ben and Ira shook hands in their semi-friendly, we're in-the-same-boat-here, brother-in-law fashion. "Can I get you a drink?" Ben asked.

"Sure, Stoli and tonic?"

"Do you think you could slum it with a little Absolut?"

"Great, great, I hope I'm not drinking alone," said Ira.

"Not a chance," said Ben, and set about fixing stiff drinks for the both of them.

When Sheila got through hugging Grace and Ira, she pulled Roxanne over, who had suddenly become very interested in pruning one of her houseplants.

"So, would you recognize your own sister?" Sheila said, gripping both of Roxanne's shoulders. "Did I lie or is she stunning now?"

"Mom, cut it out," Roxanne said pulling away.

"No, you're right Mom," said Grace, looking her up and down with a deadpan expression on her face. "Roxanne, that doctor certainly did a job on you. You really had a lot done."

"Drinks ladies, drinks," Ben hastily decided that Roxanne and Grace needed the vodka tonics more than he and Ira. He placed the drinks in their hands, and ran back to the bar to fix three more.

"So, Mom tells me you got a big settlement from the accident and quit your job," Grace said.

"Well, I decided I'd take some time off to explore other career options. I'm not sure what I'm going to do next."

"Oh, I thought Mom said you were planning on making it big in show biz?"

Roxanne gritted her teeth. Grace always made light of her interest in theater. She was not about to discuss her plans with her sister. "No, not really. I just signed up for some acting classes for fun. The schedule worked out well and it doesn't interfere with any of the kids' things.

"That sounds more reasonable," Grace agreed ever so irritatingly. "I thought Sheila was exaggerating a bit," she said softly.

"So, how bout those latkes," Ben intervened again. "Honey, can I do anything to help?"

"No, no Ben, I've got it all under control," said Sheila. "You just be the wonderful host and entertain our guests."

There was so much wrong with those two sentences, Roxanne felt as if her head would explode. *There is no control here. Ben never signed on to be the host. Who was Sheila including in "our," this was still Roxanne's home, and finally, her sister didn't exactly fit her definition of "guest." Unwanted interloper was more on the money.*

"Mommy, Mommy, Allison said we could keep these," Emily and Ashley ran downstairs, each clutching two Beanie Babies.

"Oh, aren't you lucky to have such a generous cousin," said Grace. "Allison, these will probably be their favorite Chanukah gifts, thank you."

Despite her resentment toward her sister, Roxanne couldn't help but melt in the presence of her twin nieces. Emily and Ashley were right out of central casting. Their shoulder-length auburn hair gleamed and the ends curled up in sweet, natural waves. Their bright blue eyes and button noses topped perfect little lips that were always grinning. *They were incredibly delightful and Grace didn't deserve such treasures for a minute,* Roxanne thought.

"Hey, I haven't gotten my hugs yet," Roxanne said to the twins. "Don't you have a hug for Aunt Roxanne?"

"Are you the new Aunt Roxanne?" asked Emily.

"Mommy said we were getting a new Aunt Roxanne," added Ashley. "What happened to the old one?"

"No, no it's still me, I'm really the same Aunt Roxanne, I just look a little different," Roxanne said, laughing.

"I think it's a lot different," said Emily.

"Yeah, you don't have that bumpy nose anymore," Ashley said, looking at her intently.

"And your smile is different," said Emily. "And you used to have different colors in your face. It's all one color now. But your hair's the same."

"Well, that's right," said Roxanne. "I had some changes made because I got hurt in an accident. When the doctor was fixing me up, I asked him to make me better than before."

"You look more like Mommy," said Emily. "You still don't look like twins like us, but you look more like sisters now, right Mommy? Doesn't Aunt Roxanne look more like you now?"

All eyes turned to Grace. How would she react to having her territory as "the pretty one" encroached upon?

"Well, I don't know about that, babies, but Aunt Roxanne does look very nice with her new face." Grace was getting noticeably uncomfortable, and she quickly excused herself to use the bathroom.

Ira, sensing they might be getting into dangerous territory, tried to change the subject. "And your Aunt Roxanne is still the best cook in the family. Dinner smells great."

"Aunt Roxanne, can you still do everything you could do before the new face?" asked Emily.

"Sure, honey. Why, what is it you're thinking of?"

"Chocolate malteds!" Emily and Ashley said together. "You always made the best chocolate malteds," said Emily.

"And I still do," Roxanne laughed again. "Two Aunt Roxanne Special Malteds coming up."

"Hey Mom, what are we, chopped liver?" asked Gabe. "Can you make it five?"

By the time the malteds were poured, dinner was ready and everyone sat down together at the dining room table. Focusing on the kids instead of her sister allowed Roxanne to get through the meal, and before she was quite ready, the second wave of guests arrived for dessert. The bakery had delivered that morning, and Roxanne and Sheila were putting everything out when the door swung open.

"Happy Chanukah…" sang out cousin Cydelle. Her husband Sidney followed with Nana Sadie.

Sheila rushed past Roxanne to greet them.

"Cyd, Sid, how good to see you. And how are you Sadie, you're looking well," she said loudly into the old woman's ear.

"Ach how good could I be?" Nana Sadie said. "I'm alive, that's more than the doctors expected last year."

No sooner had they taken off their coats, than Phyllis and Stu arrived. Freida, Arthur, Lydia, and Hal were right behind them. The guests filed in as if they owned the place. Allison, Justin, and Gabe were loaded down with coats and hats, which they then surreptitiously dumped in the laundry room on top of the washer and dryer.

"Roxanne, is that really you?" Phyllis was the first to make the comment.

"Darling, you look wonderful," said Freida.

"A little too thin," added Nana Sadie.

"Sadie, don't be silly, you can never be too rich or too thin, right?" said Cyd. "And with that huge settlement our Roxanne is now both, right, right?"

"You know who she looks like?" posed Freida. "Marlo Thomas."

"That Girl?" questioned her husband.

"No, not then, after she married Phil Donohue."

"I think she looks like that actress, the one who was married to Neil Simon," said Phyllis.

"Marsha Mason!" exclaimed Cyd. "I can see the resemblance, but still, that's not who I would say she really looks like.

"I know," said Grace, who all of a sudden decided to take part in this discussion with the older generation. "She looks like Valerie Harper."

"You mean Rhoda?" asked Stu.

"Yes, but not when she was on Mary Tyler Moore, when she had her own show," Grace clarified.

"That makes sense," declared Sheila. "She was real frumpy when she was in Minneapolis, but when she got to New York she was very attractive. Just like Roxanne."

"Thanks a lot, Mom," said Roxanne in her most sarcastic tone.

"What? What did I say?" Sheila looked at Roxanne, who turned away from her. "I just call it like I see it," she said and shrugged. "Sadie, come sit down. Let me get you a nice piece of chocolate cake."

The guests took that as a signal to hone in on the dessert table. Taking generous helpings of everything that appealed to them, the adults gathered around the dining room table. The kids were relegated to the kitchen where their own selection of goodies was set up. Allison was put in charge of the twins.

Conversation stopped for a time as everyone dug into their selections of baked goods. When their initial gluttony was satisfied, Cyd broke the silence.

"This is so nice," said Cyd. "Roxanne, thank you so much for having us. Sheila, you certainly know how to put together a great party, right, right? I shouldn't eat like this but…"

"Oh, it's a holiday," Freida interrupted. "And how often do we all get to see each other like this? As far as I'm concerned, everything here is fat-free and sugar-free and I don't want to hear anything otherwise."

"Well you never have to worry about that anyway, mom," said her daughter, Lydia. "I don't know why I couldn't get your skinny genes. This is all going directly to my thighs."

"Just more of you to love, dear," said her husband, Hal. "Enjoy yourself, like your mom said, it's a holiday."

"I only wish Dad were here," said Grace.

Roxanne felt the tips of her ears turn red hot in response to Grace's statement. Up until then she had been handling having Grace in her home by concentrating on the present and trying to forget about the past.

"Yeah, sure you do," Roxanne said snidely.

"What's that supposed to mean?" Grace was not about to let that comment pass.

"Girls, girls we're all having a good time here," said Sheila. "Let's try not to be sad. We all miss Jack."

"Ach, my poor Jackie," Nana Sadie moaned. "So young, too young. Remember how he loved to make the latkes?"

That seemed to be too much for Grace to hear. She burst into tears, and then moved away to the sofa. Sheila followed and sat down close beside her.

"She's so sensitive," said Sheila. "She loved Jack so much, she still can't talk about him."

"She is full of crap!" Roxanne shouted.

Freida and Arthur, Lydia and Hal, Phyllis and Stu, Cyd and Sid all stopped eating, their forks in mid-air. Ira dropped his chocolate-covered matza, and Ben coughed up a piece of mandel bread, which went flying across the table.

"What did she say?" asked Nana Sadie.

"I said, Nana, that Grace is full of crap," Roxanne repeated, rising out of her chair.

"Roxanne!" Sheila raised her voice, too. "What's the matter with you? Ben, is she still on medication? Could she be having a reaction?"

Ben stood up and put his arm around Roxanne. "The reaction has nothing to do with medication. Roxanne is reacting to Grace's typical play for attention."

"Ben! I'm surprised at you," Sheila said.

"Sorry, I just call it like I see it," said Ben.

"Thanks honey, I can handle it from here," said Roxanne, more calmly now. "Excuse my language folks, but I've had enough of Grace's 'pity me act' whenever Dad is mentioned. When we were at the cemetery, Grace stayed on the beach at Bermuda! Where were her tears then?"

"Daddy wouldn't have wanted me to cancel my vacation," Grace sniffed.

"It's not about what Daddy would have wanted. Sure, Dad would have sat up in his coffin and said, 'Don't worry about me, just get a good tan,' but that's not the point. You could have shown the respect he deserved and some consideration for your mother for that matter, and put someone besides yourself first for once in your life!"

"Well, it's not always so easy to change a flight," said Freida, hoping that practical matters might help diffuse the tension.

"That's true, we had such a hard time getting a flight home early from Disney World when Freida's mother was rushed to the hospital with appendicitis," added Arthur.

"Yeah, but you *did* get home," said Roxanne triumphantly. "You cut your vacation short for Freida's mother's illness. But Grace couldn't be bothered when our father *died*."

Roxanne's words painted a vivid image for all the relatives. They remembered the funeral too, and at the time, many words had been whispered about Grace's absence. The room was silent, except for Grace's sniffling.

Freida and Arthur, Lydia and Hal, Phyllis and Stu, Cyd and Sid exchanged looks and nudges. At once, they all got up and went into the kitchen.

"Allison, dear," said Lydia. "We've got to get going. Where did you put our coats?"

Hastily buttoning up, the group went back into the dining room. Sid held out his hand to Nana Sadie. "Come Sadie, it's time to go," he said.

"But I didn't finish my cookies," she protested.

"I'll wrap it up for you," offered Ben. He grabbed one of the empty bakery boxes and filled it up with cookies and pastries. "Here you go, bring these back for your friends."

"Ach, half of them are too senile to enjoy it, and the others are on restricted diets," said Nana. "But I'll give some to the nice nurses. Thank you, Ben."

"Roxanne, we have to go now," said Freida, speaking for the group. "Thank you for a lovely party. And congratulations on your new face. Doesn't she look lovely?"

"Oh yes, yes," the relatives all agreed.

"Now no more accidents, dear," said Phyllis. "You stay away from buses."

As they edged down the path, careful not to step on any ice, Cyd commented, "Funerals and weddings. These are the two situations that cause the greatest tension for families right, right? I've seen more enemies made at funerals and weddings than anywhere else, right?"

"You know, dear, you're absolutely right," agreed her husband, Sid.

When the guests were gone, Sheila turned on Roxanne with venom.

"I hope you enjoyed humiliating me like that," she said. "Never was I so ashamed of my own daughter."

Roxanne took a deep breath, and remembering Ann's advice she said, "Mom, you've been ashamed of me my whole life. What's the big deal now?"

TWENTY

SHEILA DECIDED TO SPEND the rest of the week with Grace and her family. She hastily packed her things and retreated with them to the Holiday Inn. "I can't take this kind of conflict at my age," she declared. "I've got a mitral valve condition. I'll switch my flight to Newark so that Grace and Ira can take me to the airport."

"Right, we wouldn't want them to have to travel out of their way," Roxanne said sarcastically.

Later, in bed, Roxanne kept going over the scene line by line with Ben. "And can you believe she had the nerve to start crying over Daddy?" she fumed.

"Your sister will never change," Ben sympathized. "If she's not the center of attention, she'll do anything to get there. You do realize of course, that your outburst will be the topic of conversation for months and months. It will probably make it all the way to your distant cousins in California."

"I know. Well, there's nothing I can do about that now. Do you think they'll at least spread the word about how good I look?"

"I think you can count on that. I'm sure they'll report every detail."

Roxanne and Ben spent New Year's Eve keeping their own, personal tradition. Eschewing parties or expensive restaurant feasts, they cooked their own lobsters, opened a bottle of champagne, and watched the ball fall in Times Square. Allison was invited to sleep over a friend's house, but the boys stayed home, and the four of them played a very competitive game of Monopoly.

On New Year's Day Roxanne could hardly sit still for a moment, thinking about her reunion plans with Ricki and Jenny. In order to prepare them, she had sent the following email:

> *"Hi. I'd love to see you both on January 2nd.*
> *I booked us a room at the Marriott Marquis.*
> *You may not recognize me at first. I haven't*
> *spoken to either of you in a long time. In*
> *September I had an encounter with a school*
> *bus that pretty much squashed my face. Well,*
> *there was no way I was going to have them*
> *put me back the same as I was before, so I had*
> *a bit of reconstruction done. I look different,*
> *but it's still the same old Roxanne underneath.*
> *I'll meet you both in the hotel lobby at 7:00*
> *p.m.*
>
> *Love,*
> *Roxanne"*

Roxanne changed outfits about seven times getting ready for her reunion with Ricki and Jenny. Again, it was a case of wanting to look good, but not so good that they'd think she was conceited or trying to impress them. The safest way to go seemed to be once again velvet pants, but this time she opted for a silk top that better showed off her weight loss, which she had been so careful to maintain. While she was getting ready,

Allison came into her room. It was rare that the sixteen-year-old initiated conversations with her.

"Hey Mom, are you excited about seeing your old friends?"

"I'm excited and a little nervous. I'm not sure how they'll react to my new face."

"Well, you haven't seen them in ten years, right?"

"Yes"

"In ten years everyone can expect to change. So instead of looking older, you just look a little better, right? Is it that big a deal?"

"Not when you put it like that," admitted Roxanne.

"I can't imagine what my friends will look like when we're middle aged."

"Hey, go easy. I prefer the term 'mature adult'."

"The great thing is that you're getting together. I'm sure it'll be sick."

"Sick?"

"That's sick in the good sense of the word. It'll be great."

"Thanks, honey."

"Oh, and Mom,"

"Yes?"

"How long are you going to be fighting with Grandma and Aunt Grace? I know you don't like them much but I like having more family around."

"Oh Allison, I don't dislike them. I love them. But I got to the explosion point with them. I've already spoken to Grandma and she's pretty much over it. She'll keep it in her arsenal of things to hold over my head. We'll call this one: 'The time I humiliated her in front of the cousins.' But we'll be as fine as we ever were. Grace and I will get past this. I'll give her a call soon."

"Promise, New Year's resolution? Make up with your sister?"

Roxanne looked at Allison and thought, *who's the mother*

here? How did my kid get so wise? She hugged Allison close and said, "I promise. Thanks Allison, now I'd better finish putting on my makeup and get going."

At 6:48 p.m. Roxanne arrived at the Marriott Marquis. Clutching her purse and a small overnight bag, she went to the reservations desk to check in.

"I have a reservation for Thornton," she said.

"Very good ma'am, just a moment. How many keys will you need?"

"Three," said Roxanne.

"That's the THICKHEAD THREE!" shouted Jenny and Ricki, sneaking up behind Roxanne.

"Oh my God!" Roxanne spun around and the three friends fell into a jumping, squealing three-way hug, which was looked upon with both amusement and disdain by the other travelers in the lobby.

"Room 303, just sign here," said the clerk.

Finally relaxing the embrace, Jenny held Roxanne at arm's length.

"Wow," she said.

"Yeah, wow," said Ricki a little less jubilantly than Jenny had. "You said you'd had some reconstruction but… I guess I didn't know what to expect."

Roxanne blushed deeply. "Yeah, modern medicine and all that. What do you want to do? Shall we go up to the room?"

"Yes, definitely," said Jenny. "We've got a lot to talk about."

They stepped aboard a waiting elevator together and then started talking all at once.

"You look fantastic," said Jenny.

"Jenny, you've lost weight, haven't you?" said Roxanne.

"This is going to be so much fun," said Ricki. "I have a special surprise for you guys."

After fiddling around with the card key, they entered the

luxurious hotel room. There were two queen-size beds made up with overstuffed comforters and four pillows on each bed.

"I call the single," said Ricki. "You two can share."

Roxanne and Jenny looked at each other knowing they'd once again been beaten by Ricki's quick wit and tongue. Ricki was always the one to lead the way for the three of them, and it looked like now would be no exception.

Just then someone knocked on the door. "Room service," said a voice.

"We didn't order room service," said Jenny cautiously. Turning to her friends, she whispered, "You never know what scam people will use to rape and rob you in your hotel room."

"A Mr. Ben Thornton called and ordered champagne sent to this room," the voice explained.

Roxanne pulled open the door and the waiter entered pushing a cart with an ice bucket stuffed with a bottle of champagne, a plate of fresh chocolate-covered strawberries, and three crystal goblets. "Oh, wasn't that sweet of Ben!" she exclaimed.

"You certainly have Ben trained well," said Jenny. "This is amazing."

"This is a great way to start off the New Year," said Roxanne. "I can't believe we're all here together. It's, so, so great…" suddenly overcome with tears at the emotion she felt, Roxanne couldn't finish her sentence.

"Hey, don't cry," said Ricki.

"You haven't changed at all, have you?" said Jenny. "You're still the same sappy Roxanne."

"Well, the doctors couldn't do anything about that part of me," said Roxanne, wiping her eyes. "Sappy removal wasn't covered by insurance."

Ricki finished rummaging in her purse. "Look what I have," she said, holding up a joint. "When was the last time either one of you got high?"

"I can't believe you," said Jenny. "Where did you get that?"

"Hey, I live in a college town," said Ricki. "It's like the stuff grows on trees," she laughed loudly at her own joke.

Ricki found an ashtray and matches, lit the joint, and took a deep drag before passing it to Jenny. Jenny shrugged her shoulders, "just don't tell my kids," she said, and followed suit. Roxanne took her turn and held in the smoke for as long as she could.

"You know, I think this is just what I needed," she said, exhaling.

"Why is that?" asked Jenny, who was always the one who liked to examine everyone's feelings and hidden motivations. At the same time, she popped open the champagne and poured each of them a glass.

"To the Thickhead Three!" they said in unison. They clinked glasses and sipped the champagne enthusiastically.

After the joint had gone around three times, Roxanne said, "This stuff seems a lot stronger than it used to be, doesn't it?"

"It is stronger," Ricki explained. "That's why we shouldn't let our kids get their hands on it. The stuff we smoked as kids was much milder than what they're selling now. Remember how we used to pass around a bong for an hour and go through so much pot? Now, one joint will do three people in for the night."

"And we've got champagne too," said Jenny.

"I have a feeling we're never going to make it out of here tonight," said Roxanne. "Do you want to order room service for dinner? It'll take at least an hour to get here."

"Oh, that's a great idea," said Ricki.

"I never get to order room service when we travel with the kids," said Jenny. "I always tell them it's too expensive. Let's do it!"

Forgetting all diets, and putting all New Year's resolutions to start new ones on hold for another day, the women ordered Caesar salad, stuffed shrimp scampi with risotto, and Roxanne's favorite, crème brulee for dessert.

"We're a bit busy tonight," the operator had told her. "We can have that for you in about 45 minutes."

"Perfect, fine, we're in no rush," Ricki said magnanimously to the operator, then popped another chocolate-covered strawberry in her mouth. "Roxanne, tell Ben I love him, these are delicious."

"So really, Roxanne," said Jenny, getting back to her earlier comment. "Why do you think you needed the joint to relax tonight?"

"Well, I wasn't sure how you guys would react to the plastic surgery. I only did it because my face was a total wreck from being run over by the bus."

"Still you did have some extra work done, didn't you?" said Ricki with a slight hint of accusation in her voice. "It's not like you just had them put you back together. You really went for major improvements."

"Well, sure. You two know how I hated being ugly my whole life."

"You weren't ugly," said Jenny.

"Oh c'mon, I had a face only a mother could love, unless of course the mother is Sheila."

"Well, you were never ugly to me," said Jenny. "And Ben certainly didn't think you were ugly."

"Ben is a saint," declared Roxanne, lifting her second glass of champagne. "I do believe we were meant to be together, but the truth is, no one ever attempted to take me away from him, did they? If it weren't for Ben I'd probably be an old maid."

"Roxanne, how un-PC of you to say that," protested Ricki. "Anyway, as soon as you fell in love with Ben you built a wall around yourself that no other guy would dare try to climb."

"You're kind of right about that," Roxanne admitted, feeling tipsy. "Once I was going out with Ben, I think I started every conversation with a guy with the words, 'my boyfriend,' so there'd be no chance of anyone ever asking me out."

"I'm not judging you, Roxanne," said Ricki, "and probably some of this is the pot and the champagne talking, "but I think you did do a bit of a disservice to the majority of women in this world who are not beautiful but are still wonderful, successful people, including yourself."

"Funny, I thought you weren't judging me," Roxanne said quietly. "See, this is what I was afraid of. You'd see my surgery as a betrayal of you both, the Thickhead Three. I'm sorry, but I'm no hero, and I have no interest in being the poster girl for the plain of face. I had an opportunity to for once feel pretty and I took it. I hope that you can accept my decision."

"We do. We DO," said Jenny, giving Ricki a kick in the foot.

"Of course, we do," said Ricki. "Roxanne, you can be as beautiful as you want to be. You'll always be the ugly duckling kid to me," she said, laughing. "Joke, joke, c'mon, Roxanne. I still love you. It's really great to see you and I *am* happy for you."

Room service then arrived with dinner.

"Good evening madams," said the waiter. "I have a marvelous dinner for you. I'll just set up the table for you over here. Is there anything else I can get you?"

"No, thanks, that looks wonderful," said Ricki.

"Just leave the dishes on the cart outside your door when you are done. Thank you."

For the next hour they concentrated on enjoying the food and sharing stories about their children. Jenny had four kids, three boys and then the girl she had been wanting so desperately. Ricki had boy-girl twins, now 15 and according to Ricki, the cause of her "premature gray hair."

"Didn't you ever get tempted to have a third baby once the twins were in school?" asked Jenny.

"No way. I did just what I intended. I had a boy and a girl

together to get it over and done with as quickly as possible. And, the secret is, that if you have twins, no one questions your right to an au pair. I love being a mother, but I have to admit, I'm counting down until they go off to college."

"Well, what if they decide to go to your husband's school? Isn't it free for them?" asked Roxanne.

"Yes, but we have a consortium of schools that the faculty kids can go to gratis," explained Ricki. "They can go away, it will be free tuition, and it won't be that far. It's one of the best things about Jerry being an academic."

"That is great," said Roxanne. "I used to have nightmares about college tuition, but now…"

"You don't have to worry about it anymore, do you?" asked Jenny.

"No, I got a very nice settlement from the accident. We've put away enough for each of the kids to go to the school of their choice," Roxanne said, blushing.

"I remember when you swore you'd never have any children," said Jenny.

"Oh, so do I," said Roxanne. "I can tell you guys without you holding it against me. Having those kids was the best thing I ever did. They are each great in their own individual ways. And they're all great looking. They don't look like me at all."

"Oh shut up," said Ricki, pelting Roxanne with a feather pillow.

"You know, it figures I'm the one of us who has the most kids and I'm the one who gets stuck paying for tuition like all the rest of the Joe Schmoes."

"Umm, as I recall you are Mrs. DOCTOR Joe Schmoe," teased Ricki. "How's Matt's practice?"

"It's pretty busy," Jenny admitted. "You know, for the bottom of the social strata of our junior high class, the Thickhead Three are not doing half bad, wouldn't you say?"

"So Roxanne, what's next? What are your plans for your new face?" asked Ricki.

"How does it feel to finally like the way you look?" asked Jenny. "You are happy with the changes, aren't you?"

"It's taken me up until now to really get used to it," Roxanne, said, answering Jenny first. "Last week I faced my mother, sister, and a whole bunch of relatives, and now I'm seeing you guys. Before that I was pretty much staying home, nursing my wounds and not wanting to deal with the world yet."

"But are you happy with the way you look now?" Jenny persisted.

Roxanne took a deep breath, let it out, and finally for the first time out loud said "Yes, I think I am now pretty."

"Pretty woman, walking down the street, pretty woman," Ricki started singing after pouring herself another glass of champagne.

"Well, not Julia Roberts pretty, but yes, I do like the way I look now and I'm going to go out and see what difference it makes in my life," Roxanne continued seriously. "Don't laugh, but what I've decided to do next, since I'm taking time off of work, is to take acting classes. I'm hoping I'll even get to play an attractive woman. In all my years of community theater I've never been cast in anything but a character role. Fuck it, there are *too* such things as small roles, and they always go to the actors with the quote character faces."

"Umm, Rox… I don't know how to break it to you, but I think the ship has sailed on your playing the ingénue," said Jenny.

"I know, I know, I'm not 22 anymore, but I still think I'll have better opportunities for roles in community theater, and who knows, with classes I may even get good enough to go for regional theater. Imagine starring at the Goodspeed Opera House." Roxanne lay back on the queen-size bed and stretched her arms up over her head. "Oh, I know it's a crazy dream, but I'm giving myself some time to go for it. After that, I'll see about doing something else…or give myself some more time."

TWENTY-ONE

IT HAD TAKEN HER a while, but Roxanne was fully "out" now. Her bruises were gone, her ankle healed, and she'd even bought some new clothes to fit her slimmer body. Regardless of how she had resented Sheila's warning about gaining back her weight, she had taken it seriously and been determined not to put back those pounds that never should have been there in the first place. She was a size eight for the first time in ten years and she loved it.

"This is how my body likes to be," she explained to Ben. "This is the weight I am most comfortable at." Although she still had a sweet tooth and could never give up ice cream, she found that she was satisfied with eating smaller portions, and she adjusted the amount of food she bought and cooked to prevent her from overeating.

Finally, she decided to consider changing her hairstyle. "Let's take away some of this excess length," suggested Vinny, when she settled in his chair. "You have a new look, and you need a hairstyle that flatters your face. Are you ready to lose some of your security blanket here?"

An hour later, Roxanne walked out of the salon feeling her transformation was complete. Her shorter hair curled more easily without the excess weight, and she felt it bounce on the back of her neck when she walked quickly. She was so focused on how different the haircut made her feel she almost walked right past Marge Karp and Claire Goldrich, who were leaving the restaurant next door with their husbands, Harvey and Sandy.

"Roxanne, look at you," Marge squawked. "I love your new haircut."

"You look great," added Claire. "How are you feeling?"

"Oh, hi. I didn't see you," said Roxanne. "Thanks, I'm feeling good as new."

"Oh, you're much better than new," said Marge. "You've completely changed."

"Well, that was pretty much my goal," Roxanne laughed nervously.

"You know, Roxanne," said Claire. "My Hadassah group is having a plastic surgeon as a guest speaker this month. He's going to talk about different types of cosmetic surgery. I know the women would love it if you could join that meeting and give us your views, as a patient, you know."

Roxanne stared at Claire as if she had invited her to eat worms. "I'm sorry, Claire," she said when she had regained her composure to speak. "I can't make it."

"But I didn't give you the date," Claire persisted.

"It's a bad month for me. Nice seeing you all, bye," and Roxanne hurried away as quickly as she could without breaking into a full sprint.

"Who was that?" Harvey asked.

"You remember Roxanne Thornton, the woman who was hit by the bus at the soccer game," said Marge.

"Are you kidding me? That was the same woman?" asked Sandy.

"Well, she's had a lot of work done, as you can see," said Claire, getting annoyed at his sudden interest. "It's all artificial."

"But she looks great," Sandy said.

"Yes, but she looks that way because she had *plastic surgery*," Claire emphasized. "Granted, the bus did smash her face, but I think she went a bit overboard with the alterations, don't you?"

"It looks like they did a great job to me," said Sandy. "Why do women always focus on the negative?" he turned to Harvey.

"I know," Harvey agreed. "Every time we walk past a nice set of boobs, Marge says 'fake, fake.' I say if they are there, they are real. What do I care how she got them, nature or nurture?" he laughed.

"Exactly," Sandy agreed.

"You two are impossible," said Marge.

"C'mon Sandy, we should get home. It looks like snow," said Claire.

TWENTY-TWO

"So, ARE YOU READY for the first day of school?" Ben asked as they got under the covers that night. "Nervous?"

"Oh no," said Roxanne. "I'm not nervous at all, just a little terrified. Ben, you don't think I'm totally deranged taking acting classes at this time of my life, do you?"

"No, not at all," said Ben, putting his arm around her and drawing her close to him. "You're allowed to do something you love. I'm proud of you. I'd never be able to do something like that."

"What do you *mean*, something like that?" Roxanne said sitting up and looking at him accusingly.

"Nothing, nothing," he soothed, pulling her back and laying her head on his chest. "I just meant that I'm not as brave as you to put myself in a whole new situation with new people. You know I hate change."

"Well, it's not that I love it, but there's no other way I can see to do this," Roxanne explained.

"Rox, that's what's so great about you," Ben said. "You're willing to go for what you want. Really, I'm very proud of you." He rolled over and kissed her. As his hands moved down to her hips, Roxanne grasped his wrist and pulled it up.

"No way, honey, not tonight. I'm too nervous. I need to

get a good night's sleep and you know that sometimes keeps me awake afterwards."

"I never noticed you staying awake."

"That's because you're snoring so loudly. Good night, Ben, love you." Roxanne turned her back to Ben, inched away a little and pulled the covers up under her chin to emphasize she was serious about sleeping. Ben was defeated. Heaving a sigh, he rolled over to his side and before long he was sound asleep.

Despite her anxiety, Roxanne slept soundly through the morning routines of Ben, Allison, Justin, and Gabe. By the time she woke, 9:17, according to her digital clock, everyone was gone. Even Clarissa was being unusually quiet, curled at her feet and not even clamoring for food. Her train left at 10:48 and got her into Penn Station at 11:22, in plenty of time for her to make her noon class. The class ran until 1:50 and she could make it back home without having to ride in the rush hour "peak fare" time.

This time, getting dressed was a little easier for Roxanne. Casual, very casual, was the only way she could see dressing for a class in Physical Acting. She pulled on her favorite jeans, a velour top, matching wool socks, and suede sneakers. She forced herself to have a cup of hot tea and a toasted bagel, figuring she could always grab something else to eat in the city if she was still hungry.

She had gone over her subway route many times with Ben. It seemed easy enough; she just had to make sure to get on the downtown local train. Once she got out of the station it would be just three blocks to the school, assuming she could figure out which direction to turn. No matter how hard she tried to orient herself, when Roxanne came up out of the subway she had no idea if she was facing, uptown, downtown, east, or west. Her eyesight was never good enough to read the street signs a block away, so she invariably would end up walking almost the whole short block out of her way until the sign came into focus. Roxanne had worn glasses for nearsightedness since the third grade, and her vision had gotten worse each year for almost her entire life. Now, she was also getting farsighted as well. Instead of that working to improve her distance vision, as she had hoped, the farsightedness meant that in addition to not being able to see things far away, she also couldn't read a book or a menu without extending her arm. Getting fitted with multifocal contact lenses helped somewhat, and she always seemed to have wonderful vision at the optometrist. The doctor would show her how well she could see both near and far, and she certainly couldn't argue that the letters on the screen weren't clear. But walking around on a daily basis, Roxanne felt things were perpetually blurred. She knew she couldn't see signs as clearly as Ben, but she didn't want to make too much of a big deal out of it or Ben might start questioning her driving.

Roxanne left in plenty of time to find a parking spot in the very furthest lot. It was almost not worth driving, she thought, but she drove anyway. If the weather turned, she'd appreciate the half-mile or so it had saved her from walking. She waited for the train, clutching her ski jacket against her to keep out the extra wind she felt on the exposed platform high above the street. There was a heated shelter available, but she would rather bear the cold than be warm and breathe in the smells of urine and smoke and the unwashed homeless person who would certainly be there, pretending to wait for a train. The benches lining the shelter had metal armrests between seats to prevent any loiterers from sleeping comfortably, but there was always someone just slumped over on the bench who looked as if he hadn't seen the inside of a house in many months.

The train arrived right on time, and Roxanne settled into a window seat facing forward. She never liked when she had to ride on a backwards seat into the city. It was just disconcerting to her sense of equilibrium. She checked her makeup in her compact, applying more lipstick to fill in what she had bitten off of her lips. She wiped off the mascara that had run when her eyes had teared up in the cold wind and quickly brushed a new layer on. Then she looked at herself again in the tiny, round mirror. Here she was, the new Roxanne, starting off on a new adventure in her life. The world looked at her differently now, that she was sure of. Men smiled at her more often, and women looked at her more carefully than they ever had before. *This is a face that can do whatever it wants,* Roxanne silently told her reflection. *This face won't be prejudged as plain or uninteresting. This face is going to step forward with a self-confidence that Roxanne had never had before.*

"Penn Station, last stop," announced the conductor. "Please make sure to take all your personal belongings and dispose of trash in the station receptacles."

Roxanne zipped up her jacket and arranged the strap on her purse so that it crossed diagonally across her chest. That was how the news articles said was the best way to protect yourself from purse snatchers. She clutched the Metrocard that Ben had given her, and headed toward the subway. Even in the middle of the day the crowds at Penn Station were large enough to make walking an obstacle course of getting out of the way of slow movers, hurrying commuters pulling large baggage, people handing out unwanted flyers, mothers herding young children and trying to keep them moving and close by, and men in suits swinging their briefcases and computer laptops. It seemed as if every person had a cell phone to his or her ear and was busy communicating with someone distant. Even when people were traveling together in couples or groups, it seemed as if someone needed to be in constant phone contact with an unseen party, as if all these people swarming around her were receiving instructions from a higher authority, and none of them were capable of deciding on their next move without confirmation from the disembodied voice on the cell phone.

It made Roxanne feel simultaneously superior and insecure

that she was on her own, charting her own course (even if it had been spelled out by Ben). She headed in the direction of the downtown local Ben had told her to take, and strode with false confidence that she hoped would turn into the real thing. In her head, she sang, "Whenever I feel afraid, I hold my head erect, and whistle a happy tune, so no one will suspect, I'm afraid," and just as Anna had when heading to meet the King of Siam she put on her bravest face and swiped that Metrocard through the turnstile with a flourish. The unyielding steel bar caught her hard in the stomach. "Please Swipe Again," read the turnstile display. And, with a little less flourish and a little more determination, she swiped the Metrocard and was rewarded with access to the subway.

Ready or not, here I go, she thought, as she rushed down the stairs to catch the train.

Following Ben's directions to the letter, Roxanne arrived at the Actor's Studio in plenty of time to go to the restroom, pace nervously, and scope out the other students before they came in. Everyone around her looked as if they knew just where they were going, and they all looked right at home, even though it was the beginning of a new semester. *Well, I wore the right clothes*, Roxanne thought. Jeans, wool pants, sweaters, sweatshirts, sneakers, and boots were worn by the other acting students, teachers, and whoever else was there. Roxanne located the room for her class, but decided to wait until she saw a few other students arrive before entering. She pretended to read the bulletin board with great interest.

APARTMENT TO SHARE,
NONSMOKERS ONLY
VEGETARIAN PREFERRED, CATS
WELCOME

Cast Call:
NYU Film Student seeking Black or

Asian woman 18-28 who is willing to perform with snakes. Small salary provided. Plus all the mice you can eat (Someone had written in afterwards.)

MUSICIANS WANTED
To form a Goth-Rock-Folk Band
Must own amplifiers and mics
Call Spike or Daisy at 555-666-9090

RIDE NEEDED TO LA
Going out to make your fortune in films? Take me along. Willing to share expenses and driving. I know plenty of places we can crash for free along the way.

Does Your Life Have Meaning?
Find out how you can achieve inner peace. Join us at a free introductory meeting and learn how you can qualify for a discounted membership

SUBJECTS WANTED FOR RESEARCH
Psychology PhD candidate will pay individuals to participate in a sleep experiment. Must have the following qualifications:
Male, aged 22-37
European Ancestry (Scandinavia or Iceland, okay)
Raised by either a single mother, two mothers, or grandparents
No history of drug addiction

Must maintain carb-free diet for 3
weeks
Ability to tolerate extreme
temperatures (both heat and cold)

FLATMATE WANTED
Male or female, student preferred
Must be willing to share food and
expenses and not be all obsessive-
compulsive about labeling food,
possessions and space. If you can chill
out and live and let live, Call Angel at
555-727-8888

When she had memorized all the notices on the bulletin board, her fellow acting classmates began to straggle in. Solo, in pairs, and one group of six wildly laughing people emerged from the elevator at the end of the hall and entered the classroom. Roxanne took a deep breath, headed for the door, and then quickly made a detour for one last trip to the rest room.

When she had stalled long enough, Roxanne made her way back to the classroom. The room was arranged with about twenty molded plastic chairs in a semicircle and there was a one-step-up platform that evidently was used as a stage. The six laughing people had dumped their coats and bags in the center seats. There were four women and two men, all who looked to be in their very early twenties. The two seats at each end of the semicircle were taken by pairs of friends (one set of men, one set of women) who were both engaged in serious discussions and not one of the four seemed to be aware of anyone else present in the room. There were four other students who appeared to be operating on their own. Each one was busying him or herself in some way so that they did not look to be waiting for class to begin with nothing better on their mind. To the right of the six laughers there was a 30-something man of enormous stature who was intently reading the *New York Press*. Next to him, a very sexy looking young black woman with multiple earring studs that traveled the entire outer edge of her ear was whispering loudly into her cell phone.

"No Nelson, I can't discuss this anymore with you. No means no!" But Nelson was obviously not taking no for an answer because the woman remained on the phone. Roxanne wondered if those studs ever give her interference with the cell phone.

To the left of the laughers an extraordinarily thin Asian woman of about 22 was deeply engrossed in updating the calendar of her PDA. Using a tiny little stylus she poked and jabbed the electronic gadget in her hand, alternately shaking her head when she had successfully made a change, or stomping her foot when she made an error. One seat over, a middle-aged man of about 45 with thick, dark curly hair showing just a few wisps of gray, a trim beard and mustache, and wire-rimmed glasses sat with an open novel in his lap. He didn't appear to really be reading it, and Roxanne surmised that the novel was merely a prop so he would have something to hold and to pretend to read if need be. Deeply relieved that she might not be the oldest member of the class, Roxanne decided he was the closest to a kindred soul she was going to find in this class and slid into the seat next to him.

"Hi, how are you?" she said in her friendliest please-like-me-I'm-a-nice-person voice.

He looked up, pretending not to have noticed that she had sat down. "Hello, I'm Garrett," he said, extending his hand.

"Roxanne," she said, and shook his hand warmly. "This is my first class here. Have you been coming here long?"

"Oh, off and on all my life," he said and smiled showing

her teeth that had recently undergone a whitening treatment. "Don't worry, it's great here. You'll enjoy it."

"I'm so glad to see that there's another grown-up here. Everyone else is so much younger."

"That's okay, there are some advantages to being the 'mature' members of a class like this," he assured her.

"You look familiar," said Roxanne.

"Oh? Well, picture me about two inches tall and sailing in a boat inside a bathroom bowl. Now can you place me?"

"Oh My God, it is you!" said Roxanne. "I love you in the toilet. It's a great commercial."

"Yes, well it's one of my most lucrative. Of course, the one that puts my son through private school was the dancing banana. They pay extra for the dancing talent, you know."

Roxanne was about to answer when the last student entering the classroom distracted her. He wore a helmet and a rather tattered messenger bag slung across his shoulders. He was carrying the front wheel of a bicycle, and he clumsily tripped over Roxanne's foot trying to get to the windowsill to place the wheel out of the way.

"Excuse me, I'm such a dork," he said.

"Oh, that's okay, no problem," said Roxanne, resisting the urge to rub her foot.

"I hope he's better at maneuvering in traffic," she whispered to Garrett.

Before Garrett could reply, in burst a muscular man of about 35. His bold stride and his dancer's body could only mean that he was the instructor. It was also a dead giveaway that he immediately placed himself in the center of the stage, facing the class. His hair was bleached platinum blonde, and he had a tan that in January was meant to leave the impression of a holiday in the Caribbean. *I bet that's a Century Village Boca poolside tan he got visiting mom and dad over Christmas,* thought Roxanne.

"Hello, hello people," he said. "I'm Erik and if you've

registered for Physical Acting then you are in the right place." Erik was dressed completely in black stretchy clothes that emphasized his great physique.

"Okay, this is Physical Acting, so let's get physical. Everyone up," he clapped his hands and grinned.

The class looked around at one another and rose to their feet.

"Now, push those chairs back so we have some space," continued Erik. "Step forward, spread out so you have some room to move. We're going to begin with some stretching and loosening up exercises." Erik turned on some fast music with a strong beat.

"Ready, here we go. Start with the head. Slow circles… around, around, around we go. Now the shoulders. Shake them out. No, really shake them out. That's it, up, down, up, down. Now, let's bend at the waist, follow me. To the right, and bob, one, two, three, four. To the left, and bob, one, two, three, four. And stretch up your arms above your heads all the way up on your toes. Now jump, one, two, three, four, five and shake out your arms, kick out your legs. Are you getting loose?"

Treating it as a rhetorical question, the class gave no response.

"I said, people, are you getting loose?"

"Yes," they answered, simultaneously stopping their shaking and kicking.

"Okay, now stretch backward as far as you can without falling over. Hold it, hold it, hold it."

Roxanne felt the blood rushing to her head as she bent backwards. *Oy, what did I get myself into,* she thought. *I don't know if I can do this.* She stole a sidelong glance at Garrett, who gave her a smile and a thumbs up.

"All right," Erik clapped his hands loudly. "Now that we've warmed up, everyone take a seat and let's see who we have here."

He pulled a yellow Nerf ball out of what seemed to be thin air to Roxanne and tossed it in the air.

"Okay, introductions are always a little weird, but we have to know who we all are if we're going to work together," he said. "Bring the semicircle in at a sharper angle so we're all a little bit closer."

The class obediently slid their chairs forward so that everyone could see everyone else. They formed a tighter horseshoe around Erik.

"Okay, let's make a little game of this, shall we? When I toss you the ball tell us your name and something about yourself. It could be what brings you to this class or something else you want to share. Then you toss the ball to whomever you want. Ready?" He didn't wait for a response and tossed the ball to the enormous 30-something man.

"I'm Joe, but my friends call me Tiny," he said. "Believe it or not I get typecast a lot. I want to expand my skills to be able to go out for a wider range of roles." He tossed the ball over to the thin Asian woman.

"Ming," she said. "I can relate to being typecast. I'm always asked to play truckers," she said with a laugh. "Honestly, I've been in New York for a year answering every cast call I can. I just want to continue learning the craft."

Ming threw the ball a little too high to the bicycle messenger, who caught it in his helmet. The class laughed and clapped. "David," I'm a bike messenger slash struggling actor. I've been in the city for two years. I've done two way-off Broadway shows, I mean, they were in Brooklyn."

David tossed the ball to one of the laughers. "Jeremy," he said. "I'm a Libra and I do some modeling on the side." He threw the ball across to the friend of his with long, curly red hair.

"I'm Carla. I don't know what to say. I'm happy to be here," she said, laughed again and flipped the ball over to the woman next to her.

"Mona. I just got cast in my first television commercial."

The ball flew through the air to one of the men in the end pair. "Matthew. I'm a vegetarian and I have two cats and a gecko." He then aimed the ball at Roxanne. She tried a little too hard to catch it, and nearly fell off her seat.

"I'm Roxanne," she said. "Umm, I've loved acting all my life but I never had time to pursue it. I've got the time now, so here I am." She breathed a deep sigh of relief and imagined she saw a few of the laughers exchange glances, perhaps in judgment of her. *No matter,* she thought to herself. *I'm twice their age; they don't intimidate me one bit.*

The ball continued making its way around the class and Natasha, Leigh, Caitlin, Jeremy, Garrett, Evan, Carolanne, Guillermo, and Jeanine introduced themselves in turn.

By the end of class Roxanne's head was spinning. Other than Ming, Tiny, Natasha, David, and Garrett, she still couldn't match the names to the faces of her classmates. Erik had taken them through a few exercises that Roxanne felt were much like charades. The two hours passed quickly and Erik was soon bidding them all a good afternoon.

"Where are you headed?" Garrett asked her as she gathered up her bag, book, papers, and coat.

"Penn Station. How about you?"

"I could go that way," he said, not revealing his final destination. "How about a cup of coffee first?"

Roxanne had just about gotten all her things together, adjusted her coat, distributed her bags, and the whole process had her feeling a little pooped. "You know, a cup of coffee would definitely be a good thing now. Where do we go?"

"In New York all you have to do is spin around twice and you'll hit a Starbucks. Let's see how close one is to this building."

They boarded the elevator, crowding into the last spaces available, and then spilled out into the lobby crowded with other students.

"C'mon, let's head north," said Garrett. "I think there's a Starbucks on the next corner."

Sure enough, the Starbucks appeared and Roxanne and Garrett got on line, ordered, and after waiting for their custom coffee orders for "a New York minute" they found a table for two in the corner.

"So, how did you like your first class?" asked Garrett.

"I haven't quite figured that out yet," said Roxanne. "My head is still spinning a little, especially after those neck exercises."

He smiled and waited quietly for her to continue, all the while looking directly into her eyes.

"It was good, though. It's just going to require a little time to adjust."

Again Garrett looked into her eyes and smiled. Was he flirting with her? Roxanne wondered how she could tell if that were so. City people were a different species entirely than suburban types like her, she thought.

"So, have you really been away from the stage since you were a kid?"

"Well, I do community theater periodically. But as I said I've never had time to really devote to acting between working and raising three kids."

"Three kids, nice. Married?" he asked.

"Twenty-two years. And you?"

"Divorced."

"Ah."

"Yes, ah."

"I'll bet you had the leads in all your high school shows, right? The lovely ingénue?"

Roxanne smiled and then with all the self-restraint she had resisted her natural instinct to spill all. There was no reason to tell Garrett her sad story about all the character roles and old ladies she played in her youth. He'd never check. He'd never know the truth. She felt a secret thrill at the realization that a completely objective fellow thespian had assumed she'd been used to obtaining the lead, the female object of desire. *So this is what it feels like to be viewed as attractive by even the casual observer,* she thought. Garrett didn't know her or love her. He just saw her as a leading lady type and assumed that she had always enjoyed the privileges that such good fortune bestowed upon that race of good-looking individuals. "Well," she said, looking down and stirring her coffee. "It was a pretty competitive program. I wasn't the top diva, but I guess I did okay."

TWENTY-THREE

"ARE WE GOING TO have pizza every night from now on?" Justin asked hopefully.

"No, of course not," said Roxanne. "I just wanted to celebrate making it through my first acting class. I promise tomorrow night I'll make dinner."

"Well, really, don't strain yourself, Mom," said Justin trying to show deep concern. "We can survive on pizza."

"How kind and considerate of you, dear. I know you're only thinking of me."

"Hey Mom, I think you're acting already," quipped Allison.

"I still don't get it," said Gabe. "Why is Mom going to school now? Didn't you graduate when you were, you know, young?"

"Gabe, Mom is taking acting classes. It's not like the fourth grade."

"Yeah, there's no math," said Justin.

"But Mom, you already know how to act. You were great as that ghost in the temple show last year," said Gabe.

Roxanne smiled. Playing Fruma Sara in "Fiddler on the Roof" had been a lot of fun. Sure it was a small role, but it was a great featured part. She had even gotten to fly in on cable wire. Her kids had loved seeing her do that. They'd even talked some of their friends into coming on the second night of the show. She had definitely gotten "cool Mom" points for that one.

"Ben, do you want to meet me for lunch tomorrow?" asked Roxanne. "I have an hour off between classes from twelve to one."

Ben paused, pizza slice in mid air. "Doesn't the old saying go we married for better or worse but not for lunch," he said laughing softly. "Seriously honey, I don't think that's a great idea. I always take lunch from one to two, anyway."

"But you're a manager, can't you change your lunch hour if you want?" Roxanne wasn't expecting to be brushed off so nonchalantly.

"I could, but Rox, the department eats together and we actually get things settled over lunch pretty often. If I don't eat with them, then I'm usually taking care of errands in the city. And my office is pretty far from your school, by the time we got together we'd be very rushed to get served and eat. Anyway, absence makes the heart grow fonder."

"Well, you're full of clichés tonight, aren't you?" Roxanne said, obviously annoyed.

"Oh come on, don't take it like that. It's not you, it's me," he said, hoping that Seinfeld line would make her laugh.

"Forget it," she said. "Maybe I'll just have lunch with one of my classmates. I wonder what Garrett's schedule is like tomorrow."

"Who is Garrett?" asked Ben.

"You know the guy who sails the boat in the toilet bowl in that commercial?"

"Mom, you know that guy?" Allison, Justin, and Gabe were incredulous.

Hmm, more cool Mom points for me, thought Roxanne.

"Yes, I met him in class today. He's really very nice. He gets along quite well for someone who is only four inches tall."

The kids and Ben all laughed at Roxanne's joke.

"He's not really four inches tall, is he Mom?" asked Gabe.

"I'm just kidding. But he was in my class today, and he was very friendly."

"Great," said Ben. "It's good for you to make friends in your classes. Really Roxanne, I'd just get in your way."

Roxanne was certainly not going to beg. If he didn't want to meet her for lunch tomorrow, that was fine. She'd explore the neighborhood. There was always recreational shopping to keep her busy for the hour.

Ben reached for another slice of pizza, feeling Roxanne's resentful stare burning into his neck.

"What?" he said, "Rox, I really do believe it would be better for you to be on your own during the day. You can't expect me to be threatened by a guy who navigates toilet bowls for a living."

TWENTY-FOUR

TUESDAY, ROXANNE AWOKE AND showered before all the kids in order to help them get ready for school and have time herself to make a 9:05 train. Ben had been considerate to let her sleep in on Monday, but that party was over. She supervised the shower shuttle, as each kid, oldest to youngest, took their turns in the bathroom and she put out breakfast foods for the kids to choose from. Allison was into Special K this year, Justin liked to start the day with a peanut butter and banana sandwich, and Gabe ate frozen waffles, straight from the toaster, no butter, syrup, or jelly. Roxanne couldn't understand how Gabe could eat the waffles like that, but since it made it that much easier for her to provide, she didn't complain about his culinary preferences.

The school district staggered the building openings to allow for the most efficient use of buses. Although they each attended a different school, Roxanne's kids waited at the same bus stop at specific intervals each morning. Allison's bus to the high school came at 7:38, Justin's middle school transportation came at 8:05, and Gabe had to be there for the elementary school bus by 8:20. Roxanne put her own breakfast of a light English muffin in the toaster before helping Gabe into his winter coat and boots. As the door shut behind him, the toaster bell rang and the tea kettle began to whistle, indicating that her water was ready to make tea.

She spread the hot muffin with light butter and lo-cal fruit jelly compote and dangled the tea bag up and down until the water was just the right amber color. Watching the Today Show while scanning the headlines, she gave herself the luxury of a 15-minute breakfast. By 8:45 she was in the car and headed toward the train station.

Her Tuesday/Thursday schedule had two classes. She had Voice and Speech from 10:30 to 12:00 and then Improvisation from 1:00 to 2:50. After making great subway connections, Roxanne arrived at school with more than a half hour to kill before her class started. She decided to take a walk around the area and scout out places for lunch and shopping for later.

It was a cold, but clear morning. The weather didn't seem to make any difference to New Yorkers, and the sidewalks were full of people with places to go. Dogs of all shapes and sizes led their owners on leashes, and many people pushed strollers with babies so bundled up you had to have faith that they were actually there. When Roxanne got to the corner she looked up and down the street to see which way looked more interesting. When she turned to go uptown she found she had to quickly dodge one of the over-bundled strollers, which was heading right for her foot. She stepped back and looked at the woman pushing the stroller.

"Jo!" she exclaimed. "Jo Glickman?" she said to the mother who looked at her with surprise and bewilderment.

"Yes, hello," she said. Her expression showed no sign of recognition, and she waited for Roxanne to give her a hint as to her identity.

"So you don't recognize your own college roommate?" Roxanne teased.

"Roommate?" Jo's face was still a blank.

"It's Roxanne. Roxanne Klein Thornton. Relax Jo, you're not going crazy. I really have changed."

Jo stared hard at Roxanne. "What, what, how, who?" Jo didn't know how to ask without sounding insulting.

"I had a bad accident last fall and I ended up having a lot of reconstructive plastic surgery on my face. As long as I was going under the knife, I had them do a few improvements."

Jo's jaw hung open in classic astonishment. *I can use that expression in my physical acting class,* Roxanne thought.

"I can't believe it. You look incredible. Wow, it's good to see you. It's been so long," and Jo reached out and gave Roxanne a loving hug.

Roxanne took in how little Jo had changed. Sure, she had a few lines in her face, but she was still gorgeous. Not a strand of her shoulder-length blonde hair was out of place. Long thick lashes and carefully sculpted brows set off her wide-set blue eyes. Her complexion was flawless, and even with a winter coat on, Roxanne could see that she was probably still an almost perfect size six. The "almost perfect" part was that Jo had sometimes had trouble fitting her ample breasts into some styles. Of course, Jo got absolutely no sympathy on that complaint from Roxanne or any of the other women in the dorm.

"I don't think I've see you since Justin's bris," said Roxanne. "I had a third kid, Gabe, who's nine. And who is this?" she said trying to peek into the blankets in the stroller.

"This is Tai, my daughter," Jo said proudly. She gently pulled back the blanket to reveal the face of a beautiful little girl with huge eyes that gazed intently into Roxanne's. "She's eighteen months old. I adopted her from China when she was eight months old."

Now it was Roxanne's turn for her jaw to drop and to feel astonishment. "Oh, Jo, congratulations," she said. "What a beautiful child. Gee, we have a lot of catching up to do, don't we? Do you live near here?"

"Yes, but you were out in the burbs, last I heard. You and Ben didn't…?"

"No, Ben and I are still together. I'm here taking some courses at The Actor's Studio. What are you doing at about 3:00 today?"

"That's naptime," Jo answered quickly.

"Does that mean you're home with Tai?"

"Yes, I'm working from home these days so that I can be with her."

"Could I come by after class? I have to get back soon, but I'm done at 2:50."

"That would be wonderful. Here's my card, it has my address and phone number. You can walk to my apartment from here."

"Well, then I'll see you around three o'clock?" Roxanne asked expectantly.

"Absolutely. Hey, are you sure it's really you? How can I be sure?" she said, only half kidding.

"Let's see. Freshman year you slept with a pink elephant named Peanuts. You're allergic to radishes; you sneak chocolate kisses in the middle of the night when you think no one can hear you; you lost your virginity at 17 with your brother's best friend; and your favorite book is *Black Beauty*. Now do you believe it's me?"

Jo laughed and gave Roxanne another hug. "I'll see you later," she said. "We're on our way to Mommy and Me."

As soon as they separated, Roxanne pulled out her cell phone and dialed Ben's office. She got his voice mail. "Hi, it's me. I probably won't be home for dinner tonight. You'll never believe who I bumped into on the street. Jo Glickman, my college roommate. She has a Chinese baby. I'm meeting her after class and I may stay with her a while. There's a baking dish of chili in the refrigerator you just have to nuke for the kids. I'll call you later. Bye, love you."

There were no familiar faces from Physical Acting class in Voice and Speech. This time the students filed in rather quietly and sat around a big conference table. The teacher was already seated at the head of the table, studiously writing in a leather-bound notebook. She was an older woman with long gray hair held back with a carved wooden barrette. She wore a gray cowl-neck sweater that matched her hair and gray pin-striped pants. In the center of her chest, just below the scoop of the cowl neck, she wore a huge turquoise-stone and silver pendant in the shape of a sunburst. *She could use that as a spare hubcap*, thought Roxanne.

"In this class you will learn to talk and use your voice as an instrument," began the instructor without so much as introducing herself.

"Gee, and here I've been talking since I was two years old," remarked a young man in a red sweatshirt with the hood on.

"Stand-Up Comedy is down the hall," the instructor said severely.

Red sweatshirt slunk in his seat.

"Now, are we ready to begin? My name is Veronica Lodge," she said. Then in a loud, stern voice, "No, I never married Archie Andrews so stop thinking it."

Her declaration startled the class, and no one dared to say a word. Then, she threw back her head and laughed. Roxanne and her classmates figured she was either very funny or quite insane, and opting to believe the former, they laughed along with her.

"Ha, gotcha," she said. "But my name really is Veronica Lodge. And just as a name can bring to mind all sorts of images, so can the tone of your voice, the manner of your speech, and the phrasing of your words greatly influence your portrayal of a character, your interpretation of a role. This is a beginning class, so before we recite any lines we will explore the basics of how to use and train your voice to give you depth and range as an actor."

Roxanne found class to be both interesting and challenging, and, unlike physical acting where she feared that she might not have the flexibility or stamina that her younger classmates had, speaking was something she had plenty of experience in. The class was small enough to fit around the table comfortably, and the students were a diverse group of individuals who each added something unique to the mix. Roxanne was surprised at how quickly noon and the end of the session came.

She followed a group of people onto the elevator down and then felt a tap on her shoulder. It was Garrett, the toilet bowl captain.

"Hi Roxanne, how are you? Where are you headed?" he asked.

"I'm just going to get some lunch."

"So am I. Would you like to go together?"

"Sure, I'll bet you know all the good places to go, too."

"What's your pleasure? Deli, Japanese, Chinese, Indian, pizza, salad bar, bagels, burgers, Mexican…?"

"Whoa, too many choices. I eat anything. You pick this time."

"How about French soup and salad?"

"Sounds perfect, is it far?"

"No, not at all, let's go."

He took her arm companionably and led her to a little café that was filled with the aroma of hearty soups and fresh baked bread.

"This is great," said Roxanne. "How did you know this is just the kind of lunch I love?"

"I guess because it's what I like," said Garrett. "I had a feeling we'd be compatible," he said, smiling and again making that direct, twinkly eye contact.

They ordered crocks of onion soup and decided to share a salad and a serving of quiche.

"Will you join me in a glass of chardonnay?" asked Garrett.

"Gee, I don't think we'd fit in there," said Roxanne.

"Very funny. Was that a toilet bowl reference?"

"Well, maybe a little. But seriously, I don't know if I should have anything to drink. I have another class at one."

"It's okay, you're a grown-up. You won't get in trouble for drinking at school."

Roxanne laughed. "I've still not used to this yet. But what the hell, I've got Improvisation next. A glass of wine may be just what I need to loosen up for the class."

"I'm in that class, too. And I fully concur. A glass of wine is a great way to get ready for class, but let's keep it to one apiece. We don't want to embarrass ourselves in class." Garrett signaled the waiter to bring two glasses of wine. He raised his to a toast and said, "Here's to new friends," and clinked his glass lightly with hers.

"I'll drink to that," said Roxanne. "And thank you, Garrett, I think having a friend is going to help me in this new chapter of my life."

Garrett looked as if he was about to say something else when the waiter came back with their food.

"This looks great," said Roxanne. "Thanks again for picking such a perfect place."

"The pleasure is all mine," said Garrett. "Bon appétit."

TWENTY-FIVE

AFTER IMPROVISATION, ROXANNE HEADED directly to the address on Jo Glickman's card. It was just six blocks uptown and one avenue east. On the way, she stopped to buy a bunch of flowers for Jo and was thrilled when she found a stuffed elephant for the baby. It was a different color than "Peanuts" had been, but Roxanne was sure Jo would appreciate the gesture.

A doorman seated at a reception desk with an intercom console and closed-circuit security camera system buzzed Jo to announce a visitor. "Four D," he said. "Make a left out of the elevator."

Jo was waiting at the door of the apartment. "Come on in," she whispered. "I just put her down so we have to be a little quiet for a few minutes. If she hears there's someone else here she'll want to see who it is."

Roxanne removed her boots and walked softly into the living room, where amidst toddler toys, Jo had cleared off the couch and set a coffee pot and cups in the middle of a glass coffee table whose edges were fitted with foam rubber secured by duct tape. Roxanne smiled at Jo's child proofing efforts.

"It's the latest in interior decorating, you know," said Jo. "All the biggies are into foam and duct tape this year."

"It's quite lovely," said Roxanne. Then she pulled the

stuffed elephant out of the bag. "I thought Tai should have her own Peanuts."

Tears welled up in Jo's eyes. "I can't believe you," she said. "That is the sweetest thing I've ever seen. Oh, Roxanne, I'm so glad we bumped into each other. It's so good to see you. I'm so sorry we lost touch for all those years," and she started to really cry.

"Hey," Roxanne put her arm around her and comforted her. "That was a long time ago. I'm just glad to see you now. Come on, fill me in. Tell me everything." The truth was that Roxanne had resented Jo for years. She had believed that Jo had pulled away from her because she wasn't interested in putting up with all Roxanne's motherhood priorities, and she thought Roxanne had become a big bore. But seeing Jo as she was now changed all the feelings of resentment she felt to compassion. It always shocked Roxanne when life didn't work out perfectly for the beautiful people.

Jo blew her nose and tried to stop the flow of tears. "I'm sorry to be blubbering. I'm just overwhelmed to see you, on top of being about to collapse from sheer exhaustion. Single motherhood is ten times harder than you could imagine. Oh, don't get me wrong, I adore Tai. She's the best decision I ever made and she's my life. I just…"

"Jo, you don't have to make any excuses to me. Just relax, sit back and tell me how you got here. Last time we were in touch you were going out with that lawyer who had political aspirations. Whatever happened to him?"

"Oh you mean Charles. You know, it's not even worth going into. Charles was just one in a long line of men in my life who either liked me more than I liked him, or liked me less than I liked him. I've just never been in the same amount of like—not to even mention, love—with the right guy at the right time. I could never find anyone perfect for me like Ben was for you. My shrink says I set impossible standards."

"Well, don't you?" said Roxanne as gently as she could.

"I used to. That's certainly true. But somewhere around thirty-five, thirty-six, I got a little less picky. By then it was too late. The men my age were either all married or committed commitment-phobes. I had several offers to be a trophy wife, but I'm not into older men, you know what I mean? Then when I hit thirty-eight that biological clock started keeping me up at night it was ticking so loud. For my fortieth birthday I filled out the adoption forms, and now I have Tai. I'm crazy for her, but my life has certainly turned out different than I ever thought it would. I guess I always thought that by this time of my life I'd be more like, well, like you."

"You mean, the husband, house, three kids scenario?"

"The truth is that after taking care of one baby I don't know if I'd have ever gone for three kids, but I certainly thought there'd be a husband in the picture. I sometimes feel guilty that Tai doesn't have a father. I worry that it was selfish of me to adopt her when a two-parent family could have taken her."

"Jo, don't talk like that. Don't even think like that. Tai is very lucky to have a mother like you. You're warm and loving and fun and smart. You can give her a wonderful life."

"I hope so," Jo said sadly. "I just hope I'm as good for her as she is for me. She's incredible. Now, not to change the subject, but how the hell did you get to look like this? What were you, run over by a bulldozer?"

"A school bus, actually."

"No! Really? Ouch, that must have hurt."

"It was bad. But because the facial reconstruction was covered by my medical insurance I got to get an extreme makeover. Look, even the doctor wanted to do it after seeing my old face."

"Stop, you're terrible. I'm sure he never said anything."

"Actually, you'd be wrong. But even though it's been a big adjustment, I'm very glad I did it. I also got a big enough settlement to quit my job for a while, and that's why I'm in the city. I'm taking acting classes because I really love it."

"That's amazing. Do you realize how amazing you are?"

"It's just amazing circumstances I've found myself in. I do give myself some credit for taking advantage of what's happened. You know, making lemonade out of lemons?"

Jo sipped her coffee. "Well, I think it's a little better than lemonade you've made. Roxanne, you're my new hero."

Roxanne laughed at Jo's words. "I'm the same person I always was. I am definitely no hero."

Knowing that Ben and the kids would be fine with the chili for dinner, Roxanne allowed herself the luxury of staying for hours and catching up with Jo. Once Tai woke up from her nap, Roxanne couldn't tear herself away from the baby. They took in Chinese food and Roxanne and Jo felt almost as if they were back in college together. Promising to come back soon, Roxanne left and took a cab to Penn Station just in time to catch a 9:27 train. Ben was already in bed when she got home.

"Did you have a good time with Jo?" he asked, rousing himself from his almost-asleep state of consciousness.

"I really did. I think for the first time in my life I wasn't jealous of Jo's beauty. In fact, she actually seemed a little jealous of what I have."

"And what exactly do you have that she doesn't?" he asked, raising his eyebrows in a mischievous manner.

Having changed into a nightgown, Roxanne playfully jumped onto the bed and dove under the covers. The room was a little cool, but she knew Ben would warm her up quickly enough.

"Well, a wonderful husband, for one thing. Jo doesn't have that."

"Aww, well, you could lend me out if you really feel so badly for her."

"Oh no, I shared a lot of things with Jo when we lived together, but I'm keeping you all for myself."

Roxanne was bubbling with energy, and looked at Ben with renewed appreciation, thinking about Jo going to bed alone tonight. She hugged Ben tightly and then moved her hand inside his shirt, tickling his chest hair gently, knowing he was getting aroused and that he was now quite glad that he had waited up for her to come home.

Ben was pleasantly surprised when Roxanne disappeared under the covers and began kissing his belly and working her way down to his now throbbing penis. He was tempted to say something, but was afraid to break the spell. This was a rare move for Roxanne, who usually gave the excuse "Jewish girls don't do that, well not <u>married</u> Jewish girls."

She teased his penis with her tongue, licking, sucking, and blowing her hot breath on the moist member. When Ben started to moan, she finally took him in her mouth until she felt he was ready to explode. With acrobatic agility, she grabbed her own panties that she had shoved under the pillow, and caught his cum. Giving head was one thing, but having to change the sheets now was more than she was willing to do.

"I definitely think you should visit Jo more often," Ben said after Roxanne had come out from under the covers and was snuggled in his arms. He lifted her up and placed her on top of him so that he could suck on her breasts and cradle her tush in his hands.

Still flushed from her uncharacteristic adventure down under, Roxanne rubbed her body against Ben's until she felt on the verge of climax. Knowing just how to get her over the edge, Ben massaged her left nipple and sucked deeply on the right breast. He then worked his finger into just the right spot, and Roxanne was overcome with the pleasure of a breathtaking orgasm.

When she had recovered enough to talk, Roxanne said to Ben, who was starting to drift off to sleep, "You really like making love to the new me, don't you?"

Ben turned fully towards her and rested his head on his bent-elbow arm. "Rox, I'm not making love to the new you, I'm making love to my wife, who is now happy with the way she looks, and is finally allowing herself to enjoy being the sexy, wonderful woman she's always been."

"Well, that's sweet of you to say, but c'mon doesn't my new face make a difference in the way you think of me?"

"Rox, when you and I make love--have sex--do the nasty--whatever you want to call it, I see you in my mind, not in my eyes. I mean, my eyes are usually closed most of the time, right?"

"Yes, and I guess mine are too."

"Tell me, is it this 44-year-old body that turns you on, or is it me, the man you've spent your life with for the past 24 years? When I make love to you, I'm making love with the girl I fell in love with in college, the new mother exhausted to her very bones who nursed our babies and sang Broadway show tunes to put them to sleep, and yes, to this more confident woman you've become since the accident. I do like the way you look now, but it doesn't make me love you more. It's the way you feel about yourself now that is the real gift to me. If you're happy, Roxanne, then I'm happy too."

Roxanne was stunned. It was so unlike Ben to be so introspective. But he was right. It was the Ben of the past, present, and the future that she made love to in her mind while her body responded in the physical manner. They had lived their entire adult lives together and the bond they shared was the kind that made marriages like theirs strong.

"You know Ben, there's one real problem I have with you,"

"Oh?"

"Yeah, sometimes you're almost too good to be true."

TWENTY-SIX

"So how's it going?" Ann asked to begin the therapy session Roxanne had put off for the past three weeks. "Tell me what's been happening and how you've been feeling."

"Well, I started my acting classes."

"Great! Is it great?"

"It actually is," Roxanne admitted. "I'm still getting used to it but those classes are so freeing to me. When I'm there I'm totally absorbed. It's as if I have no other life outside those classes during the time that I'm there."

"That's an interesting observation."

"Well, it's what I've always loved about acting. You can't do it half-assed. It requires your complete focus and you just have to block out anything else that might be on your mind."

"You look wonderful. How do you feel about your appearance now? Are you happy with the results of the surgery?"

"Oh, I'm definitely happy with how I look now. I'm especially thankful that I've been able to keep off the weight I lost. I never want to go back to size 14 again."

"And have you seen a lot of changes in the way people treat you?" Ann pushed the issue.

"Yes and no. My family doesn't treat me any different, well, with the exception of my mother, but I do get a different reception from strangers. It's pretty much what I expected… but,"

"Yes?"

"My husband said something interesting the other night. It was after we had, you know, had sex. He insists that the change in my appearance doesn't affect how he feels about me sexually or romantically. He said when we're being intimate he sees me in his mind, not with his eyes."

"That's pretty amazing. Ten points to Ben for that," Ann said with a big smile. "How does that make you feel?"

"Well, I feel like it *should* make me very happy, but the truth is that a part of me wants him to be as shallow as the rest of the world and find me more attractive than he did before."

"You know, I don't think Ben was saying that he doesn't find you more attractive. I'm sure Ben would agree that outwardly you have improved your appearance. I think what he said, and in such a loving way, is that he's always been attracted to you because he loves you. Correct me if I'm wrong, Roxanne, but you've always said that Ben is your biggest fan. Do you really need more from him?"

"Not *need*, no, but I kind of *want* more. Oh I'd never admit that to anyone else, but if I can't be totally honest in therapy, where can I?"

"Do you think you may still be trying to justify to yourself having the reconstruction done?"

"What do you mean?"

"You're saying that Ben insists it doesn't make any difference to him. That must mean you did it entirely for your own benefit. I think you may have some feelings of guilt about taking such measures to please yourself. You'd feel better if it wasn't a wholly selfish act, and you could justify it better if you believed you were doing it to make Ben happier, too."

"Yeah, but the whole thing was more of something happening **to me** than **by me.** I mean I really didn't have much of a choice to make. I had to have the reconstructive surgery.

I think making the improvements was a no-brainer. Wouldn't I have been crazy to pass up the opportunity I was given by the accident?"

"I think so. But then I'm a lot more accepting of Roxanne than you are."

"Oh," said Roxanne. "I see you what you mean. New face, same self-image."

"Well, let's just say it's easier to change the outside than the inside," Ann said. But you're getting there, Roxanne. I know you'll make it there."

TWENTY-SEVEN

ROXANNE TURNED THE CALENDAR page to look at what was ahead for February. There it was, February fourth, Grace's birthday staring her in the face. She still hadn't spoken to Grace since she had practically thrown her out of the house (at least that was the way Sheila described it). Her promise to Allison that she would make up with Grace rang in her ears. *If she didn't follow through on this, how could she ask Allison to keep her own promises? Besides,* she told herself, *she was getting tired of fighting with Grace. She really didn't have to feel jealous of Grace anymore.* Roxanne had loved it when Grace's daughter had pointed out that the sisters now looked alike.

Of course, there was still the matter of Grace's abominable, selfish behavior when their father died, but Roxanne was hopeful that her Chanukah tirade had made an impact on Grace. In any case, there was no way Grace could make up for that now, although an apology would be nice.

I guess I can afford to be the magnanimous one. After all, I did get two million dollars, she thought, breaking into a grin. She wondered which bothered Grace more, the new face or the settlement money. Nevertheless, blood was blood. Grace was the only sister she had and it was time to make amends.

Roxanne was just about to pick up the phone when it rang and startled her.

"Hello," she said.

"Honey, listen, I just got a call from Cydelle. Nana Sadie is gone," said Sheila.

"Gone? Is she missing or did she die?"

"She passed away this morning. They said she went in her sleep. Don't get upset honey, after all, you can't complain about living to 92."

"I know, I know but it's still sad. You know it's coming, but it's always a shock. Well, at least we got to see her last month. Umm, have you spoken to Grace yet?"

"No, I called you first. Why? Roxanne, please don't start making trouble now." Sheila's voice went up in her most threatening way.

"I wouldn't, I swear. Actually, I was just about to call Grace and see if we could, well, bury the hatchet. Why don't you let me call her and tell her about Nana Sadie? Have there been any arrangements made? Who's doing that anyway?"

"Cyd and Sid have it all worked out. They're making the service on Sunday. The rabbi is letting them wait a few days so that family can fly in. You know, Sadie outlived her children and all her brothers, there's no one to sit shiva for her, but we should give her a good sendoff."

"So you're coming up?"

"Much as I hate to come north twice in one winter, I feel I should come. You'll pick me up at the airport tomorrow if I can get a flight?"

"Sure, go make your plans. I'll give Grace a call."

"Are you sure you can do that without getting into an argument? What if she can't come to the funeral? Are you going to attack her?"

"Mom, I'm worn out. Grace can do whatever she wants. I promise not to pass judgment. Call me after you make the plane reservations. And Mom, you know you really don't have to come up if it's too difficult. I'll go and represent our family. She's on the Thornton side anyway."

"When I married your father I erased all the sides. Family is family. I'm going to try to come. It's a mitzvah. Goodbye Roxie, I'll talk to you later."

Well, at least I have an icebreaker, Roxanne thought as she started to dial Grace's number. Grace answered on the second ring.

"Hello?" said Grace.

"Hi, it's Roxanne."

"Oh, who died?" Grace said coldly.

"Nana Sadie, this morning."

"Oh my God," Grace was truly shocked. "I guess that's why you're calling?" she asked, quickly going back on the defensive.

"Grace, I was going to call you anyway, but believe it or not, just as I reached for the phone Sheila called to tell me about Nana Sadie."

"Oh? What did you want to say to me?"

"Listen, I'm tired of fighting. I want to end this hostility between us. I'm willing to forget Daddy's funeral if you'll forget my screaming at you in front of the relatives."

"That *was* incredibly rude," said Grace, not yet letting go of her indignant anger. "And to add insult to injury I wound up getting Mom for the rest of the week. Are you sure that wasn't your motive all along?"

Despite herself, Roxanne had to laugh. No matter how much the sisters disagreed, they could always unite on the trials and tribulations of dealing with Sheila.

"No, really, that was just a lucky break for me. But she's coming up for Nana Sadie's funeral and staying with me, so can we call it even?"

"Are you going to stop picking on me for every little thing?" Grace asked.

Roxanne took a deep breath and told herself, *Remember your promise to Allison.*

"I promise to try. C'mon, let's try acting like sisters who

are also friends. I can even pass for one of your old crowd now, I guess."

"What are you talking about?"

"You know, you always hung out with the pretty, popular crowd. I didn't exactly fit the part."

"And your friends were the top students. I couldn't quite make it into that group either, now could I?"

"But, but that was different," stammered Roxanne.

"How was that different?"

Because I was jealous of you and your friends and you were never jealous of me, thought Roxanne. But she couldn't say it out loud to Grace.

"I don't know, look can we change the subject please? Do you think you'll be able to come to the funeral? It's not until Sunday. If you want to bring the girls, I'm pretty sure Allison would watch them while we're at the service. No one is actually sitting shiva, but Cyd and Sid are having everyone back to their house afterwards. But honestly, if you're busy this weekend, or don't feel up to the drive, it's okay. I will not be mad."

Grace decided that she really couldn't miss another family funeral without becoming the subject of more gossip. Although she'd never admit it, she knew she had messed up when their father had died. In her own mind, she blamed it on the shock of the news interfering with her judgment.

"No, I'll come. I think I'll leave the girls home with Ira, though. Can I stay with you Saturday night? I don't like to make the drive back and forth in one day."

"That'll be fine. Sheila's going to try and get a flight in Friday. I'll put her in the guest room, and you can have Justin's room. He'll sleep with Gabe."

"Great. Your boys are so easy-going. You're lucky. So I guess this is going to be another debut of your new look. Other than the Sids and Nana Sadie, you haven't seen the Thornton side of the family, have you?"

"No, I guess you're right. Not since Dad..." Roxanne broke off, not wanting to get back into that territory again.

Grace quickly cut her off. "Okay, then, I'll see you Saturday around six. Let's just bring in pizza for dinner, you don't have to cook."

"Thanks, I'll see what I feel like doing. But pizza is always a safe solution. Goodbye Grace, and listen, I'm glad we're talking again. I'm looking forward to seeing you, even if it is for a funeral."

"Yeah, me too. Oh, I've gotta go, Emily just came in soaking wet from the snow. Bye, see you Saturday."

TWENTY-EIGHT

SINCE SHE HAD NO classes on Friday, Roxanne had most of the day to prepare for Sheila's visit and then Grace's arrival on Saturday. She decided it would be nice to make a real Friday Sabbath dinner. Even though they weren't observant and they never lit candles, it still gave Roxanne a warm feeling to bring the whole family together for a comfort food dinner of roasted chicken with mushroom gravy, mashed potatoes, and sweet baby carrots. She got out of the house early and even went to the bakery for a loaf of challah and a fresh apple pie to serve warm with vanilla ice cream. Sheila's plane was arriving at 2:30, and if they were lucky, and Sheila stuck to her plan of bringing only carry-on luggage, they'd be able to miss rush hour traffic.

Roxanne did all that she could for the dinner ahead of time. Everything was ready to pop in the oven when they got home from the airport. She had it all under control. She headed to the airport in plenty of time to meet Sheila. She took along a book of scenes to try to find something to work on for Physical Acting. She had already accepted Garrett's offer to do the scene together, so now she had to find a scene that they would both like.

She plopped down on one of the seats in the baggage claim area. Being at JFK always made her think of her father, and she felt a pang missing him. She used to go with her mother and Grace to meet him at the airport after he'd been on a week-long business trip. In those days you were allowed to go to the gate to meet the passengers. She and Grace would try out all the different chairs in the waiting room, then bored, they'd beg Sheila for money to buy candy at the gift shop and Sheila would let them walk down the huge corridor together if they'd promise to come right back and not touch anything if they had to go to the bathroom.

The baggage claim area felt closed-in and gloomy compared to the spacious departing gates. There were no windows to see planes arriving and departing. There was nothing much to look at except unclaimed luggage circling around and around on the conveyor belt and a lot of very tired and cranky people. There was something incredibly annoying about waiting for luggage and it showed on the faces of those waiting. A group of people congregated at the opening chute, their eyes intently focused as if looking away for a second would mean they would never find their suitcases. Logic dictated that one could stand anywhere along the baggage carousel, but many people had no patience to wait for the luggage to come to them. They seemed to feel that by stationing themselves at the beginning, they would get their stuff much, much sooner. This made it quite perplexing that with so many people desperate to get their hands on their things and leave, you always saw a bunch of the same luggage going around and around the carousel unclaimed, while your own suitcases stubbornly refused to surface.

Roxanne amused herself by watching the faces of the suitcase seekers. It was fun to watch a person's facial expressions if you could catch them at the exact moment of recognition. Their dull, glazed eyes would open wide, they'd smile involuntarily, and when they had their luggage all accounted for they looked as if they'd just won the lottery. What satisfied looks were on the faces of those who could load up their luggage carts and head off on the next leg of their journey!

After watching the scene play out over and over with its rotating cast of characters, Roxanne became aware that she, too, was being watched. An attractive man dressed in a business suit was leaning against the wall, seemingly unconcerned about snatching his luggage as soon as it appeared. When she looked at him to see if he was poised to grab his luggage she saw instead, that he was gazing at her with an expression of admiration and perhaps a bit of longing. When her eyes met his, he winked!

Oh my God, did he really wink at her? Roxanne panicked that she had somehow given this total stranger the impression that she was interested in him. She got up on the pretext of checking the flight arrival schedule and then took a seat out of the man's line of sight. Sure enough, the man in the suit moved his position against the wall so that once again he could watch Roxanne while also keeping an eye out for his bags.

Now feeling worried that he might try to approach her, Roxanne moved to a seat closer to the security guard. The "terrorist stalker" (he had now become that in her mind), smiled at the move and continued to watch her from a distance. She refused to look back at him and was happy to hear an announcement that Sheila's plane was on the runway. Within moments, her cell phone rang and Sheila was repeating the announcement for herself.

"I'm right in the baggage claim area, Mom," she said. "I'll see you in a few minutes."

"Excuse me," the stalker was now standing beside her, his smile even wider. "I noticed the book you were carrying. Are you an actress?"

"Um, um I'm waiting for my mother," Roxanne said. *Did she really say that? Was she in high school?*

"My name is Raymond Micelli. I'm in advertising. We're holding auditions for a new series of commercials and we're looking for a pretty, new face like yours. Here's my card. If you're interested, call my office on Monday and make an appointment." He pressed the card into her hand and gave it an extra squeeze.

"Oy, what a flight," Sheila moaned, coming in close and sticking her cheek in Roxanne's face to be kissed. "Do you have my warm jacket, I'm freezing."

"It was nice meeting you, Miss...? May I give your name to my secretary?" said the stalker AKA Raymond Micelli.

"Oh. Thornton, Roxanne Thornton."

"Does that mean you'll call?" he asked, ignoring Sheila's gaping stare.

"I don't know, I mean, I'll think about it, maybe."

"It's a good opportunity, Ms. Thornton. I have an eye for talent and I see something in you."

Roxanne swallowed hard and tried to think of something intelligent to say. "Thank you," was the best she could do.

"Well, goodbye for now," he said and turning to Sheila, he bowed sharply and said, "Madam, you have a lovely daughter."

"Yes, dear, you certainly do." A tall, elderly gentleman had joined Roxanne and Sheila. Roxanne looked at Sheila and saw immediately that Sheila was not at all shocked by this comment from a stranger. In fact, she was smiling.

"Roxie, this is Herb Seckendorf. He's a friend of mine. When he heard I was flying up for the weekend, he decided to come up and see his daughter, too. He hates to fly alone, you see."

"Really?"

"Would you mind dropping Herb at his daughter's house? Believe it or not she lives just off the exit before yours. We thought it would be silly for both of you to have to drive here."

Herb took Sheila's bag from her and the three of them

headed for the car. Roxanne was surprised to see her mother get into the back seat of the car with Herb Seckendorf.

"You don't mind if I sit back here, do you Roxanne? Really, your driving makes me so nervous I'm better off not seeing where we are going."

"What, since when?" Roxanne was used to her mother's remarks, but this one was completely out of left field. Uncharacteristically, Sheila chose not to respond.

Throughout the drive home Sheila kept up a travelogue describing all points of interest: the hospital where Jack had died, the mall that charges higher tax than Florida, the diner with the best blintzes. Herb appeared to be fascinated by it all, and added some of his own anecdotes about the garage that fixed his daughter's flat for free and the bagel place with the best herring in cream sauce.

Roxanne pulled into the driveway of the white split-level Herb pointed out, and after putting the car into park she popped open the trunk, expecting Herb to take out his suitcase and leave. A tall red-haired woman came running out of the house.

"Dad, Sheila you made it!" the woman exclaimed. "How was your flight?"

Roxanne was surprised to see her mother get out of the car and embrace this woman with the red hair. They had clearly met before, in fact, they seemed to be quite well acquainted. She sat with her hands still on the steering wheel, waiting patiently as any hired taxi driver might.

"Beverly, come meet my daughter," said Sheila, taking the redhead by the hand and walking around the car to the driver's side.

"Roxanne, aren't you going to get out of the car?" Sheila said.

Seeing no alternative, Roxanne quickly obeyed her mother.

"Beverly, this is my daughter Roxanne. Rox, this is Herb's

daughter Beverly. She came to visit him and joined us at the Clubhouse for New Year's Eve."

"Nice to meet you," said Roxanne, shaking hands with Beverly. She looked at Sheila, trying desperately to tell her with her eyes that she wasn't interested in chatting and willing her by mental telepathy to get back into the car.

"Umm, Mom, We really have to go," Roxanne said, giving up on nonverbal communication.

"Okay dear, listen, would it be okay if Beverly and her husband and Herb join us for dinner tomorrow when Grace comes? She and Stan are empty nesters, so it's just the three of them."

"I wasn't planning on even making dinner tomorrow, Mom. I'm just taking in pizza."

"Great, we love pizza. I'll bring dessert. Any allergies in your family?" asked Beverly.

"No, no food allergies."

"Okay, we'll see you, what time, about seven?"

"Sure, seven should be fine. I guess you need directions to my house."

"Actually, your mom e-mailed them to me last night."

"You what?" Roxanne asked. "You actually used a computer?"

"Well, Herb really did it. What are you so shocked at, Roxanne? Aren't I allowed to keep up with the times?"

Not wanting to further this line of conversation, Roxanne turned to Beverly and Herb and said, "Okay, so we'll see you tomorrow. Come on Mom, the kids will be home soon and they can't wait to see you."

Sheila got back into the car, in the front seat now.

"Honey, I'm just going to rest my eyes on the way home. I'm feeling tired from the flight."

Roxanne had a million questions about Herb Seckendorf, Beverly, Stan, and exactly why they were coming to her house for pizza the next evening, but with her eyes closed, Sheila looked kind of old and vulnerable. There would be plenty of time for questions later. Roxanne reached in her coat pocket for the car keys and felt the card with Raymond Micelli's phone number. Meeting Herb had pushed the encounter with Raymond from her mind. She fingered the card and then pushed it deep into her pocket for safekeeping. *Would this be her big break, or was the guy merely coming on to her?* She'd never had to ask herself these questions before.

TWENTY-NINE

"HI GRANDMA, WHAT'D YOU bring me?" asked Gabe.

"Gabe, I thought you were old enough to know better," said Roxanne sharply.

"Oh, he's just being honest," said Sheila. "Actually, I did bring you some chocolate from the airport, but you have to share it with your brother and sister." Sheila dug into her tote bag and came up with a two-foot plastic candy cane filled with Hershey's kisses wrapped in red and green. "They had the Christmas candy on clearance. Don't eat it all at once."

"Oh, I won't," said Gabe, as he tried to break open the package.

"Hey, wait until after dinner," said Roxanne. "I made a special dinner for Grandma and we're all going to eat together when Dad gets home."

Justin and Allison, chocolate-sniffing hounds that they were, came bounding down the stairs to greet their grandmother. Before Roxanne could get a chance to ask Sheila about Herb Seckendorf, she and the kids were setting up for a game of hearts in the living room.

"Mom, do you want to play?" asked Allison.

"No thanks, I'm going to finish making dinner," Roxanne replied. Seeing that everyone was engrossed in the card game, Roxanne pulled the business card out of her pocket. Raymond

Micelli's office was midtown, an easy subway ride from Penn Station or from her school. She wondered if Garrett had ever worked for him or knew anything about him. After all, Garrett did do commercials. He'd be a good person to talk to before she called the number on the card. *I can't deal with this now,* she thought; *I've got to get through this weekend first.*

Roxanne's dinner was a hit with everyone. Even Sheila had praise for the meal, and exclaimed, "You just can't get a good challah like this in Florida."

Once everyone had filled their plates, Roxanne was ready to put Sheila on the spot. She couldn't rest her eyes or start a card game now. What better place than the dinner table was there to talk and catch up?

"So Mom, what's the story with you and Herb Seckendorf?" she asked, rather bluntly.

"No story, I told you, he's a friend of mine."

"Well, he seems like more than a friend, to me," Roxanne persisted.

"Grandma, do you have a boyfriend?" asked Allison. "That's so cool."

"I did not say he was my boyfriend!" Sheila said defiantly.

"Okay, okay, calm down," said Roxanne. "By the way, did you make reservations for a flight back? I was just wondering if I would need to miss any classes to get you to the airport, or maybe Beverly could drive you and Herb back, you know, like a carpool."

"Well, actually we're not flying back together," said Sheila.

"Oh. I thought you said he doesn't like flying alone?"

"That's true. Actually, Beverly is giving Herb her car. She just got a new job that comes with a company car. Herb's car is on its last legs so we're going to drive back. You know, see the sights along the way."

Roxanne was somewhat stunned by this news. Making a

three-hour flight together back and forth to Florida was one thing. But driving twelve hundred miles and stopping to see the sights meant something else—it meant they were going to stay in motels. She shot Ben a look that told him she was struggling with how to react to this announcement, and he quickly jumped into the conversation.

"Well, that sounds like fun," said Ben. "Would you like me to get you an itinerary from the Triple A, Sheila? I could get some guidebooks for you, too. Where are you planning on stopping, DC, Williamsburg?

"Maybe, but we're planning a little side trip to Myrtle Beach. I've heard so many nice things about that area."

"Mom, you certainly know how to make the most of a funeral, don't you?" said Roxanne. "How did you plan all this so quickly?"

"Oh, it wasn't really me," said Sheila. "Herb is just one of those people who like to take action. He sees an opportunity to make an unfortunate situation into—well, into an adventure, and he just gets it all figured out. I'm just going along for the ride. I mean, why not? I can miss a few tennis games and some cards."

Roxanne decided that she didn't want to discuss the trip with the kids at the table. "Sure, that makes sense," she said. As soon as the kids had finished dessert she strongly suggested that they go upstairs and finish their homework. Justin and Allison knew when they weren't wanted, but Gabe wasn't as easy to get rid of.

"I finished my homework," he said, not moving from his chair.

"Great, then you can go clean out the litter box," declared Roxanne.

"Umm, actually there is a book report I need to work on," said Gabe, and before Roxanne could say the words "litter box" again, he was gone.

"So Mom, you're really traveling around with a strange man?" Roxanne was beyond being delicate anymore.

"What strange man? I've known Herb for a long time. Your father knew Herb, too."

"Really? What do you think he would say about this little trip of yours?"

"Roxanne, your father is not here to give his opinion. If your father were here, then THAT would be a story! You're not the only one in this family who is allowed to make some changes in her life, Roxanne. You know, you didn't ask my opinion when you made some pretty major decisions of your own. I don't think I need to ask you for your opinion about this. I've had enough of this subject. We don't need to discuss it any further—and that includes at our dinner tomorrow night. Do I make myself perfectly clear?"

Not waiting for an answer, Sheila turned her back on Roxanne and Ben, went directly to the guest room, and closed the door firmly behind her.

"I'm sorry, but she's right," said Ben. "Whether they are just friends or more than that, really isn't your business. You're just going to have to get used to the idea, Rox."

With a heavy sigh, Roxanne looked at Ben. "I know. I did act like an ass just now. I'll go apologize. You're right, it's really all good, isn't it?"

THIRTY

GRACE ARRIVED SATURDAY AFTERNOON with presents for the kids and a little awkwardness for Roxanne and Ben. Sheila quickly stepped in to take over the conversation and before too long Roxanne and Grace were able to put down their defenses and enjoy being together without feeling tension.

"Do you know anything about Mom's friend Herb?" Roxanne asked Grace when Sheila stepped out of the room.

"No, other than that he exists, why?" asked Grace.

"Because he and his daughter and her husband are coming here for a pizza party tonight. Sheila is taking a road trip with him back to Florida after the funeral."

"What do you mean by road trip?"

"The two of them—Sheila and Herb—are driving together back home, and they're making stops in several places, including a few days at Myrtle Beach."

Grace let that sink in for a few moments.

"Do you think there's something going on with them?"

"I don't know, what do you think?"

"I don't want to think about that. But, really, I think it's good Sheila has a gentleman friend. She's not dead yet, you know."

With the Monty Python's Spamalot song, "I'm Not Dead

Yet," playing in her head, Roxanne reluctantly agreed with Grace.

"Well, you're taking this much better than I did. I'm afraid I kind of freaked out on her."

"Why?"

"I'm not sure I could know without deep Freudian analysis. And my therapist doesn't do that."

"I don't either, but something about our mother having a so-called relationship with a man gives you trouble. I don't think it's anything to worry about, though. It's probably the best thing that could happen for her and for us."

"You know, you're probably right."

At seven on the dot the doorbell rang announcing the arrival of Herb Seckendorf and Beverly and Stan Mergenthal. Beverly carried two huge cake boxes, Herb toted a gigantic bottle of Chianti, and Stan wore a somewhat embarrassed look on his face. Roxanne sensed that he was not any more comfortable with the sudden joining of these two families than she was, and immediately decided that she liked him the best. Roxanne had expected Sheila to rush ahead of her to get the door, but when she turned around, Sheila was nowhere in sight.

Introductions were made all around as the kids came downstairs to see who had arrived. Roxanne was just about to send Gabe to find Sheila when her mother appeared at the top of the stairs. She had changed from her black wool pants and white sweater into what Roxanne presumed to be a "hostess ensemble" of brilliant turquoise velvet with silver studs adorning the collar, cuffs, and the hems of her billowing pants legs.

Everyone turned to watch Sheila float downstairs on her cloud of turquoise. "I'm so glad you're here, dears," she said. "Did you have any trouble finding us?"

"Sheila, what a beautiful outfit," Beverly gushed.

"Oh, thanks. I just picked it out of a catalog. It looked

like something very comfortable to wear," Sheila said. "Well let's not all stand around in the hallway, come on into the living room."

Roxanne grabbed Ben and asked him to quickly call in the pizza order. "You better order salad and garlic knots too, and tell them to rush it. Don't let them deliver, pick it up. It'll be faster."

Roxanne didn't have to worry about making small talk. Beverly and Herb seemed to know everything about her and Ben, their kids, and also about Grace and her family. They both showed tremendous interest in everything they were doing, asking about Roxanne's classes, Ben's business, and the kid's school activities, even knowing what grades they were each in.

"And Gabe, how's the soccer game going?" asked Herb. "I understand your mother suffered the most injuries of any player."

Gabe laughed at Herb's remark. "Yeah, Mom tried to play defense against a bus," said Gabe.

Having finished her second glass of Chianti, even Roxanne was able to laugh along with the others. Herb was diligent about refilling all the adults' wine glasses. By the time Ben arrived with the pizza, the red wine had mellowed Roxanne out of feeling uncomfortable entertaining her mother's "new best friends."

The evening passed quickly, and at 11:00 Sheila announced it was time to turn in. "We've got Nana Sadie's funeral tomorrow at nine. We don't want to be bleary eyed for the service," she said.

The next morning Sheila had transformed herself back into the woman Roxanne knew best. Her turquoise splendor had been replaced with her black tailored wool suit and pumps, and she breakfasted on tea and toast while waiting for the rest of the family to rise.

Ben and Roxanne had decided to bring the kids to the

funeral. "They've never been to a funeral and I think it's best if the first time they go it's for someone they were not that close to," Ben said. "A lot of my family will be there, and it will be good for the kids to see them."

Roxanne had to admit it was a good life lesson for the kids, even though she predicted they would be pretty miserable for most of the day. Still, this was one of those, whoever said life was all fun and games times where the kids would learn the virtue of paying their respects to an elderly relative. Like it or not, Allison, Justin, and Gabe were directed to put on their temple clothes and be ready to leave by eight a.m.

The funeral was almost enjoyable. With no official mourners, and Nana Sadie's having lived to an undeniably ripe old age, it turned out to be a pleasant time for family members to see one another and catch up on what was happening since they last met. For an elderly widow's funeral, the turnout was unusually large. Everyone who had known Nana Sadie wanted to show by their presence that she had been special to them, too. Several family members shared Nana Sadie stories at the service, and more tears were shed from laughter than in sorrow.

"Nana Sadie was truly the Grande Dame of her family. Her mind and her wit were sharp until the very end, and she lived her life seemingly without regrets," said Cousin Kay. "She had her share of sorrow, and outliving her husband and sons was tough on Nana Sadie, but she never asked for any sympathy, she kept on going and going like the battery bunny. She certainly served as a great example of strength and good humor for us all. I know she'd be very pleased to see so many of us here today, and she'd probably say something like, "What's all the fuss about? Eat, enjoy, life is short. Nothing made her happier than seeing her family together."

"The last time we saw Nana Sadie was at Roxanne and Ben's house for Chanukah," said Cyd when it her turn to speak.

Roxanne tensed as she tried to anticipate what Cyd would share about that holiday with the rest of the family.

"On the way home, we were all remarking on how Roxanne looked so great after having been through such a serious accident," she said. "My Sid said something like, 'Roxanne is quite attractive now, don't you think?' And Nana Sadie, said, 'Roxanne was a beautiful girl from the day she was born. Look at her beautiful children, could they come from a mother any less beautiful? Of course not.' It struck me then, that one of the reasons we all loved Nana Sadie was for the way she loved all of us. We were all beautiful, talented, and brilliant in her eyes. We're going to miss seeing her shep nachas every time one of us has a simcha, but I like to think that she'll be watching us, and smiling every time we have a personal success. I think she'll be there during our low times too, but she'll be telling us, 'have a bite, relax, this too shall pass.'"

Roxanne had expected to undergo blatant scrutiny by her relatives at the funeral. They had all heard about her accident and subsequent transformation and she knew they were eager to form their own opinions on how she looked now.

"So, how does it feel to be a beauty like your sister, finally?" asked Cousin Kay, who could never be accused of being subtle. "What do you think Grace? You two look much more like sisters now, don't you think?"

Grace didn't quite know how to respond to Kay. Opting out of the discussion, she laughed lightly and excused herself to call Ira and the girls.

"Did you get to choose how you wanted to look, or do they just promise to make an improvement and you hope for the best?" asked Kay's sister, Gwen.

"I see you had a little work done below the neck too," said Eileen. Was the boob job part of the package or did you have to pay extra? I'm just asking because I have a friend who might be interested."

"Don't be crazy, Roxanne didn't have a boob job, did you dear?" Kay said. "Please, Eileen, they wouldn't bother if you were going to keep them small like that."

"Hey, wait a minute," Roxanne felt the need to clear up some facts. "First of all, I did not have any plastic surgery on my body at all. Everything was done to reconstruct my face, which was severely injured by the school bus."

"Well, it was more like *new* construction than *re*construction wouldn't you say?" quipped Cousin Alexa.

"I guess you could say it was a bit of both," answered Roxanne.

"Well I think you look lovely," said Cousin Florrie. "Not that you weren't sweet looking before, Roxanne. But I think the doctors did a very nice job. They've managed to bring out your eyes. The eyes are the windows to the soul, they say, and Roxanne, you have always had a beautiful soul."

"Why, thank you Florrie. What a nice thing to say," Roxanne was touched to receive such a sincere compliment from Florrie.

"I mean it. I just hope all this has made you happy," said Florrie, and gave her a friendly squeeze.

"Yes, that's all that's important, right, right?" added Cyd.

"Of course, Cyd, you are absolutely right," said her husband.

When they got home from the funeral the message light was blinking on the answering machine. It was Herb calling Sheila. He wanted to know if she could be ready to leave on their trip at 5:00 that night.

"Herb was tracking the weather, and he thinks we'll miss a bad rainstorm if we leave tonight instead of tomorrow. He'll be picking me up soon," said Sheila, after returning his call.

"Are you sure he's okay driving at night?" asked Roxanne.

"Oh, he's fine. He told me he took a long nap this afternoon and he's ready to go. I'm just going to change into my traveling clothes."

When Herb arrived, Roxanne saw Sheila's face light up as she greeted him. He was clearly excited at the prospect of their trip, and hustled Sheila out the door before she could launch into her customary drawn-out goodbye. Herb seemed to be the one in charge, so different from how Sheila and Jack had been, Roxanne thought. Jack had always looked to Sheila to make the plans. Roxanne supposed that might be one reason that Herb appealed to Sheila. Maybe she's actually tired of being the one always in the lead. Maybe she really can change at this point in her life.

Even after they had pulled out of the driveway, Roxanne looked down the dark road imagining she could see them on their way. She was surprised to feel a tear run down her cheek.

THIRTY-ONE

"So what do you think, Garrett? Have you ever heard of this agency? Have you ever met this guy Micelli?" Roxanne asked her new friend on Monday, showing him the business card before class began.

"Sure, I've heard of them, but I've never met Micelli. You should definitely call. Go on the audition, you've got nothing to lose."

"But I don't know if I'm ready."

"Roxanne, please. It's a commercial. They'll probably have you read two or three lines of script. You can do it. The fact that he asked you to call must mean that you have the look they want. It's 95 percent about physical appearance with commercials."

"Isn't it 95 percent about physical appearance with everything?" Roxanne said.

Garrett laughed. "I guess you could say that. So make the call."

"Now?"

"Yes, right now. I'll sit with you for moral support."

Garrett pulled her over to a quiet corner of the student lobby. Encouraged by his enthusiasm, Roxanne pulled out her cell phone, cleared her throat three times, and punched in the number.

"Mr. Micelli's office," said a crisp, efficient, secretarial voice.

"Hello. My name is Roxanne Thornton. Mr. Micelli asked me to schedule an appointment for an audition. He said he's doing some commercials that I might be…"

"Oh, you're the airport actress, right?"

"Yes, I guess so."

"Mr. Micelli told me to expect your call. He's interested in your reading for the GlimmerGlo Cleansers account. The auditions are being held Thursday afternoon. Can you come in at 2:45?"

These people certainly work fast, Roxanne thought. She'd have to miss half her Improv class but she wasn't about to make waves at this point.

"Yes, that will be fine."

"You have the address?"

"It's the one on Mr. Micelli's card?"

"You've got it. We'll see you tomorrow. Have a good day. And be sure to bring a headshot."

Roxanne snapped the phone shut and looked up to see Garrett grinning at her.

"Congratulations, you have your first audition. We have to celebrate. Lunch is on me today."

"Oh, you don't have to do that, Garrett," Roxanne protested.

"But I want to," he said. "Please let me."

Roxanne felt somewhat embarrassed at his intensity, so she just made light of the situation. "Well, if you insist, I guess I can't stop you. Thanks. Wait a minute—she said to bring a headshot. I don't have any."

"Relax, I've got my digital camera with me. I'll take a few shots and print them out in the computer lab on the third floor. It won't be Annie Leibowitz, but it will do for now."

"Okay then, let's get to class. Those warm-ups are the best exercise I get all week."

Erik was in an especially exuberant mood, even for him. "Let's have some fun today," he said. "I know, let's start with a good death scene. How does an actor portray dying?"

"They don't move?" offered Tiny.

"Well, obviously, when it's all over, you have to be still, but the fun is in getting there. After all, there are so many different ways to die. Let's see how many ways we can come up with. You'll do your death scene, and the class will try to guess the cause of death. When you finish your turn, call on one or two people to go next. No cheating, now. I'll just put out some floor mats to cushion any falls. Is everyone game?"

They nodded at the purely rhetorical question, and Erik lined the stage with foam rubber matting. There was no tolerance for hesitance in Erik's class. David, the bicycle messenger, was first.

"Run over by a garbage truck," shouted Roxanne before David had a chance to do anything.

David just smiled and gave a little salute to Roxanne acknowledging her joke at his expense. He then placed a chair in the middle of the stage and sat down, his hands gripping the armrests and his feet firmly planted on the ground. Staring straight ahead, without saying a word, David communicated a range of emotions with his eyes and the position of his body. First, he feigned nonchalance then, he expressed a fear that grew quickly in intensity and barely audible whimpers escaped from his lips. Finally, his body shook violently as he conveyed the force of 50,000 volts of electricity surging through it. He was so convincing in the agony he was portraying, that Roxanne found her eyes moisten and felt her heart thumping by the time David slumped over "dead."

Once recovered themselves, the class burst into applause.

"Excellent, you had us all on the edge of that electric chair with you," said Erik. "Now, choose two people and let's see what they can come up with together."

"Okay," said David. "Roxanne and Garrett, you're up."

"Can we consult first?" Garrett asked.

"Two minutes prep—that's it," said Erik.

"Let's try falling off a mountain," Garrett whispered to Roxanne.

"I don't know. I'm not sure what to do."

"Don't worry, just follow my lead." Garrett removed his belt and handed one end to Roxanne. "Here, we'll use this as the climbing rope."

Garrett began his imaginary ascent up the mountain and Roxanne followed, separated by the length of his belt. At first, she just mimicked what Garrett did, but as she got further involved in the exercise through her movements and expressions and gasps for air she and Garrett showed the class that the mountain was getting steeper and the oxygen was thinning. Then, giving Roxanne a nod to warn her, Garrett shrieked. He stumbled and fell backward, trusting Roxanne to catch him.

Playing her part, Roxanne instinctively reached to grab onto Garrett, and then, holding onto each other, they tumbled across the stage until they came to a stop at the foot of the "mountain." Roxanne chose to die immediately from a head wound, but Garrett took his time, deciding that he would expire from internal bleeding. He dragged his broken body back over to Roxanne and embracing her, proclaimed his love for her with his last breath.

Roxanne, still playing dead, lay perfectly still. She was very aware of Garrett's tenderly caressing her face, her hair, and laying his head upon her shoulder before he allowed himself to succumb to his wounds. She felt herself beginning to blush, and very suddenly, she sprang to her feet and took a sweeping bow. Garrett looked up in surprise and then jumped up and took his own bow by her side. He grabbed her hand and genuflected as if they were the leading man and lady taking their final bows after a standing ovation on Broadway.

"Wonderful, wonderful," Erik applauded. "Now that's

real drama. You gave us an entire show there. Thank you, good work."

When class was over, Garrett took his camera out of his knapsack.

"We can do the headshots here in the classroom when everyone clears out. I know there's no one in here for the next hour," he said.

Roxanne felt very self-conscious at the thought of posing for him. "Maybe I can get away without it," she said.

"No, you really have to bring something. Don't worry, I promise I'll be very quick. It'll only hurt a little."

Roxanne knew she had no choice. "Okay, I'm ready for my close-up Mr. DeMille."

Garrett had her sit on the desk and made silly jokes that elicited a real smile. He moved around the room to get some different angles. In just ten minutes he was satisfied. Taking her by the arm, he led her to the third floor computer room where he swiftly located the necessary photo paper for the printer. He inserted the memory card in the correct slot in the computer and the images of Roxanne came onto the monitor.

"Hey, these are great," he said. "They need to be in black and white, though, I'll put them into Photoshop and we can pick the best one."

Garrett certainly knew his way around a computer; in a few seconds the color photos had been drained of color. "What do you think?" he asked, grinning.

Roxanne stared hard at the screen. She had never seen herself look quite like that before. The black and white eliminated any skin-tone flaws, and Garrett had captured her looking very natural in several poses. She swallowed hard, not sure she could speak.

Garrett didn't notice Roxanne's reaction. He was quite pleased with his photography.

"I'm better at this then I thought," he said. "Of course,

I knew the photos would come out great. How could they fail with a model like you? So, which one is your favorite? I'll print a bunch of eight by ten glossies for you."

Roxanne compared the shots with one another. They were all pretty good, but one stood out. Her eyes had a happy shine to them and her smile was just right.

"I think I like this one the best," she said.

"I am in complete agreement. Ten copies coming right up."

Garrett gave the computer the command to print and the printer lights began to flash.

"So, where can I take you to lunch?" Garrett asked.

"Garrett, I think I'd better run over to Macy's and see if I can find something to wear to that audition," said Roxanne. "I guess something that makes me look wholesome and clean."

"Oh. Okay, do you want me to come with you? Give you a guy's opinion?"

"No thanks. You're really sweet, but I definitely do better shopping alone, especially when it's speed shopping. I'll see you tomorrow. Thanks for everything, for the photos and all your encouragement, and, oh, it was fun dying with you," she said.

Garrett found a manila envelope for the photos and handed them to Roxanne. She gave him a very quick kiss on the cheek and hurried away before he had a chance to come up with any more suggestions.

Macy's Herald Square "The World's Largest Department Store" could be extremely confusing if you didn't have a plan. Roxanne, however, headed straight for the Petites Sportswear. Here, her choices were limited, but at least they would fit her. Ever since the accident and losing weight, shopping had been ten times easier than it had been since her post-Gabe years when she was at her heaviest. She reasoned that an audition for a commercial for GlimmerGlo called for a clean, crisp outfit with style but no flash. As always, she was drawn to the medium blues that complemented her eyes. They were already showing spring clothes, but Roxanne didn't want to show up with lightweight clothes under her winter coat.

Eventually she found just what she was looking for. A periwinkle blue sweater with matching wool slacks. Both the sweater and pants were trimmed with a woven-in floral design in neon green. She realized that Allison had green shoes she could borrow that would match almost perfectly. How fortunate that her daughter's feet had stayed small even after she surpassed her mother in height! The fitting room mirror was kind and in less time than she had expected, Roxanne was on her way home.

On Thursday morning, Roxanne decided to skip classes altogether and instead visit Vinny for a blow out. She realized that she would be too nervous to get anything out of her classes, and she knew that if she went she'd find herself blabbing about the audition to people in her classes, and she felt that she'd probably regret that in the end.

Vinny was surprised to see her. She never came in between cuts and he immediately asked what was the special occasion.

"I'm afraid to talk about it, but I'm going on an audition for a commercial," Roxanne admitted, knowing she couldn't keep it from him. "I just want it to look good, but natural, not as if I just left here. Can you do that?"

"Sure. What's the commercial for?"

"Some kind of cleanser, so don't make it glamorous. Just make me look like someone who can clean her house without any exertion because I use a miracle cleaning product."

"Aha, I know just what to do."

In twenty minutes, Vinny had done his magic. Roxanne was very pleased with the way she looked. She gave him a peck on the cheek and promised not to forget him when she was famous.

THIRTY-TWO

BACK AT HOME, ROXANNE did her makeup with extra care and then put on her new "audition outfit." Pleased with her reflection in the mirror, she was confident that she had made an excellent choice at Macy's. Still, she needed a little encouragement, so she hit the speed dial to call Ben at his office.

"Hi, it's me," she said.

"Hi, you. Did you have the audition yet?"

"Ben, I TOLD YOU the audition was 2:45! It's only 10:30 now!" Roxanne said exasperated with his lack of attention to the details of her big day.

"Oh, right, right I knew that." Ben tried to cover up his negligence. "So, how are you? Nervous?"

"Yeah, a little."

"Well, don't be. Just pretend it's one of your community theater auditions. You've always said that you had no reason to be nervous. It's not as if you need this job to put food on the table."

"I know, but I can't help but feel different about this. I feel like this is going to foretell my whole future."

"C'mon Roxie. That's not even logical. Hey, would you like me to meet you for lunch before the audition?"

"I thought your office lunch was sacred."

"I can make a one-time exception."

"Thanks, but I'll be too nervous to eat. I would love it if you'd meet me after the audition though. Could we go out for a drink to drown my sorrows?"

"You mean to toast your success?"

"Well, either way. The agency is not far from your office."

"You've got it. I'll just take a quick lunch at my desk and then leave here early. What time do you think you'll be done?"

"I have no idea. Why don't we say four o'clock?"

"Okay, and break a leg, sweetie."

Roxanne hung up the phone and did feel a little better. At least now she had something to look forward to after the audition. Win or lose the job, she'd enjoy her mini-date with Ben. She left a note for the kids, telling them she'd be home a little later than usual, but would still be home in time for dinner. Assuming she was able to meet Ben at four, she figured they would grab a drink and then catch a train no later than six pm. The kids would be fine until then.

Roxanne arrived at Mr. Micelli's office at 2:30 for her 2:45 appointment. The receptionist checked her name off a long list and gave her a form to complete.

"Photo and resume?" she asked.

"Oh, I'm sorry I don't have a resume, just a photo," Roxanne stumbled. "You see, Mr. Micelli asked me to come in for this. I'm, umm, I'm the airport actress?" she said, hoping that would jog the woman's memory.

With a face as blank as before, the receptionist gestured for Roxanne to take a seat. It was just like so many movies and television shows she had seen. The waiting room was filled with chairs and the chairs were filled with women in their thirties and forties. All of them were made up impeccably, but not glamorously. All of them playing the part of a GlimmerGlo girl. Three of them wore clothes almost identical to Roxanne's. *Well at least she had chosen the right outfit.*

Clutching the clipboard with the form she was to fill out, Roxanne checked out the competition. How did she compare? Without really being conscious of what she was doing, Roxanne began to mentally separate the women into two groups. The first group was women who were better looking than she and the second was women she felt that she had the edge over. The latter category, Roxanne eliminated as competition. Counting up the women remaining with whom she felt she was reasonably in contention, she saw that she had eliminated a little less than half the hopefuls there. In just a matter of minutes she had sized up everyone in the room and placed herself almost squarely in the middle.

She completed the form and checked her watch. Two forty-two, she wondered if they went by appointment or by the order in which people had arrived. She looked around and saw that everyone else was noting the time and sitting up straighter, expectantly. Roxanne guessed that they all had the same 2:45 appointment.

"May I have your attention please," the receptionist stood up and addressed the group. "In the top right-hand corner of your form you'll see a number. We'll be calling you in a few minutes five at a time, according to those numbers. Please bring the form into the office and return the clipboard and pen to the reception desk when you are called."

By Roxanne's count there were thirty women waiting to audition for this ad campaign. She was number 12—two groups of five would go in before her.

By the time her group was called, Roxanne had changed from being optimistically confident to feeling near panic. She tried to tell herself that this was not in any way going to be a rating of her acting ability, but she didn't believe her own unspoken messages. Along with numbers 11, 13, 14, and 15 she was ushered through the waiting room to a large, brightly lit conference room. On one side of the table sat Mr. Micelli, two other men in business suits, and one woman of indeterminate older age with a suit so tailored its lapels looked like they could cut glass. She was definitely the one to win over, Roxanne thought. Roxanne's side of the table had no seats, and she stood in a line with the others, all of whom she believed had been through this kind of ordeal before.

She gave Mr. Micelli a nervous smile, and he gave her a noncommittal nod in return. The woman spoke first.

"Thank you all for coming in. We're looking for a new face to represent GlimmerGlo Products. We'd like to hear you speak. Would you each tell us your name and oh, just for fun, try giving us a line that you think would be appropriate for a GlimmerGlo girl."

Fun? Shit, why couldn't I be number 15? thought Roxanne. What the hell am I going to say? She hoped desperately that number 11 would take her time and then screw it up.

"Thank you, next," came the prompt, signaling Roxanne to speak.

"Hello, my name is Roxanne Thornton. I used to dread cleaning until I tried GlimmerGlo," she said with forced cheer. "Now, I don't even mind when the kids track mud onto the kitchen floor." Ah, inspired if I do say so myself, Roxanne thought.

"Thank you, next," came the response. Roxanne searched the faces of the four executives for some sign of appreciation, but not even Mr. Micelli returned her glance. *Could she have been that bad?*

Number 15 took her turn and then Roxanne and the others stood up straighter, smiles plastered on their faces, still giving their full efforts to conveying through their body language and a little attempted mental telepathy that they were each the obvious clear choice to represent GlimmerGlo.

Mr. Micelli stood up. "Thank you. We'll be contacting you tomorrow morning if we need you for the callback audition. I'm sure you've all given your contact information to the receptionist at the desk. It was a pleasure meeting each of you." The other two gentlemen stood, and the woman gave a sharp nod and a smile as the women filed out.

A secretary showed the group out through a back entrance that prevented their re-entering the waiting room. Their coats had been moved onto a rack outside the conference room. There was nothing for Roxanne to do but claim her coat and leave. Numbers 11, 13, 14, and 15 all seemed to have other places to go, people to see. They checked appointment books, got on cell phones, and beat it hastily out the door. Roxanne watched them all disappear onto the elevator, but hung back. She waited by herself for the next one, checking her watch to see that it was only 3:30. She still had a half hour to wait for Ben.

The elevator doors opened into the lobby and there, waiting expectantly for her with a single rose was Garrett. *Garrett! What was he doing here?*

"Congratulations, you survived your first audition," Garrett said, handing her the rose.

"Thank you. This is quite a surprise. A shock, actually. How did you know where I'd be?"

"I was stalking you."

"What?" Roxanne looked at him sharply. *He was kidding, wasn't he?*

"Relax, Roxanne, I'm just playing with you. I remembered the name of the ad agency you were going to, and when I didn't see you at school I just decided to meet you here and see how you did. I know I can always use a friend after an audition, no matter which way it goes. So how was it?"

"I have no idea," said Roxanne. "There were, like, thirty potential GlimmerGlo girls crammed into the waiting room. We went into the conference room five at a time, told them our names, gave an impromptu GlimmerGlo pitch, and left. That was it. I would have felt used and abused, but it happened so fast and was so impersonal I don't really feel anything."

"Ouch, that sounds painful to me," Garrett sympathized. "How about going for a drink to numb the pain?"

"I'm planning on it. Ben is meeting me here in…" she checked her watch, "about twenty minutes. We can all go together."

"No, I don't want to intrude on your plans. I'll see you in class." Garrett turned away, but Roxanne grabbed his arm.

"Don't be ridiculous. It was very sweet of you to stalk me like this," she stopped and smiled, waiting for him to give her a smile in return. "I want you and Ben to meet." Garrett didn't look convinced that he should stay. "I absolutely insist you join us and I will be horribly insulted if you don't," she said in her best Scarlett O'Hara imitation.

"Well, you give me no choice then, do you?" said Garrett. "I can't horribly insult my scene partner, can I? Where were you planning on going?"

"I don't think we discussed it. Let's see what Ben says when he gets here. Do you know anyplace nice around here?"

Before Garrett could answer, Ben came from behind and kissed her cheek. "Hi, how'd the audition go? Wow, they must have really liked you—they gave you a rose?"

"No, no Ben, this is Garrett, from my classes. I told you about him, remember?"

"Oh yeah, the toilet guy, right? Did you have an audition here too?" Ben and Garrett shook hands politely.

Garrett smiled and shook his head. "No, I just came to give my fellow thespian some support. I've been to enough auditions to know that they can be hard on your ego."

"Garrett's going to join us for a drink. Do you know where you want to go?"

"Well, we usually just go over to McAnn's from work."

"I know a place I think you'll like," said Garrett. "It's just a few blocks from here, but unless someone tells you about it, you'd never find it."

"Oh, that sounds intriguing. Ben, do you mind if we follow Garrett?"

"No, why should I mind?" Ben asked, sounding a bit petulant. "I'm always willing to try a new bar."

"Let's go then," said Garrett.

The bar was just three blocks away, but as Garrett had said, it was hidden from sight up a narrow flight of stairs.

"It's kind of stuffy in here, don't you think?" said Ben, looking disappointed.

"No, I think it's charming. Oh, they have old theater posters on the wall, how cool," said Roxanne.

"I thought you'd appreciate it," said Garrett. "Joe told me there's a table in the back for us. What can I get you?"

"That's okay, I've got the drinks," said Ben.

"You can get the next round, Ben, I'll start us off," said Garrett.

"Well, we may not have time for a second. We do have three kids waiting at home for us," Ben replied.

"Ben, relax. Allison can take care of the boys for a little while. I'll have a vodka tonic, Garrett, and Ben would like a Bloody Mary, wouldn't you, honey?"

"Make mine a martini, straight up with an olive," said Ben.

"Ah, my kind of drinker," said Garrett. "Go ahead and claim that table, I'll be right there."

"Ben, what's your problem?" asked Roxanne in an annoyed voice.

"No problem, I just wasn't expecting this to be a threesome."

"Well, I'm sorry, he just showed up. What could I do? I had to ask him to join us."

"You did?"

"Didn't I?"

"Why didn't you just tell him we were meeting to take the train home together? Then we could have gone someplace nice, just the two of us."

"That's ridiculous. It wouldn't kill you to be nice to a new friend of mine. Now cut it out, here he comes."

On the train ride home, Roxanne feigned sleep rather than have an argument with Ben. He had been uptight and unfriendly with Garrett, acting more possessive of her than he had ever been.

He's never acted possessive or jealous of me before, Roxanne thought. She supposed this change in his behavior was because of her change in appearance. *He probably thought no one would ever be interested in me before.* Roxanne didn't want to even acknowledge his "immature" attitude. *I'll just avoid any conversation about this*, she told herself. *I can make myself quite busy when we get home.*

When the train pulled into their station, they got into their separate cars. "I've got some food shopping to do, I'll meet you home later," said Roxanne.

THIRTY-THREE

THE CALL DIDN'T COME. Roxanne was showered and dressed even before the kids had to get up for school. After nine o'clock she sat with the cordless phone in her lap, and watched the television with the volume lowered so that she could not possibly miss the phone call from Micelli's office.

At noon, Roxanne told herself they still might call. *They might not have meant it literally when they said morning,* she rationalized. They could still call. By two o'clock her hope was almost gone. She called herself on the cell phone to make sure the phone was working, even though she knew it was.

At three o'clock the phone rang, startling Roxanne so that she dropped it behind the couch cushions and had to disturb Clarissa's nap to retrieve it.

"Mom, can you pick me up?" asked Allison. "I missed the bus."

It took Roxanne a few moments to shake the disappointment out of her head. In the thirty or so seconds that had lapsed between the first ring of the phone and when Allison's voice had come out of the receiver, Roxanne had held an entire conversation with Mr. Micelli in her mind.

"How'd you like to be the new GlimmerGlo girl," he'd said in her imagination.

"Me, really? Thank you Mr. Micelli. I'd like that very

much," she'd answered him, and had even pictured herself on a giant billboard that greeted everyone crossing the Queensborough Bridge on the way into the city.

"Mom, are you there? Are you coming to get me?" Allison shouted impatiently.

"Sure, no problem," said Roxanne. "I'll pick you up in the side parking lot."

"Christy and Mallory are with me. We're going to Ryan Schwartz's party tonight, okay?"

The three girls piled into the backseat of the car and flung their backpacks over the front into the passenger seat. "Thanks for getting us Mom," said Allison. "Thanks Mrs. Thornton," chorused Mallory and Christy." For the rest of the ten-minute drive home the girls discussed what they would wear to the party. Christy and Mallory had each brought a choice of tops and pants with them. From what Roxanne could tell, they wanted to all dress the same but still look different.

Back home, the message light on the answering machine was blinking. Roxanne's heart beat faster. Could it be Micelli? Before playing the message, she forced herself to hang up her coat and get a pen and paper ready in case she had to take down a phone number. She took a deep breath and pushed the button.

"Hi, it's me. I'm going to be late getting home tonight. Don't wait for me for dinner. I'll have something here."

Allison and her friends would be eating at the party. With Ben coming home late, Roxanne figured she and the boys could make do with just one pizza for the three of them. She called the pizza place and ordered it to be ready for pick-up when she dropped off the girls.

Justin and Gabe were very happy with their dinner. The three of them pulled apart the slices, still hot enough that the cheese stretched into long strings. To Roxanne's surprise, Justin noticed that she was more quiet than usual.

"Is something wrong Mom?" he asked.

"No, why?"

"You look kind of sad. What is it?"

"Well…" Roxanne hesitated to admit what she was thinking, but then she remembered something she'd read in a magazine recently. The article had advised parents that it was good for them to share some of their own disappointments with their children in order to show them that even parents couldn't control everything that happened to them, but that they could learn to accept disappointments and go on with their lives.

"What is it?" now Gabe was interested, too.

"It's really nothing. I'm just a little disappointed because I didn't get a job that I auditioned for yesterday."

"Oh, that sucks," said Justin. "Was it a good part in a play?"

"Don't say sucks. No, it was for an ad for GlimmerGlo." Even as she said it, Roxanne realized that losing the job sounded nothing like the tragedy that had played out in her head.

"I thought you were going to school to be an actress," said Justin. "Do you really want to do ads for GlimmerGlo? That doesn't sound so great."

"You're right, honey. I never even thought about that. I just wanted them to want me."

"They're the losers, not you," proclaimed Justin.

"Thanks."

The boys finished their pizza and disappeared to the family room for a Friday night video game tournament. Since Mallory's mother had promised to pick up the girls from the party, Roxanne decided to make herself a hot bubble bath and soak away all remaining self-pity. Justin was right. She wasn't taking acting classes to sell soap. Her two million dollar settlement was carefully invested to ensure that money would not have to be a deciding factor in these things. Her disappointment was really about those all-too-familiar feelings of rejection. She poured herself a glass of red wine and took it with her into the bathroom. *If I'm lucky,* she thought, *Ben will stay out long enough for me to enjoy my bath and get into bed early before he gets home.*

THIRTY-FOUR

Roxanne was straightening up the kitchen Monday morning when the phone rang.

"Please hold for Mr. Micelli," said the voice.

Before Roxanne could get her mind around what could be happening, a new voice came on the phone.

"Hello Roxanne, this is Ray Micelli," he said. "I'm sorry we couldn't offer you the GlimmerGlo account."

"Oh. Well, thanks for calling."

"Look, I know you're new at this, and I feel somewhat responsible for pushing you into something you weren't quite ready for."

Roxanne wasn't sure where he was going with this, but her warning radar started beeping inside her head.

"We did all agree that you had a lovely quality about you. I think with a little coaching you could have some real success in this field."

"Well, I'm in acting class now," said Roxanne.

"I was thinking about a different kind of coaching. I've been in this field a long time. I think with a few private sessions I could really help you develop your style."

"I don't know, Mr. Micelli..."

"Ray, it's Ray."

"I just, I'm not sure if I really want to get into the

advertising field. I'm more interested in theater, even if it's not on Broadway."

"Do you know how many legit theater people either started out as pitchmen or at least supplement their salaries by appearing in ads? It's all part of the business, Roxanne. Listen, I had a last-minute cancellation of an appointment at 3:30 this afternoon. Would you come to my office so we can talk in person?"

Roxanne hesitated. Was this customary? Was she about to make an appointment for a session on a casting couch? Oh what the hell, she thought. If I don't go I'll always wonder whether I should have. After all, not much can happen in his office.

"Sure, I can be there at 3:30 today," she said.

"Great. I'll see you then."

"Yes, see you then. Goodbye now."

Shit, now what do I wear today? Roxanne wondered. She'd already picked out a sweater and corduroy jeans for class. If she put on business clothes her classmates might notice (well, Garrett would) and she wasn't sure she wanted to discuss this with him. She decided to keep the sweater, and switch to a dressier pair of slacks. No one would notice anything, but she'd feel better about what she was wearing to meet Micelli.

When she got to Physical Acting she saw that Garrett wasn't there. She was surprised to notice that she felt a little relieved by his absence. Still worried and feeling that she was getting jerked around by Micelli and perhaps pushed into something she didn't really want but was too weak to object to, Roxanne realized that Garrett's absence meant she could participate in the class without having to smile and joke with anyone. *Why were all these strange men suddenly complicating her life,* she wondered.

Since her class would be over at two, Roxanne decided to see if Jo wanted to meet for a quick cup of coffee so that she could get some advice about these men from someone with a little more experience than herself. She hit the button on her cell phone for Jo. She answered right away.

"Hi, it's Roxanne. I was wondering if you and Tai wanted to meet me at Starbucks for coffee and milk and cookies later today."

"What time?"

"That was a fast answer, don't you have to check your busy schedule?"

"Nope. What time?"

"Two o'clock at the Starbucks across from my school."

"We'll be there. How'd you know Tai loves Starbucks?"

"Just a lucky guess. Bye Jo."

"Bye, and hey—thanks for calling."

Jo and Tai were already seated at a table when Roxanne got to Starbucks. Jo had grabbed the one and only high chair available and was letting Tai amuse herself with arranging coffee stirrers in different designs.

"Don't you know she can poke an eye out with one of those things?" Roxanne said as she sat down.

Jo looked hard at Roxanne. "Are you serious?"

Roxanne laughed, "No, of course not, I'm just busting your chops. How are you?" she said, and gave Jo and Tai each a hug.

"We're fine. So, why aren't you rushing home to suburbia? To what do we owe the pleasure of your company?"

"Well, of course I wanted to see you, but I did have some time to kill between class and a business appointment. I thought you could give me a little advice on how to handle this appointment."

"Well, I'm intrigued. What's it all about?"

Roxanne told her the story of how she met Ray Micelli at the airport, the cattle call casting session, and the follow-up phone call. "What do you think? Do you think he could really be interested in helping me break into the business or is he looking for umm, you know, umm sex?" whispering the last word so Tai wouldn't hear it and repeat it.

Jo laughed. She always spoke her mind aloud. "All men are looking for sex, aren't they? The question is really is that his primary or secondary motive for calling you."

"What do you mean?"

"There are pretty much two things that drive all decisions men make. Money and sex. In this case, he could see you as a potential commodity that will bring him money; or he could find you a delightful challenge to add to his repertoire of conquests. Of course, it's probably both. If it's just the money that is motivating him, you're fine. Take the meeting and see what he has to say. If it's just the sex that he's after, you should know that soon enough. But like I said, I'll bet it's both. Now, what does this guy look like? Is he worth the sex for a shot at stardom?"

"Jo, I'm married! How could I do that to Ben?"

"I'm not suggesting you do anything to Ben…but could you stand leading him on until you get what you want? What does he look like?"

"Actually, kind of like a young Dean Martin. You know, that good-looking Italian type with the expensive suits."

"Ooh. Is he married or single?"

"I'm not sure, does it matter?"

"It matters to me. I'm still looking you know."

"Jo, I really need you to focus here. I've got to meet him in an hour. What do I do? Should I even go?"

"Of course you should go. What's he going to do, attack you in his office? Go, and listen to what he has to say. But watch for signs that he's more interested in play than work."

"What kind of signs?"

"Roxanne, where have you been the past twenty years?"

"Married."

"I'm talking about physical signs. Does he lean in close to you? Is there touching or penetrating looks that make you wriggle? Does he want to continue the meeting someplace else? His apartment, perhaps? Dinner at a dark restaurant?"

"Jo, you're the one who is making me wriggle. Do you think any of that could really happen to me?"

Jo shrugged. "Those things happen to all beautiful women. Face it, you've joined the club and you may be getting initiated here. But don't worry, he could also be strictly interested in the money and he could even be a very happily, married, completely faithful husband."

"Right, there are plenty of men like that."

"If you say so. I haven't met any. Good luck honey. You'll be just fine."

THIRTY-FIVE

MONEY AND SEX, SEX and money—was that really what all men were after? Roxanne understood that she'd been sheltered for many years by more than just a comfortable marriage. Her own self-image prevented her from ever considering that she'd get hit on by other men. *Was she really ready to be a player in this game?*

Ready or not, you're going to see what happens with Micelli today, she told herself. She arrived at his office exactly on time, but decided to wait a few minutes before going up in the elevator. After waiting a full five minutes, she pushed the up button.

"Mrs. Thornton, how nice to see you," said the impeccably dressed receptionist not a day over 25 or a pound over 105. "I'll just let Mr. Micelli know you're here and you can go right in."

Roxanne couldn't believe that the young woman actually recognized her from the cattle call. *Micelli must have told her I was coming.*

"Go right in," she said after a quick buzz into her boss.

Ray Micelli looked the very picture of the overworked executive. His jacket was off, his sleeves rolled up—just one cuff—revealing an expensive watch on one wrist, and his hair looked as if he had been scratching his head in frustration.

She noticed that even with the advance notice of her entrance he hadn't straightened himself up. He was definitely playing the role of a friendly advisor rather than strictly a business associate.

"Hi," he said with the familiarity of someone who knew her better than he did. "It's good to see you. Have a seat. He rose, walked out from behind his desk, and indicated a leather couch for her to sit down. So this is an official casting couch, she thought. She sat down on the left side of the couch, and to her immediate relief, Micelli perched himself on the corner of his desk.

"So, Roxanne, I'm guessing you're a little confused about why I asked you here. Maybe even a little suspicious of my motivation. Am I right?"

"I wouldn't say suspicious. More like curious. It's certainly nice of you to take an interest in my career. If that's what it is you're doing."

Micelli let out a full-bellied laugh. "I love your candor, Roxanne. As I said, you have a very special quality about you. You're real. There's nothing fake about you. That's what I first noticed at the airport."

"You like the real thing, then?" said Roxanne.

"It's refreshing. You're refreshing," he said and before she could blink he had moved onto the couch beside her.

"If I'm so refreshing then why wasn't I chosen for GlimmerGlo?"

"Well, to be completely honest, the client wanted to go a little younger, but you had my vote," he said.

"So…"

"So?" he responded.

"What did you have in mind? On the phone you mentioned coaching sessions." As soon as she said the words aloud it sounded like a come-on line. She looked him directly in the eye and tried her best to look all business and not at all gullible. "Are you going to coach me to look younger?" she added in somewhat of a challenge.

"No, no. I just want you to emphasize your natural qualities," he paused, then changed the tone of his voice and began to sound tired. "Roxanne, you'll have to forgive me. I've had one of those days and I'm not operating at my best right now. I could really use something to pick me up. How do you feel about cheesecake?"

"Cheesecake?"

"Yes, I've discovered that cheesecake and a cup of coffee at precisely 3:47 can give me the energy boost I need sometimes. There's a little coffee shop in this building that has excellent cheesecake. Do you mind if we continue this discussion there?"

That's not fair, thought Roxanne. *He's not following either of Jo's scripts—or is a coffee shop the same as a dark restaurant, only cheaper.*

"Actually, I love cheesecake," she said.

"Great, let me hang up your coat here, and we can go right down."

Before Roxanne knew it he was guiding her by the arm into the elevator. They walked into the street level coffee shop and the hostess greeted Micelli with a big smile.

"I'll bet I can predict your order," she said. "Will there be two for cheesecake?"

"Thanks Molly, that's right. Coffee, Roxanne?"

"Yes please."

Roxanne and Micelli—Ray, he insisted, were settled into a comfortable booth in the corner. In no time, cheesecake and coffee appeared. Ray took a forkful, closed his eyes and let the dessert slide down his throat."

"Ahh, it always hits the spot. Now you try it."

Roxanne dug her fork into the cake and sampled it. He was right. This was fabulous cheesecake. *Maybe he really didn't have ulterior motives,* she thought.

"So, Roxanne, will you tell me your story?"

"What story do you want to hear?" Roxanne hoped she sounded less clueless than she felt.

"Well, you're studying acting. I'm guessing this is a second career for you, or is it a first one, after taking time out to do the mommy thing?"

"First of all, I'm still doing the mommy thing," she bristled. "That never stops whether you have an outside job or not. Once you have kids, if you're lucky, they are here to stay. I happen to have three. But you were right the first time. I did make a career change recently. I used to work for a consulting firm."

"And so why the switch?" he asked, looking at her expectantly, and completely ignoring the indignant tone in her voice.

There was no way Roxanne was going to tell him what had really happened. "I came into an inheritance and it gave me the money I needed to leave a boring job and do something I've always loved doing—theater. So I signed up for acting classes and I'm giving myself some time to see if I can go anywhere in the business at this point in my life. I'm past the ingénue stage, but I don't think I'm over the hill yet."

"Well, I'm sure you had your fill of ingénue parts when you were a girl. But as I said before, you have a very genuine quality about you that I think might do well in commercials."

"It's not exactly why I made this career switch, though. I'm really not sure I should pursue it."

"No, you definitely should," he said emphatically.

Roxanne sat up and looked at him for several seconds before speaking.

"How can you be so certain about what I should do? You don't even know me."

"Please Roxanne, don't get angry at me," he said, and reached over and held her wrist over her sweater. "You may think I'm just an egotistical know-it-all, but the truth is that even though I don't know you as well as I'd like to, I do know this business. Do a few commercials and it will open doors for you. Just the experience of shooting alone will help you make the transition from a wannabe to someone on the inside."

Roxanne took back her wrist and grasped her coffee cup. "Well, no offense intended, but you couldn't get me the GlimmerGlo account. What makes you think you can get me something else?"

"Oh, I can't get you anything."

"No? Then why…"

"No, you'll have to get the jobs yourself. But as I told you yesterday, I think I can help you in that area."

"How?"

"First, finish your cheesecake."

Roxanne shrugged. So far, he hadn't done or said anything out of line. She was beginning to feel more comfortable with the situation. If nothing else the cheesecake was delicious, and the coffee was damn good, too, considering it was decaf. They ate and sipped their coffee slowly and before Roxanne realized it, the waitress had refilled her cup twice. The hot decaf relaxed her and outside the day had turned into evening.

Ray drained his second cup of regular coffee, black with one sugar, and seemed to have gotten the caffeine/sugar rush he had been after in the first place. "Okay, that was just what I needed. Ready to go back to my office?"

"I don't know. I really should be going," said Roxanne. "It's getting late."

"Well, your coat is upstairs, and I'd like to show you some examples of what I think you can do to get your first break."

Oh shit, here it comes, thought Roxanne.

Having no alternative, Roxanne followed Ray back to the elevator. The secretary was just putting on her coat when they got off.

"Remember I told you I had to leave early today?" she said to Ray.

"Sure Pamela, have a good night," he said to her.

"See you tomorrow."

Roxanne noticed that the offices next to Ray's were empty. It was only 4:30. "Did everyone leave early today?" she asked Ray.

"There's an account meeting at a client's office that I didn't have to attend. That's why it's so quiet here now. Believe me, there are plenty of nights the place is buzzing until very late. Come in and sit down. I want to show you something."

"It really is getting late."

"Give me another 15 minutes. Please. After all, I did buy you cheesecake," he teased.

Roxanne sat down on the couch and Ray pulled out a portfolio from a shelf on his wall and sat down next to her opening it across both of their laps. On each page were photos of women. They were pretty, but they didn't look like high fashion models.

"This is the type of look that you can offer. These women can all get steady commercial work. You just need to learn how to relax and let your inner spirit come out. I can show you how. Ray turned the pages again and revealed photos of the same women, but in these photos the women were much more scantily dressed.

"Oh, no you've got the wrong girl," Roxanne said and pushed the portfolio onto the coffee table in front of them. With the book off of his lap, it was obvious that Ray was fully aroused. His zipper bulged with what looked like a huge hard-on. For the second time that afternoon he took hold of her wrist, but this time he held it tightly.

"C'mon Roxanne, I'm a good guy. I'm not going to do anything you don't want. I can't help being attracted to you.

With her free hand, Roxanne made a fist and then with all her might she slammed it into Ray's crotch. He doubled over, releasing her wrist.

"Don't bother seeing me out," she shouted as she grabbed

her coat and bag. "I won't be coming for any more coaching sessions."

"You're overreacting, it's not what you think," he said, still trying to recover from the power of her punch.

Afraid of being caught in the elevator with another pervert, Roxanne ran down the five flights of stairs and was out on the street before Micelli could straighten up.

THIRTY-SIX

A MAN WAS JUST exiting a cab in front of the building, and Roxanne jumped in to the backseat before the cab driver could move. "Penn Station, please," she said.

Roxanne's head throbbed painfully as the cab inched along Madison Avenue, and she was afraid she might throw up. Rush hour had just begun and it would have been quicker to walk to Penn Station, but she really needed to sit just now. By the time she was finally on her train headed home, Roxanne had recovered her nerves enough to feel proud of how she had handled the situation. She took out her cell phone and called Jo.

"You were right it was the sex he was after," she blurted out when Jo answered.

"Oh. So not exactly the golden career breakthrough?" asked Jo. "Tell me what happened."

Roxanne was beginning to feel embarrassed about the whole thing now. "Let's just say that he made a pass and I responded with a hard sock in the balls."

"You're kidding! Roxanne! I didn't know you had it in you."

"Neither did I, but I seem to have very strong self-defense reflexes."

"What do you think Ben will say?"

"Nothing. I'm not going to tell him. I want to just forget this whole thing. I won't be hearing from Micelli again, and I don't want to upset Ben. Please, don't say anything to anyone about this."

"Who would I tell? Tai? I guess you didn't get a chance to give him my number, huh?"

"Jo, you are not that desperate. Listen, I'm coming to a tunnel. Gotta go. Bye."

The boys were in the living room glued to the television when Roxanne got home. "Where's your sister?" she asked.

"She called to say she's eating at Mallomar's house," said Gabe.

"What?"

"Mallory—she's eating at Mallory's house," explained Justin. "Just ignore him."

"Fine, I'm just going to take a quick shower."

Roxanne made the shower as hot as she could stand it, and squeezed out a big dollop of her vanilla mint aromatherapy body gel. She rubbed it in and inhaled deeply to get the full benefits of the gel. The label promised that its combination of natural essences of vanilla, peppermint, aloe vera, and honey extract would calm the soul, relax tense muscles, and invigorate the spirit. Wanting to give it every opportunity to fulfill its promise, Roxanne then laid down in the bath, first directing the showerhead so that the water would rain down on her body from her breasts to her knees. She closed her eyes, gave another squeeze of the gel bottle, and did her own form of tranquil breathing—pretty much the same breathing she had learned in her Lamaze classes, only without the excruciating pain.

Fifteen minutes later, feeling cleansed and pampered, and still smelling a bit vanilla, Roxanne put on her at-home comfy clothes and then went to the kitchen to start making dinner. She had decided that morning to bake some chicken breasts in cream of mushroom soup and serve it with leftover take-out

Chinese food rice. She had just put the chicken in the oven when Ben arrived home.

"Hey," he said, stopping for a quick kiss. "How's everything? How was that meeting you had with the advertising guy?"

"Oh, he had to cancel," Roxanne said, without looking at Ben and instead searching in the cabinet for a rice bowl.

"That's too bad. Did you reschedule it?" he asked.

"No. I decided not to. I was beginning to get a bad feeling about the whole thing."

"Really?" Ben was very surprised. "I don't understand. You were certainly positive about it this morning."

"I just changed my mind. Honey, I don't want to talk about it. Just forget about it. I already had."

Ben shrugged and picked up the unopened mail on the hall table to take with him into the bedroom.

That's two firsts in one day, Roxanne thought. *My first lewd pass and my first time lying to Ben about anything significant. It's the best way to handle it,* she told herself. *I don't need Ben feeling that he should somehow defend my honor. It's over and I won't let myself get in that kind of situation again.*

Roxanne was just finishing up in the kitchen when the call from Sheila came.

"How's my beautiful daughter?" Sheila began.

"I don't know Mom, I haven't talked to Grace in a while," said Roxanne.

"You're such a comedian. Maybe you should try stand-up comedy instead of this acting stuff. We could always use some new acts at the Clubhouse."

"You win. I'm fine, Mom. How are you?"

"Oh, not bad for a blushing bride of 75."

"Excuse me? What did you say?"

"I said, I'm about to become Mrs. Herbert Seckendorf."

"I…I…I don't know what to say."

"Say, *Mazel tov*! We made all the plans yesterday. We booked rooms for all the family at a "Kosher for Passover"

resort in Coral Gables. You know, I don't usually keep
Pesadicka, but for a wedding, I think it's only right. Besides, I
understand the food is fabulous, and other than a little matza
on the table, you won't even know you're keeping the holiday.
The kids won't have to miss any school; it's during their spring
vacation. Herb is paying for all the rooms and meals; all you
have to do is get your family down here. So you should book
your flights for the Saturday before Pesach, which starts on
a Monday—we'll have the ceremony on Sunday afternoon.
And, Rox, make sure the kids have some nice clothes to wear.
This is a classy place."

"Umm, Mom, could you hold on a minute," said
Roxanne. She covered the mouthpiece tightly with her hand.
"BEN! BEN! Come Here NOW!"

Ben came running in from the living room. "What's the
matter?"

"My mother is getting married!"

"No kidding? That's… news."

"She wants us all to come down to Florida for the wedding
over Passover."

"Let me talk to her," said Ben, and he gently took the
receiver from Roxanne's sweaty grip.

"Sheila, Roxie just told me your news. Congratulations,"
he said.

"Hello, Ben. So what do you think of your mother-in-law
getting married again?"

"We're very happy for you. I hear we're all going to come
down over Passover for the ceremony."

"That's right. I was just telling Roxanne the details. So
you'll be able to get the time off of work? Ben, I want you to
walk me down the aisle."

"That's great! How often does a guy get to give his mother-
in-law away? I would love to." He turned to Roxanne, smiling
at his own joke, but she responded by sticking out her tongue
at him.

"Ben, did I ever tell you what a mentsch you are? My daughter is a lucky woman."

"Ahh, I'm the lucky one. Well, I think my wife's recovered from the shock of your news now. She looks about ready to speak again. I'll let her take down all the details. Don't worry about anything on our end. We'll be there with bells on."

Roxanne looked at Ben as if he had grown a second head. "When did you get so agreeable to my mother?" she said in her strongest, angriest sounding whisper.

Still covering the phone, Ben answered, "Look, your mother's getting married. She sounds very happy, so we're going to go and be happy for her. Why put up any fight? Could there possibly be any other outcome? Talk to her, be nice, she's entitled to a second chance at happiness. Your father would approve."

THIRTY-SEVEN

THE ALARM JOLTED ROXANNE out of a fitful sleep. She shut it off, made a quick decision to ignore it, pulled the comforter up over her head and tried to go back to sleep.

"Mom, where's my red sweatshirt?" Justin asked, bursting into the bedroom. "I need it for gym today."

Resisting the urge to scream, "I don't give a FUCK where your red sweatshirt is," she sat up and forced herself to respond sanely to her son. It wasn't his fault she felt so rotten. "Did you check the hall closet?"

Justin looked at her as if the hall closet was a whole new concept to him. "Okay. Umm, aren't you getting up, Mom?"

"Sure, I'm just a little off today. I didn't sleep well last night." Roxanne threw off the covers, found her fuzzy slippers and bathrobe, and resigned herself to facing the day. She listened at Allison's door and was relieved to hear her daughter muttering to herself about having nothing to wear. She went into Gabe's room, sat down on his bed, and gently pulled back his blanket to reveal one boy, fast asleep, thumb in mouth.

"Gabe, time to get up sleepyhead," she said, prying his thumb out and then gently rubbing his head to wake him. Gabe was in such a deep sleep it took him longer than usual to open his eyes. He stretched his arms up over his head, and then smiled at Roxanne.

"Mom, I was having the best dream. I dreamed I had my own horse and we kept her in a barn in the backyard. I rode her to school every day. Her name was Sugar."

"That does sound like a nice dream, honey. But it's time to get up now. C'mon, go brush your teeth and get dressed." She gave him a quick kiss on his forehead, and proceeded to the kitchen. Justin was staring into the hall closet waiting for his sweatshirt to jump out into his arms. She stepped in front of him, pried the tightly packed coats and jackets apart, pulled out the sweatshirt, tossed it to Justin, and went to the kitchen to make the kids their usual breakfasts.

"Mom, aren't you going to school today?" asked Allison, who was first down for breakfast. "Why aren't you dressed?"

Roxanne cleared her throat and gave a weak cough. "You know, my throat is scratchy. I think I should stay home today. Actually, I might go in later for my second class." As she spoke she silently chastised herself for succumbing to the trauma of the meeting with Micelli and not being strong enough to put it aside and go ahead with her regular schedule.

By 8:20, when Gabe was on the bus headed for school, Roxanne had mentally gone back and forth a dozen times over whether or not to go into school late or get back into bed. The final decision: the bed. The house was deliciously empty, except for Clarissa, who rubbed against her ankles mewing softly for some fresh cat tuna, and Roxanne's final rationalization—that she really hadn't gotten the sleep she needed during the night—won out. She decided to allow herself another three hours in bed. She also decided that perhaps she needed a little help sorting out the feelings she was having. She punched in the number for her therapist.

It had been a while since she'd been to see Ann. They'd agreed to put their bi-weekly sessions on hold, but that Roxanne could call any time and make an appointment if she felt the need. She figured she would get the answering machine and just leave a request to see her soon.

But Ann answered the phone on the second ring.

"Oh, I wasn't expecting to get you in this early," said Roxanne.

"I have an 8:30 on Tuesdays, you got lucky," said Ann. "How are you?"

"I'm okay. I was wondering if I could come in to see you."

"Let's see, I had a cancellation this afternoon. Could you come in at one?"

"Yeah, that would be great. I didn't think I'd be able to see you so fast."

"You got lucky. I'll see you later, okay?"

"Okay, bye." That settled, Roxanne reset her alarm for 11:30 am. She'd indulge herself in a morning nap and deal with her demons in the afternoon.

It wasn't much easier getting up at 11:30, but with the appointment scheduled, Roxanne knew she had no wiggle room. She was ready to go at 12:30, and as always, she arrived at Ann's office with plenty of time to pretend to read a magazine.

Ann's office was in a suite of several therapists that shared a waiting room. A sound machine was parked outside each door, but it was quite common to hear shouts, sobbing, or other signs of despair, anger, and hysteria coming from inside the offices. Not furnished especially comfortably, there were vinyl and metal chairs placed along all four walls, and stacks of outdated magazines on several end tables. Roxanne had decided that the therapists probably didn't get along with one another and they showed their veiled disdain by refusing to make any investment into improving their common space. Ann's own office was quite inviting, soothingly decorated with soft but cheerful colors and cushioned seating.

Roxanne usually spent her time in the waiting room flipping through *People*. It didn't matter what the issue date was they were all pretty much the same. She scanned an old story about the Brad-Jennifer-Angelina nonsense, and smiled wryly to herself. "These are three of the most gorgeous people on earth, and all they do is make each other miserable," she thought.

At one o'clock, a couple in their thirties emerged from Ann's office. The woman was still dabbing at her eyes with a tissue, and the man looked straight ahead, his mouth set in a hard line. They'd certainly be back for more sessions.

"Come on in, Roxanne. It's good to see you. Would you like some tea?" said Ann. Roxanne hung up her coat and settled into the chair opposite Ann's. Even after almost three years of therapy on and off, she still felt uncomfortable and self-conscious at the start of a session. Ann always tried to come across as a sympathetic friend, but it just didn't work with Roxanne. She always felt a bit ashamed of herself for having to pay a stranger to listen to her problems.

"Well, it's been a while since I've seen you. You're looking great," Ann began. "How is everything going?"

"Things are pretty good, but obviously not perfect or I wouldn't be here."

"Okay. So what happened? Was there a specific occurrence or is it more a general feeling of depression?"

"I think we'd have to go with column A. You see, last week I auditioned for a part in a commercial for GlimmerGlo products."

"Uh huh…"

"Well, to make a long story short, I didn't get the job. But yesterday, the account executive called and asked me to come in. He said that even though the client hadn't chosen me, he thought I could have a future in the business, and he wanted to give me some help in getting started and in presenting myself better."

"That sounds promising," Ann said, trying to keep Roxanne moving ahead with the story.

"Well, after acting the part of the perfect gentleman, he

takes out this photo album of women he says are all successful commercial actresses and says that he thinks I could be one of them. Then, then…" Roxanne's face flushed brightly.

"What happened?" Ann leaned forward.

"Oh my God, it was gross," Roxanne began to cry, surprising Ann and herself at the same time. She hadn't realized how upset she really was over the encounter with Micelli. She blurted out the rest of the story amid a flood of tears.

Ann handed her a box of tissues and waited for her to calm down. "Roxanne, it sounds like you did a great job of getting away from him, and that you let him know exactly how you felt about his behavior. Can you tell me what is making you so emotional about this? This can't be the first time you've been in a situation where a man has made unwanted advances?"

"Yes it can," said Roxanne. "I never got hit on before my surgery. And the truth is, I'm not sure if he hit on me because I'm attractive, or because I somehow led him to believe that I would go along with him. I'm actually feeling guilty because of what *he* did. I couldn't even tell Ben about it."

"Why is that?"

"I don't know. I'm just afraid Ben is going to think it's my fault, too. Maybe I did lead him on."

"Did you?"

"No, not that I was aware of. But…"

"Yes, but…" she again pushed ahead gently.

"But I did kind of like the attention. I mean, he's a good looking guy, and he was saying that I might have a future in commercial acting, and, and I don't really know what I thought would happen."

"So that's why you didn't mention it to Ben? You think you did something wrong?"

Roxanne looked down at her feet, then all of a sudden she doubled over as if in pain. Clutching her belly, she ran out of the office.

"Excuse me, I'll be right back," she called to Ann on her way out.

She made it to the bathroom just in time. She bolted the door, fell to her knees, and vomited up the entire contents of her stomach into the toilet. Then, closing the lid, she sat on the toilet and held her head in her hands. She breathed slowly and tried to determine if she was finished being sick.

Ann knocked on the door. "Roxanne, are you okay? Shall I call for help?"

"No, I'll be fine. Please, just give me a minute. Really, I'll meet you back in the office in a minute."

Ann backed away from the door, but stayed in the waiting area. Fifteen minutes later, when Roxanne came out, she took her by the arm and led her back to the office.

"Here, lie down," she said, steering her to the couch that up until now they had never used in session. Ann took a bottle of spring water from her mini-fridge, twisted off the cap, and handed it to Roxanne.

"Thanks." Roxanne sipped the water and then allowed herself to sink back onto the cushions of the couch. "Hey, this is pretty comfortable," she said, attempting a smile.

Ann pulled up a chair close to Roxanne, positioning it so that they could look at one another easily. "I think you did the right thing coming here. You're obviously quite upset about what happened yesterday. Is there anything else you're upset about? Anything else new you're dealing with?"

Roxanne thought for a minute. "Well, my mother did announce she's getting married again. Does that count?"

"Really? When did you learn this?"

"Last night."

"Last night, as in just-after-you-got-home-from-your-meeting-with-the-lecherous advertising-executive, last night?"

"Yeah, that last night."

"Well, you did have an eventful yesterday, didn't you? How do you feel about your mother's news?"

"Oh, I don't know. It's just so typical Sheila to burst in with news about herself when I'm in the middle of my own inner crisis. I haven't even had time to think about it. Actually, Ben was pretty realistic about it. He talked to her and said that whatever her plans were, we'd be there for her. Before even telling us about it, she had already booked hotel rooms for us to go down over Passover and make it a holiday wedding slash vacation. She's also paying for the hotel and all our meals. You know how she always manages to bulldoze through everyone else's plans and get it done her way. Ben pointed out that in this case the only thing we can do is go along with her. Any other response will cause World War Three. If Sheila wants to get married, that's what she'll do. Any thoughts her daughters might have on the subject are of no interest to her. So really, why should I sweat it?"

"Well, you're right. Your mother will certainly do what she wants to do in terms of getting married. And from what you're saying, she's covered all the bases to prevent you from coming up with any practical ways to throw a wrench in her plans. She's even made the plans around the kids' school vacations, am I right?"

"Yep. So we'll be spending the spring vacation in Florida."

"I could think of worse things," Ann said with a wry smile.

"That's true. Bottom line is the kids will probably have a great time, and the time away might even be good for me, too. But still…"

"Still, seeing your mother marry again may be a little hard for you to swallow?"

"Is that a pun on the throwing up?"

"Sorry, no pun intended. I just meant that even though your mother may have managed to eliminate practical matters of logistics, there is still the emotional adjustment that seeing your mother remarry will entail."

"What do you mean exactly?"

"Sheila's remarriage forces you to let go of your father all over again. That's painful, especially for someone as sensitive as you are. So even if you say you haven't had time to think about it, I suspect that your subconscious has been dealing with the news from the moment you heard it. Coming right on top of your meeting with the advertising executive, no wonder you're operating on overload."

"Ann, when am I going to be able to deal with things like this without having near breakdowns? I thought…"

"Yes, what did you think?"

"I thought it would be different, that I would be different."

"You mean because you look different?"

"That does sound stupid, doesn't it?"

"It *sounds* like you're still as hard on yourself as you ever were. And it sounds like you're expecting too much of yourself, but why doesn't that surprise me?"

"I know, I know, you always say that."

"Do you think I have a valid point, or do you think I'm just being kind?" Ann said, trying to get Roxanne to think about what she was doing.

Roxanne sat for a few minutes mulling it over. "It's not that I think you're being kind, but as you always say, you are more accepting of me than I am of myself. Still, that's…"

"What?"

"Well, that's your job isn't it? I mean, who would want to go to a therapist that berated them for their shortcomings? You kind of have to accept what I do because you're trying to help me to move forward."

"BINGO. I *am* trying to help you to move forward. And if being easy on you can help, then don't you think that it would be in your own best interest for you to also be easier on yourself?"

The gentle "ding dong" of Ann's timer sounded, indicating the session time was over. "Would you like to make another appointment?" asked Ann.

"Let me get back to you," said Roxanne. "Let me see how things go. Thank you for seeing me today. I think it helped me a lot."

The answering machine was blinking when Roxanne got home from Ann's. She hit the button and heard her sister's voice.

"Hi, it's Grace. I spoke to Mom and I know you did, too. Call me."

Might as well, Roxanne thought. She hit speed dial and Grace answered right away.

"So it looks like we're going to a wedding," Roxanne said.

"I know. I'm not sure I'm thrilled about this. What do you think?"

"I think that what I think doesn't matter, and no offense, but neither does what you think. You know Sheila, she's got her mind made up about this."

"Actually, we have no real reason for to complain about it, do we?" said Grace. "I mean, he's a wealthy man in his own right, so he's not after her money. Not that there's much of that to tempt anyone. And from what I saw, he seems to be quite taken with her. Besides, I looked up the hotel on the Internet. It's none too shabby. We might as well go and have a good time. What the hell, Herb's paying for it."

"You're right. Ben's right. Sheila has every right to be happy. So why did I run to the therapist and wind up throwing up in her bathroom?"

"You did?" Grace didn't often hear such candor from Roxanne.

"I'm not making it up. I mean that wasn't why I went to the therapist, at least not consciously."

"What do you mean? Is there something else bothering you?" asked Grace.

Roxanne realized she'd probably said too much. She could share her feelings with Grace about Sheila's wedding, but she did not want to open up about the Micelli matter. She quickly tried to cover up her blunder.

"Oh, no, I just went to the therapist as a three-month check-up so to speak. I hadn't gone there to talk about Sheila. It was just a coincidence that Sheila's news came the night before my appointment. I'd scheduled the appointment weeks ago," she lied.

"So, a whole week of family fun," Grace said, her voice dripping with sarcasm. "And now we've got Beverly and her husband thrown into the mix. How will we survive that?"

"A lot of Manishevitz down by the pool, I guess. Do you want to consider a Plan B?"

"Why, what do you have in mind?" Grace asked.

"If our wonderful family members get too irritating, we could take the kids for a day or two to Orlando and do Disney or Universal. You know, just to break up the week."

"That's a possibility. But let's play it by ear. We don't have to plan in advance for that. Worst comes to worst, if all the nearby hotels are full then we just go for the day and stay somewhere in between. One thing—we have to both agree to go before saying anything to the kids. It's all the cousins or none of them," said Grace.

"Deal. Hey Grace, you don't think Sheila would pull anything like buying us matching bridesmaid's dresses, do you? She's done everything else without asking us about it. I just got a flash through my head of pink lace princess dresses with puffy sleeves."

"She wouldn't dare. Would she? Look, just to be on the safe side, tell her you bought the perfect dress for her wedding on clearance and it was final sale. I'll tell her the same story. She can't bear to waste a good sale."

"Good idea. Grace, if we stick together I think we can actually have a good time. Thanks for calling."

"You're very welcome, Roxanne. I'm beginning to look forward to it. I love you, you know."

"You too, Gracie. Bye now."

THIRTY-EIGHT

GARRETT WAS WAITING OUTSIDE class for her when Roxanne arrived. She was happy to see him. They had become good friends.

"Hi, how are you?" she greeted him.

"Good, good, I just wanted to catch you before we start. You missed class the other day."

"I know I did. I didn't know you were the truant officer here," she teased.

"Oh, sorry, I didn't mean to sound like that. It's just that we went over the scenes we're working on."

"Was he okay with our scene?

"That's what I wanted to talk to you about."

"Is there a problem? Damn, I thought it was a good one for both of us."

"Well, he wanted me to do it, but he strongly suggested that Leigh do the scene with me."

"Why?"

"Leigh and David had also chosen a scene together. He thought the casting would be better if you and Leigh switched. You would play David's mother and Leigh would be my scene partner."

"Oh." Roxanne let that sink in for a minute. She had just been told that instead of playing a steamy romantic scene with

195

a man close to her age, she would be playing the mother of a 23-year-old (which meant she had practically been a teenage mother) and Garrett would be playing his scene with a 26-year-old hottie. *Great. She was back in high school all over again.*

"I guess it's a good thing I hadn't started to learn the lines yet," she managed to say with a weak smile.

"Oh good," Garrett seemed overly relieved to have the discussion over. "Excuse me, please, I've got to make a phone call." In a flash Garrett had disappeared down the hall.

"Hi Mom," the voice of David-the-Bicycle-Messenger sounded from above her head. (Roxanne could never separate his job from his name in her mind). Roxanne looked up at David, who was at the very least six feet four, and so slim it seemed he would bend in half over backward if the wind ever blew at him too fiercely. With his ever-present smile and horn-rimmed glasses, he reminded her of the eponymous character in the *Where's Waldo* books.

"Look, let's get one thing straight," Roxanne said in a voice she hoped he would recognize as kidding. "Not only are you too old to be my son, but you're *way* too tall."

"Hey, that'll just make it more of an acting challenge for us. We'll get points on our evaluation for it. I've got your script here. Just a minute."

David rifled through his bicycle messenger bag and came up with a wrinkled script of smudgy papers stapled together in one corner.

"I was hoping we could get together some time tomorrow and have a first reading. Do you have any free time before class?" He was so earnest, Roxanne actually began to feel a little maternal towards him.

"Sure, David. Would you like to meet at nine o'clock in the lounge tomorrow morning?"

"Yeah. I can do that. Okay, it's a date."

Wonderful, thought Roxanne. I have a date with a man-child.

When class let out, Roxanne busied herself with organizing her bag, looking through it for something of obvious importance. Out of the corner of her eye, she watched Garrett and Leigh reading together from a small script, their heads nearly touching. Garrett's fingers seemed to be lightly resting on Leigh's waist. The look on his face said it all, he was immensely enjoying being so close to this beautiful, young woman.

Just when Roxanne felt she could no longer stall without raising suspicion, Leigh broke away from Garrett, flashed him a brilliant smile, and exited. Roxanne rose from her seat and walked slowly past Garrett as he was putting on his jacket.

"Roxanne, are you going to get some lunch?" he asked her.

An involuntary flip inside her stomach rose up to catch her voice in her throat. She coughed, and then, with a gigantic internal effort, regained her external composure to answer him calmly and casually.

"I could eat," she said. *Brilliant, she told herself. You're just so articulate.*

"Do you want to try that new sushi place down the street?"

Roxanne smiled, and agreed to give the new place a chance. They walked along together without speaking. Roxanne's inner voice spoke to her. *So, you're jealous of Leigh. Why? You're married. Garrett isn't your boyfriend. Isn't the friend zone where you need to be with him? You don't want anything to happen with him. But you loved feeling that he was interested, didn't you? Leigh sucks.*

Garrett's outer voice interrupted. "…So I'm glad you don't mind switching the scenes. Maybe we can do one together next time."

During lunch, Garrett moved the subject away from acting class and told her about the latest weekend he had spent with his teenage son, Dylan. Dylan lived with his mother in

Virginia and he only came to see Garrett one weekend a month and on alternate holidays. Garrett and Connie had divorced when Dylan was four. Consequently, their relationship, said Garrett, was more like a nephew and uncle than father and son. Roxanne could sense that Garrett felt guilty about the situation, but then again, she thought, *not guilty enough to have done anything to have ever changed it.*

"He's coming up again for spring vacation and I'm worried that he'll be bored. He's at the age where he'd much rather be with his friends than with me. I was wondering if your daughter Allison might want to show him around. If she's as pretty as you, I'm sure he'd be thrilled to meet her."

"Ha, flattery won't get you anywhere this time, Garrett. My family is going to Florida to see my mother get married." She shook her head as she said it, still not entirely believing it was really destined to happen. "But maybe another time. I'd have to talk to Allison first."

"He's actually quite a good-looking kid himself. He favors Connie's family."

"Oh, I'm sure he's acceptable, Garrett. You don't need to sell him to me."

Garrett looked offended. "I wasn't selling him to you. I just thought Allison might ask what he looked like."

Roxanne's sensitivity to the subject churned her emotions. "Well, I hope she's not that shallow. But I'll tell her he comes from good stock."

Garrett seemed to know not to continue the topic. "Here, have the last piece of dragon roll."

THIRTY-NINE

FOR THE FIRST TIME in what seemed like quite a while, the entire family sat down to dinner together. The boys were excited about going to Florida for their grandmother's wedding. Allison looked anything but.

"Do I have to go?" she asked in her most petulant voice.

"You know the answer to that, Allison," said Ben. "Why are you so against going to Florida? You can get a head start on your tan for the summer."

"Mallory and I had plans. Her sister invited us to come up to see her at BU. We were going to visit some of the other colleges in Boston, too."

"Yeah, and go to frat parties," said Justin.

"Shut up Justin, you don't know what you're talking about," Allison snapped at him.

"I'm sorry honey, but you really can't miss Grandma's wedding. Why is this the first we're hearing about these plans? Didn't you think we'd have an opinion on the subject? Besides, you're only a sophomore. It's early for that. We'll definitely schedule a bunch of college visits next year—even this summer if you want."

"But you won't take her to frat parties," piped up Justin.

"SHUT UP!"

"I heard her and Mallomar talking. They were planning on passing for college girls."

Allison stood up with fists clenched and Justin took off, ran upstairs to his room, and barricaded the door.

"Did you really need to have him?" Allison said to Ben and Roxanne. "He's such a jerk."

"Look, I'm sorry to put a crimp in your plans, but I'm not sure we would have given you permission to visit Mallory's sister if we knew your reason for going was to flirt with college boys," said Roxanne.

"That wasn't it! I want to start looking at colleges. How can you listen to him? He said that, I didn't."

"Okay, okay. Look, it's a moot point. The whole family is going to Florida for Grandma's wedding. I promise we'll make it a fun trip for everyone," Roxanne said, although she now had serious doubt that it would be possible to accomplish that.

"Can we go to Universal Studios?" asked Gabe, who had been sitting quietly chewing on his fried chicken.

"We'll see," said Ben and Roxanne simultaneously.

Attempting to change the subject, Roxanne told Allison that a friend of hers from acting class had a son her age and had asked if Allison might want to show him around when he's in town.

"What does he look like?" asked Allison.

"Does that really matter?"

"Are you actually asking me that?"

"What do you mean?"

"Umm, Mom, no offense, but nobody cares more about looks than you do. Did you forget what it's like for the rest of us who haven't had the benefits of modern medicine to enhance their natural beauty, or lack thereof?"

Roxanne looked at Allison and saw for the first time a resentment that her daughter must have been harboring for a long time. She wondered why she hadn't detected these feelings from Allison before.

"Allison, I got run over by a bus, remember?" was all that Roxanne could think of to say.

"I know that Mom, but what about all the extra work you had done? You can't tell me that everything they did was just to repair the injuries from the bus."

"No, of course not. You know very well that I asked the doctor to make some improvements. I was never happy with my looks. Allison, I almost didn't have you because I was afraid to have a little girl who would have the same hurt feelings that I did when I was a child. I've always thought that your being so pretty was kind of God's way of rewarding me for having the courage to have a child, in spite of my fears."

"Yeah, right."

"It's true. When I was pregnant I used to pray that you'd look like my sister instead of like me. And my prayers were answered."

"You think I look like Aunt Grace?"

"Don't you think so?"

"No, Aunt Grace is really pretty."

"Well, so are you, Allison."

"You just think that because you're my mother. You can't really see me the way I am."

Roxanne could no longer control her feelings. Something inside her snapped and instead of reacting in the mature, calm fashion she knew she should, she turned on her daughter.

"Allison, cut the crap. When I was your age I would never have had the nerve to plan to flirt with college boys, because I REALLY wasn't pretty. So don't try to pretend you don't know that you're attractive. And don't try to make me feel guilty for taking an opportunity when it was presented to me."

"Hey, I don't see what you're getting so mad about. I was just pointing out that looks do matter, and you should be the last one to argue with that. I wasn't expecting you to go ballistic on me. Now if you'll excuse me, I have to go call Mallory." Allison started to go to her room and then stopped.

"Mom, do you think I could go with Mallory to visit her sister for a weekend after the break?" she asked.

Before Roxanne could answer her, Ben jumped in. "Now is not the best time to discuss it, Allison. Let's hold off on that."

"Can I have another chicken leg?" asked Gabe.

Ben laughed softly and placed a crispy leg on Gabe's plate. Roxanne and Ben exchanged looks that said, well at least one of our kids is not a teenager. Keep his stomach full and Gabe is happy.

"Do you think she really resents my surgery that much or was she just trying to get back at me for ruining her plans?" Roxanne asked Ben when they settled into bed later.

"I don't know, probably both," he answered.

"I never expected her to act like that. I mean I expected snide remarks from the women my own age, but not from Allison."

"Don't worry about it, honey. I think we've been spoiled by her reasonable behavior up till now. Aren't you due for some mother-daughter rivalry at this age?"

Roxanne shrugged, and rolled over to escape into sleep. But as she listened to Ben beginning to snore, she knew she'd be tossing and turning if she stayed in bed. She put on her robe and slippers and quietly went downstairs to the den. She pulled one of the old photo albums that Sheila had given to her before moving to Florida off of the shelf, settled herself in the corner of the couch, and wrapped herself in the blue and yellow afghan that Nana Sadie had made for her.

The photo album started with Sheila and Jack as young newlyweds. In black and white, with edges that appeared to be cut with pinking shears, the photos chronicled the life of the young couple. Moving into their first apartment, holding their first dinner party for the family, all dressed up for the

Jewish holidays. Before too many pages had been turned, twenty-two-year-old Sheila was smiling into the camera and posing turned to her side to emphasize the round belly that protected the soon-to-be-born Roxanne.

She really looked like Grace when she was that age, thought Roxanne. A lyric from *A Chorus Line* popped into her head: "You take after your father's side of the family. The ugly side." She laughed aloud. *Well not anymore.* "What do you think, Dad?" she whispered to the photo of the young Jack, proudly holding newborn Roxanne up for the camera. "Can you see me now? Do you think I sold out by changing my looks? Well, to be perfectly frank, I don't care if I did sell out. I like looking in the mirror without grimacing at myself. Allison can afford to call me shallow. Thank God she didn't have to relive the pain of my childhood."

FORTY

DAVID WAS ALREADY WAITING in the lounge when Roxanne arrived. She thought he might be wearing the same thing as he had been the day before, but with the nylon bicycle clothes he always wore it was hard to tell. The stretchy nylon didn't really wrinkle, but there were some spots that indicated the clothes needed washing. Roxanne wondered if he had slept in them or if he had stayed over some young woman's apartment. She had a hard time picturing him in a romantic situation.

David has his back toward her and he seemed to be deeply engrossed in reading the script of their scene. She placed her Starbucks double moccachino grande next to his Vitamin Water, and he looked up at her and smiled broadly.

"Hi, you're right on time," he said. "Thanks for coming in early."

"No problem. Do you want to get started?"

"You know, I was kind of out all night…" he began.

"Yes?" Roxanne couldn't guess why he was telling her this.

"I didn't have time to change," he explained, and then his words began to get progressively faster. "We have three hours before class. Would you mind if we rehearsed at my apartment? It's only four blocks from here. I could change into some clean clothes and we'd have more privacy than in this lounge, which is probably going to get busy soon."

Well, that might be an interesting experience, Roxanne thought.

"Sure, I'm game. Lead the way."

David heaved a sigh of relief and quickly gathered up his papers and backpack. His bicycle was chained to a pole outside the building.

"I'll just leave the bike here. It's locked up tight. You'll see, it's a short four blocks from here."

"Don't worry, David, I'm perfectly capable of walking even longer than that."

Although it was a challenge keeping up with David's long strides, in just a few minutes they arrived at his building, a Village brownstone that had been divided into four units. David was on the third floor, and the walk up was a steep one. Roxanne tried to hide her heavy breathing from David. She didn't want him to think she was old and out of shape.

The apartment was much neater than she had expected. An overstuffed red corduroy couch took center stage, grouped with a matching overstuffed armchair and a bentwood rocker. A patterned area rug further defined the seating area, and the rest of the floor was dark wood parquet. An antique-looking wooden trunk served as a coffee table, and there were magazines stacked neatly on the trunk. The kitchen/dining room nook had a small, round butcher-block table with two chairs. Framed theater posters decorated the walls.

"Make yourself comfortable," said David. In an instant, he had pulled out a bowl of fresh fruit and a plate with cheese and crackers. "You can munch on this. I'll just take a quick shower and be out in ten minutes, okay?"

Roxanne nodded, and sat down to enjoy the pleasant breakfast he had provided. She was struck by how comfortable and "adult" the apartment seemed to be—so unlike her image of David the Bicycle Messenger. After sampling the cheese and crackers, she surveyed his books and his music and video collections and saw that she recognized many of the titles. He seemed to have an appreciation of the music from her generation.

Good as his word, in ten minutes David was back. His hair was still wet, and he smelled of a very nice aftershave. Rather than the garish bicycle shirt and black pants he usually wore to class, he was dressed in tan slacks and a pale yellow cotton sweater that showed off the muscles he'd developed cycling all over Manhattan, Brooklyn, and Queens. (He said he didn't really do much in The Bronx or Staten Island.) She was startled when she saw him. It appeared that Where's Waldo had been transformed.

David sat down on the couch, script in hand. "Are you ready to do a read through?"

"Absolutely," said Roxanne, internally fighting with the nervous feeling that had come over her. She sat down on the rocker, facing David.

The dialogue started off calm. The scene involved a mother and son who had just come from burying their husband and father. At first, they spoke quietly, rehashing the funeral service and exchanging derogatory comments on the various family members and friends who had come to pay their respects. Then the drama of the scene came into play.

"Well you really pulled it off, didn't you?" David said, speaking in character. "No one but me will ever know you killed him."

"Are you mad?" Roxanne instinctively leaned back in the rocker to put some distance between herself and her suddenly agitated "son."

"Don't play innocent now, mother," David rose from the couch, shouting the words in heated anger. He leaned his hands on the arms of the rocker and pushed his face close to hers.

Roxanne reacted by leaning further back. When David

turned his back in "disgust" at her, the chair rocked back with such force that it dumped her out. She hit her head on the coffee table/trunk.

A few minutes later, Roxanne discovered she was lying on the couch with her feet up on a pillow and a baggie of ice cubes on her forehead. David was perched on the coffee table and was staring at her intently. "Shhh, don't try to talk yet," he said.

"Did I pass out?" she asked, ignoring his advice.

"You were only out a minute. You fell out of the chair and hit your head. I'm so sorry."

"It's not your fault I'm a klutz," she said.

"Shhh, listen to the doctor, well almost, I'm a trained paramedic. I'm afraid you're going to have a bump on that pretty head of yours."

Roxanne was surprised that he spoke to her so tenderly. "Thank you for taking such good care of me, David. I'm lucky to be in such good hands."

David took her hand in both of his. Although he held it very gently, she could feel how strong he was. His hands felt enormous compared to Ben's, whose hands were so small they could share gloves. He slowly rubbed the back of her wrist, and then, turned it over and took her pulse.

"You're fine now," he said. "Your heart was racing a bit before, but you're back in normal rhythm." He kept her hand in his own and looked into her eyes. Then he lowered his head to hers and put his lips to her forehead.

"No fever," he whispered.

Roxanne was transfixed. She could see where this was leading and she knew that she should stop it, but she seemed to be having a kind of out-of-body experience she told herself. *Could this be a dream?* she wondered. *Am I still unconscious?* But she knew this wasn't dreaming.

Slowly, he moved his lips onto hers and gave her the most tender and sensuous kiss she had ever had. A little voice in her head screamed, *No, what are you doing? Are you crazy?* But another little voice said, *Shut up, this is too good to stop now.*

Her lips opened involuntarily and his tongue tickled hers teasingly and then probed deeply into her mouth. Her arms went around his neck and pulled him down on top of her. As they kissed she felt her body heat up as if she were on fire.

David sat up for half a second and pulled off his sweater. Roxanne literally gasped at the sight of his incredibly hard, youthful chest. Ben had never looked like that when he was David's age. He smiled at her obvious appreciation and then reached for the buttons on her blouse.

"May I?"

Unable to speak, Roxanne nodded and slipped further into this fantastical episode. His fingers moved with the speed of an athlete and fortunately (?) she was wearing a bra with a front closure. He snapped it open with expert ease and drank in the sight of her breasts with wide-open eyes and a grin to match it.

"I see you're a little bit happy here," he said, rolling her very erect nipples between his thumbs and forefingers.

Roxanne thought she would climax then and there, but then he lowered his head again and took one breast in his mouth and sucked hungrily while continuing to play with her other nipple.

"Oh my God!" Roxanne could barely stand the excitement she felt. She reached down and frantically pulled off her own pants, and David followed her lead. He felt under the couch for his stash of condoms he kept in a carved wooden box he had brought back as a souvenir of the Great Smoky Mountains, and again, with expert precision he slipped on the condom before slipping into Roxanne.

She sneaked a peek down at him and wasn't at all sure that something so large would actually fit inside her, but she was so wet that she took him in easily. Unable to hold back her orgasm, she trembled as she came, and then, a bit better able to control herself, she pulled David close to her and rode the crest with him until he too had found release.

"Come on in the bedroom, we'll be more comfortable," David whispered in her ear.

He pulled a soft throw off the armchair, wrapped it around her shoulders, and took her into his bed. Under a fluffy down comforter, she nestled in his arms.

"David, I have to ask you one thing," said Roxanne.

"Sure, what is it?"

"Have you ever been diagnosed with an Oedipal Complex?"

He let out a delighted laugh and hugged her tight.

"Beautiful and funny, too. You're really something." One thing led to another, and he was soon reaching for the stash of condoms he kept by his bedside.

Ding, ding, ding, ding. Roxanne awoke to a gentle alarm clock bell and took a few moments to remember where she was. *OH SHIT! She was in David the Bicycle Messenger's bed. Naked! But where was David?* Singing and the sound of a shower running answered that question. She jumped out of bed but almost fell right back onto it. Her head. Ouch. The bump had formed into a round, blue-green, throbbing egg. Roxanne took a deep breath, let it out slowly, and then, with cautious, deliberate steps she made it to the living room where her clothes were strewn about the floor, the couch, and that dangerous coffee table of his.

Listening for David, she dressed quickly. *Now what? Should I run? What can he be thinking? I'm a slut. I'm a whore. Twenty-two years of fidelity down the drain. But shit, that was incredible sex. If I do it again does it count as one betrayal or two? Or am I already up to three? How did you calculate cheating?*

While she was debating herself, David appeared before her in a blue terry robe.

"Oh, you're all dressed. I guess you don't want to shower then?" he asked.

Boy, he was cool about this. How often did he do this kind of thing? He was certainly good at it, but still, how could he be so nonchalant? Roxanne didn't answer him.

"We have about 15 minutes before we need to leave for class if we're going to be on time. Are you hungry? I could make us something quick, or we can stop for take-out on the way back. How does your head feel? You've got a huge bump."

"Oh, I'm fine. I don't think I could eat anything just now."

"Okay. Just humor me and keep this ice bag on your head while I get dressed. Here, sit down on the couch." David handed her the ice bag, then grabbed a banana off the table, peeled it and devoured it in three bites. Then he disappeared back into the bedroom for a few minutes.

Dressed again in the clothes that had first transformed him from Where's Waldo? to Who the Hell is That? David sat down next to Roxanne and again took her hand in his.

"Thank you for this morning," he said. "You are an incredibly beautiful and sensuous woman. You just made our scene a little more difficult though. It will be hard to call you mother. But no worries, I'm a good actor, you'll see."

Roxanne wondered if he was acting now. There were a million questions racing through her mind, but she wasn't able to get any of them to come out of her mouth.

"I'm married," she blurted out.

"Yes, I know," he said gently, as if he were talking to a young child.

"I don't do this," she explained further.

He raised one eyebrow, saying without words, *well, you did it today*.

"Did you like it?" he asked.

"Very funny, I'm *not* that good of an actress, David."

"Roxanne, you seem upset. I'm sorry. You are just so beautiful…well, I don't have to explain to you what happened.

You were here. But I'll understand if you don't want to have any, shall we say, repeat performances."

"Oh, no. I couldn't."

"I understand. We'll just be friends. But Roxanne," he said.

"Yes?"

"Anytime you want, we can be friends with benefits. All you have to do is whistle. You know how to whistle, don't you Slim?" he said, doing a Humphrey Bogart imitation.

Somehow, Roxanne managed to make it through the rest of the day without exploding into a ball of guilt-ridden flames. In between her bouts of internal self-flagellation she relived the feelings she had experienced in David's arms. They had made it to class on time, and miraculously, no one had stepped forward and pinned a huge scarlet A upon her breast.

At the end of class, David had thanked her again for the "lovely morning," and told her he'd call her later to schedule another scene rehearsal. A note on the bulletin board announced that her afternoon class was cancelled due to a death in Veronica's family, so Roxanne decided to catch an earlier train home.

She couldn't tell anyone. This was probably the first time in her life that she couldn't confide in anyone about something that had happened to her. It reminded her of the time she had her first French kiss. She had been a CIT at sleepaway camp. One evening during free time she had been walking down by the lake when she'd bumped into Mark Veluzzi, that cute dishwasher she'd been admiring from afar. He was poorly hidden behind a huge, twisted tree carcass and he was smoking a joint.

"Hey, Roseanne, what's up," he said, clearly stoned.

"Hi Mark, it's umm, Roxanne, actually."

"You're not going to say anything are you?" he asked, taking another hit.

"No, no of course not."

"Well, then have a seat. Here," he passed her the joint.

Roxanne had sat down and taken the joint from his fingers. There wasn't much left, but she took a strong toke and let the smoke fill her lungs. Pot was quite popular with her crowd, although the rest of the school would never have believed it. It was a well-kept secret that the top students liked to get high on the weekends when schoolwork was not an issue.

A few more passes between she and Mark and the joint became a tiny "roach." They took a few sniffs before tossing it, and then it happened. Mark put his arm around her, drew her close and gave Roxanne her first French kiss with a rather slobbery open mouth.

She struggled to maintain her cool and breathe at the same time. His hands started to move down her back and then found their way inside her tank top. When she realized he was about to try to make it to second base she started to panic, but it was just then that the bell rang over the camp PA system, signaling the end of free time.

"Oh, I've got to go, if I'm late getting back again I'm going to get into trouble," Roxanne said.

"Okay, catch you later." Dishwashers didn't have to worry about those rules.

Roxanne ran all the way back to her bunk. At the top of the hill, she took a flying leap over the resting rock that they liked to lie upon for tanning and almost landed in the arms of her best friend in the group, Elizabeth.

"Hey, what are you so crazed about?" Elizabeth asked.

Roxanne had pulled Elizabeth away from the rest of the girls and told her in explicit detail what had happened with Mark Veluzzi. Her recounting of the incident in fact, took about twice as long as the actual event. Of course, later that night, when everyone was in bed, after Elizabeth hinted about it to the girls, Roxanne had shared the story with the whole bunk. That was just the way things were at camp. The telling was more exciting than the kissing had been. She finally had a story to share. Slobbery or not, the kiss had been a milestone for her.

Sitting on the commuter train, Roxanne let out a heavy sigh. *Oh, how I wish I could jump into Elizabeth's arms now and tell her what happened with David. But I can't tell anybody. Here I just got through telling my therapist how horrified I am that Micelli makes a pass and then I go spend the whole morning in bed with a teenager.*

That was no teenager, her little inner voice told her.

FORTY-ONE

THE THORNTON FAMILY WAS packed and ready to go. Roxanne went over her list of things to do before their trip to Florida one last time.

One suitcase per person to be checked containing: Good wedding clothes, good shoes, extra dress shirts for the boys, shorts, tee-shirts, bathing suits, jackets, sweatshirts, shoes, sneakers, sandals, sunscreen, various and assorted vitamins and lotions, hats, sunglasses, pajamas, underwear, socks. Roxanne did not believe in traveling light, and her family had learned not to fight her on this.

One carry-on per person containing some or all of the following (depending on who was doing the carrying): Books, magazines, Ipods, Gameboys, snacks, cell phones, sweaters for the plane ride. And don't forget the airplane tickets!

Cat sitter supplied with key. Cat food and litter in good supply. Cat automated drinking fountain cleaned and freshly filled.

Newspapers and mail stopped.

Automatic sprinkler system set.

Burglar alarm ready to be activated (Cat sitter given code and complete instructions).

Reservations for long-term parking at airport confirmed.

"Ben, I'm ready for you to start loading up the car," Roxanne shouted.

Ben emerged from his home office prepared to follow his wife's instructions. She was the one who mobilized the troops and got everything ready. He was just the soldier following orders.

"Okay, I'm all yours. Is this everything?"

"I think so. Start loading up and I'll check again with the kids."

Justin and Gabe were in the den glued to the television.

"Do you both have everything you want to take? Books? Games? CDs?"

"Yeah, whatever," said Justin.

"Well, think about it because this is your last chance to pack anything."

Allison was in her room and on the phone. Her attitude about the trip had not changed over the past three weeks.

"Mom, do you mind, this is a private conversation?" she said as soon as Roxanne stuck her head inside the doorway.

"Last call to pack anything you want to bring. We're loading the car."

Allison replied with a stone silent stare.

"We should be leaving in 15 minutes. Be ready."

Ben was performing at his most competent. He was actually afraid that his usual joking manner would set Roxanne off like a cannon, so he kept all comments to himself and without any complaints, stuffed the luggage into the minivan and slammed down the trunk.

Their airplane seats were in two different rows, two seats and three seats. Roxanne wanted very much to sit quietly with Ben and let the three kids sit together, but taking into consideration Allison's mood, she decided to give her daughter the choice.

"Do you want to sit with Daddy and me or with the boys?" she asked Allison.

Allison thought for a minute, and then smiled.

"I think I'll sit with Daddy and *you* can sit with the boys."

Rats, she got me, Roxanne thought. *She's getting too smart for me.*

"Great idea sweetie," said Ben. He handed Roxanne her carry-on and helped her get the boys settled. They had already tossed a coin for the window seat and Gabe had won.

Ben and Allison continued down the aisle to their seats.

"Have a nice flight," said Ben, still smiling at the trick their daughter had played. Allison was safe from prying questions, lectures, or any attention at all from Ben, who was notorious for sleeping from take-off to landing no matter what time of the day or night they flew. She had stolen the peace and quiet that Roxanne had been looking forward to and successfully dodged any attempts Roxanne might have made at reasoning her into being a good sport about this trip.

Roxanne sat in the aisle seat next to Justin. Luckily, the airplane had individual TV sets at each seat. The boys used their own Ipod earphones, which gave better sound and were more comfortable than the cheap hard plastic ones the airline had provided. Good enough for a mother, thought Roxanne as she tried to adjust the cheapies to her head.

Once the plane was in the air, Roxanne was glad to see that her sons were leaving each other alone and were each tuned into different channels on their TV's. After flipping through what was playing twice, she realized that she really didn't want to watch anything. She put her headset on the jazz music station and leaned back. She just might have four hours of peace and quiet.

However, as cooperative as the silenced voices of Gabe and Justin were, Roxanne's internal voices would not allow her anything she could call peace. It had been three weeks since her first encounter with Bicycle Messenger David. In that time, Roxanne had accepted her new friend's "benefits" twice more. Both times had started out as innocently as the first time, although, fortunately there was no repeat injuries to her head. She told herself she hadn't had any intentions of winding up in bed with David after rehearsing their scene again, but somehow she had done just that. The last time was just three days ago, and as the plane took her closer and closer to a week with Sheila, Grace, Herb Seckendorf, and all those others, her mind insisted on broadcasting a replay of her last indiscretion with David, moment by moment.

It was the day before they were scheduled to perform their scene for the class. After their second rehearsal had ended up in another lovemaking session, Roxanne had insisted they remain in the student lounge for practice, and those sessions had been all business, but as luck would have it that day, the lounge had been taken over by another group of students and David had suggested they go back to his place.

"Okay, but just to work," Roxanne had said, trying to believe her own words.

"Sure, whatever you say," David agreed.

They ran through the scene three times before they were satisfied with their own and one another's performances. When they finished, David took a bottle of white wine out of the refrigerator. Before Roxanne could protest, he had poured two glasses into sparkling crystal stemware.

"Here's to knocking them dead tomorrow," he said, clinking her glass with his.

"I guess I'll have to drink to that," Roxanne said.

"Let's see what else I have in here," said David, opening the refrigerator again. He brought out a plate of strawberries dipped in dark chocolate. "Now where did these come from, I wonder?" he said.

"David, you're not playing fair. How did you know I love chocolate covered strawberries?" Her mind flashed to the night that Ben had sent the same treat to her hotel room when she was meeting her friends from high school. *Ben had done it first.*

David placed the plate of berries on the coffee table and sat in the middle of the couch. "C'mere," he said, patting the couch cushion.

As she remembered what followed, Roxanne felt herself getting warm in the airplane. She glanced over at her boys. Gabe was dozing and Justin was still watching the TV. *Thank God they can't read my mind,* she thought. *Why is it that men and boys always say "c'mere" when they want to kiss you?* she wondered. *We're usually right there when they say it, but they say it anyway. It's definitely a control thing,* she decided.

And Roxanne had let David take control once again. She had sat down next to him on the couch and let him feed her a berry. Another swallow of wine and her head was feeling light and giddy. By the time he kissed her she was aching for his lips.

"Beverage?" the flight attendant was standing over Roxanne with the drink cart. Roxanne nearly jumped out of her seat at the interruption of her thoughts. Startled back to the present, she resigned herself to staying in it. She asked for a tea and the boys asked for cokes.

"Where are we now?" she asked Justin, who was following the airplane's path on the TV screen in front of him.

"We're over Georgia. We should be landing in about an hour."

Roxanne sipped her tea and cleared her head of thoughts of David. *That's finished*, she told herself. She would need to be sharp to get through the next week with her mother.

Roxanne never got used to getting on a plane in New York and stepping off in Florida and into oppressive heat and humidity. No matter what time of year it was, the heat always felt like she was being hit in the face with a hot, wet towel.

The resort had sent a shuttle bus to pick them up, along with Grace, Ira, and the girls, who were arriving fifteen minutes later on a flight out of Newark. They lucked out at the luggage carousel; their bags were in the first batch that came out the chute. In no time they were on their way to Gables Gala Spa and Resort.

FORTY-TWO

"I WAS HOPING I'D find you out here," said Grace. "Are you okay?"

Roxanne had retreated to an isolated patio far from the wedding party. She had told Ben she needed to take a walk, but had not said anything to anyone else. She'd been gone for close to an hour and Grace had followed her instincts and uncovered her place of seclusion.

"I know I'm being a brat. I should be happy for her, right?" Roxanne said, feeling the tears starting to well in her eyes again just when she thought she had finished with that.

"Hey, it's hard for me to take, too." Grace sat down on the chair next to Roxanne.

"I mean, she's acting like a silly newlywed," whined Roxanne. Doesn't she think she's insulting Daddy like this?"

"Apparently not. She's starting a new life with Herb and we're expected to be happy for her."

"Well, fuck her, she's too old for all this."

"Yeah, fuck her, she's an old bag."

"Too bad she doesn't know it."

Roxanne and Grace looked at each other and burst into laughter. It felt good to curse Sheila's new life.

Both Roxanne and Grace had been completely unprepared for the celebration that had just taken place. The sisters were expecting the two immediate families to be joined by a handful of cousins, and Sheila had said nothing to make them think otherwise.

The two families had met for dinner the night before after getting settled into their rooms. Sheila and Herb had already been installed into the Honeymoon Suite.

"Everything is all set for the ceremony tomorrow," Sheila told them. "We're all to meet the Rabbi in the Aloha Alcove at 11. It's a lovely private room away from the tumult of the rest of the resort. Don't eat a big breakfast, because we've got a great brunch being served right afterwards."

The kids were eager to watch a movie in their room, so they said good night by 9 p.m.

The next morning it took a little coaxing, cajoling, and downright threatening to get the boys dressed appropriately in their wedding outfits. Gabe complained that it was too hot to wear a jacket, and Justin seemed to have grown during the plane flight. His shirt collar was too tight when buttoned, and he could barely squeeze into his dress shoes.

"Ben, do you have an extra pair of shoes he can wear?"

"I don't have any other dress shoes, but he can wear these Docksiders."

"Well, they'll have to do, they're better than sneakers or sandals. Here Justin, wear these."

"Mom, what's the big deal?" Allison said, her voice revealing the full disdain she felt. "It's just the family right? It's not the Inaugural Ball for Chrissakes."

"I don't need that tone this morning, my dear daughter. You could be helping your brothers get ready instead of sitting there like a princess. Are you ready to go?"

"In a minute!"

Ben gave her a sharp look that said, "leave it alone, let's just get this over with." At 11:10 the family finally passed Roxanne's inspection criteria.

"Hey Mom, there's a package outside the door," shouted Gabe.

Roxanne took the package and saw that the same kind of box was sitting outside of Grace's room. She opened it up to find corsages for herself and Allison and boutonnieres for the boys and Ben. She called into Grace's room.

"Hi, I just wanted to let you know that mom sent up flowers for us to wear to the ceremony. There's a box outside your door. We're about ready to go down, shall we wait for you?"

"If you don't mind, we'll be ready in two minutes, I'll just grab the flowers, and I'll knock on your door on the way down."

"Okay, everyone, chill out for a few minutes, we'll wait for Grace and Ira and the twins and then we'll all go to the Aloha Alcove together," Roxanne told her family.

Roxanne was never so happy to have decided to wait for Grace—a habit that had been ingrained on her throughout their childhood. When they got to the lobby, they asked the concierge exactly where the room was. *It's odd that Sheila didn't show it to us last night,* she thought.

"Just follow the path outside the pool to the left, I believe the rest of the party is already down there," she said.

Alcove was certainly a misnomer for the building that was at the end of the path. Pavilion would have been a more accurate name for the stucco structure with huge glass windows and exotic flowers everywhere. It certainly seemed much too large for the family wedding. *There must be a wedding here after ours*, Roxanne thought.

Herb's daughter Beverly opened the door before they had a chance to let themselves in. "Hi, we were getting worried, come this way, Sheila and Herb want us to walk down the aisle before them."

Roxanne and Grace could hardly believe what they saw. The Aloha Alcove was filled with what looked to be 100 or more chairs, and each chair seated a smiling septuagenarian or octogenarian, with a few "youngsters" in their sixties as well. It looked like all of Leisureville had made the trek to the Gables Resort. A magnificent chuppa of white carnations, daisies, and lilies stood at the front of what looked like a very long aisle.

"Is there any way out of this?" Roxanne whispered to Grace.

"Just take a deep breath. It looks like Beverly has this whole thing orchestrated."

"Gee, do you think she ever considered letting us in on what was happening?"

"I think we can only assume that Sheila has struck again and decided that it would be more fun to surprise us."

Beverly ushered them into a small sitting room where Sheila, Herb, and Beverly's husband Stan were waiting impatiently.

"Oh, you all look so lovely," said Sheila. "Justin, that's the shoes you wear?"

"Mom, why didn't you tell me you were having a Queen's coronation?" Roxanne demanded.

"Oh, don't exaggerate Roxanne, we just invited some of our good friends. You know how these things get, we didn't want to cause any hurt feelings by excluding anyone. Besides, the more the merrier, right?"

"Okay, everyone," said Beverly, "we're going to form a nice processional. Twins, can you lead the way?"

"Lead the way where?" asked Emily.

"All you have to do is walk straight down the aisle to the big flowered canopy. Then take a seat in the very front row. There's a nice lady in a red dress who will show you where to sit."

"Sure, we can do that," they said in unison.

"Okay, boys, you're next. Just walk slowly together. Allison, you go down by yourself so that everyone can see how beautiful you are. All the children will be seated, and the adults will be standing up for the couple. Next, Grace and Ira, then Stan and I, then Roxanne, you'll be the official matron of honor, here's your bouquet, and Ben, you'll be walking Sheila down the aisle. Wait until everyone is at the chuppa before starting down the aisle. Simple, right?"

Allison was the next one to find her way to the patio. "Mom, Aunt Grace, what are you doing out here?" she asked.

"Gee, my hiding place is getting crowded," said Roxanne. "Allison you'd better get back to the party before they notice we're all missing."

"It's too late, they already have. Grandma sent me to look for you."

Grace grabbed Roxanne's hand and pulled her up. "Come on, Rox, don't make it worse. Let's go back and be good girls for Mom."

Allison took her mother's other hand and the three walked back to the party.

"Where have you been? We need you for a group photo? The music is going to start soon." Sheila didn't stop for an answer to her question. She took her daughters by their hands and led them to a cluster of palm trees and colorful flowers where the rest of the family was gathered. Gabe and Justin were chasing Emily and Ashley around a spouting fountain of cherubs. Herb, his daughter Beverly, and her husband Stan were deep in conversation with Ben and Ira; and the invited cousins, canasta partners, golf buddies, and old and new Florida friends were contentedly munching on the kosher appetizing. Although Passover had not yet begun, the hotel had already purged its kitchens of any bread products, but the fresh fruit, potato puffs, deli meats, and six different kinds of smoked fish were enough to keep everyone happy until they made their way over to the dessert table, which was full of all sorts of Pesadika cakes, parve puddings, and candies. There were even strawberries dipped in parve chocolate.

The reception went by in a blur to Roxanne. The only concession to the age of the wedding couple seemed to be the foregoing of the lifting of bride and groom on the chairs. They didn't want to risk any of their guests having a heart attack, so instead they sat on high bar stools while the guests danced around them. Beverly tossed rose petals over Sheila and Herb to "ensure a rosy future."

"She's really into this wedding," Roxanne grumbled to Grace. "Do you think she's got an ulterior motive?"

"Like what? It looks like Herb's the one with the money."

"Maybe he's got a terminal illness and she'd rather Sheila be the caretaker than be stuck with him herself."

"Roxanne, that's a terrible thought. Besides, if that were the case she wouldn't want any new wife to share in the inheritance."

"Oh I know. I just hope I'm wrong."

"You had better be."

When the reception was over and Roxanne and Ben and Grace and Ira had settled the kids in their rooms, the two sisters and their husbands met back in the bar to unwind together.

"You know, Universal Studios is looking pretty good to me now," said Roxanne. "I think we should go with Gabe's suggestion and get out of here for a few days. What do you say?"

Ben knew better than to say anything but "yes" at that point. He hoped Grace would go along with the idea so that the two sisters wouldn't clash.

"Let's do it. The twins went to Disney last year, so Universal would be fine. I think we all need to put a little space between ourselves and the happy couple."

"Right, the honeymooners don't need us," Ira agreed. Let's

leave early in the morning and stay overnight. We'll be back here before they get out of bed."

"Ira, shut up!" said Grace.

"Kidding, kidding."

"Speaking of bed, let's get in early ourselves so we have the energy for the park tomorrow."

Agreeing, they took their drinks and headed to the elevator. Grace promised to write a note for Sheila and Herb and slip it under their door right before leaving the next morning. No one wanted a confrontation with Sheila to interfere with his or her plans.

However, Roxanne and Ben were unable to escape that fate with their daughter. Allison did not want any part of going to Universal.

"Well, you guys have a good time," she said. "I'm going to stay here and work on my tan."

"What are you talking about? Since when don't you want to go to Universal Studios? We can't leave you alone here. We're staying overnight," protested Roxanne.

"I'm not going to be alone. Grandma is here. I'm not a child Mom, I'll be fine."

Ben and Roxanne exchanged looks and stepped out into the hall. Ben spoke first.

"We should let her stay here. She may be bored, but I don't think she can get into any trouble. If we drag her along she's going to make sure we regret it. Just like you need a break from your mother, I guess Allison needs a break from us and the boys, too."

"But now we have to talk to Sheila. I can't just leave Allison here without asking her first."

"Yeah. There goes our sneaky getaway plans."

"You tell her."

"ME?" Ben almost choked.

"Ben, I need you to do this for me. She loves you the best. You walked her down the aisle. You won't get in a fight with her. Just go knock on their door and tell them the kids are insisting we go to Universal Studios but Allison wants to stay at this wonderful resort with them."

"ME?" Ben repeated.

"Go, go now," Roxanne pulled him down the hall to the Honeymoon Suite. She rapped on the door and quickly darted away, leaving Ben standing there.

Sheila came to the door wearing a red satin robe and holding a glass of champagne.

"Benny!" she exclaimed. "What is it dear? Would you like to join us for some champagne."

Sheila was clearly looped, and Ben said a silent prayer of thanks.

"No, Sheila, I'm so sorry to disturb you and Herb. I just wanted to tell you that Rox and the boys and I are going with Grace and Ira and the twins to Universal Studios early tomorrow morning. The kids have been nagging constantly and we just caved in. We'll just be gone overnight."

"That's nice dear," said Sheila, swaying unsteadily.

"There's, just one thing. Allison wants to stay here with you and Herb. Do you mind?"

"Of course not, darling."

Ben could not believe how well this was going. He should ply his mother-in-law with booze more often.

"Okay then, we'll call from the road. I don't want to keep you from your new husband. Good night."

"Nighty night Benny Benny," Sheila crooned.

"How did it go?" Roxanne asked.

"Oh. Piece of cake," said Ben. "Let's get to bed, we've got a big day tomorrow."

FORTY-THREE

ROXANNE STOOD IN FRONT of the mirror getting ready for the last day of classes of the semester. There was a special Friday session during which they'd be performing final scenes and monologues. Later that evening she was going to Garrett's house for a party. Ben was coming too. He was sure that Garrett had designs on Roxanne, and when she had told him about the party he asked if husbands were included. "Sure," she had said. "If you really want to come to a party with a bunch of actor wannabees you are more than welcome." She would just have to give David advance warning to keep his distance. She knew that wouldn't be a problem. He was always discreet in public. She never asked him, but she was positive she was not the first married woman he had made a special friend.

Since her trip to Florida, Roxanne had kept her word to herself and had not agreed to any more visits to David's apartment over the past six weeks. But the connection they had with one another had remained strong. For the first time in her life, Roxanne felt attractive and had actual proof in the attentions given by such a good-looking younger man. In her mind, Ben's attraction to her didn't really count. *He just loved her because they were fated to be together. He was the exception to the rule.*

Roxanne and David had gone for lunches in cute Village

cafes and taken long walks together, just talking about everything and nothing. It felt very romantic. When she felt his enormous hand around her own it was as if she were walking on air. It reminded her of the lines from the song in "My Fair Lady." "I have often walked on this street before. But the pavement always stayed beneath my feet before." Sometimes, he would pull her close and kiss her, but she wouldn't let herself get carried away and return to his apartment with him. *This is as far as I'm going with this; just a little innocent kisses between friends. I think he's part French, anyway. The French are always kissing. We Americans are just very uptight.*

Applying her makeup, she still wasn't completely used to her reflection even now, nine months after the accident. *How would my life be different today if this was the face I had started with?* She wondered for the millionth time. The vibration of her cell phone in her pants pocket interrupted her reverie. It was Jo.

"Hi, are you busy after class today?"

"Actually, yes. Why, what's up?"

"Nothing. As usual. I'm just kind of feeling low and lonely and wanted some company."

"Hmmm, can you get a sitter?"

"Possibly. Why?"

"I'm going to an end of term party with my acting school people. Come."

"Is it an open house? Wouldn't I be intruding?"

"No, not a bit. There's always room at a party like this for a beautiful, single woman."

"You mean single mother."

"Jo, they're not mutually exclusive terms. At the party, you're a single woman. At Mommy and Me you can be a single mother. Hell, you don't have to wear any label at all. Listen, just book the sitter and meet me in the first floor lounge at five. Ben's coming too, we'll all go together."

Roxanne spent some more time reassuring Jo that

she would be welcome at the party, and eventually the conversation turned to what Jo should wear. Claiming she was going to miss her train, Roxanne ended the call so that she could make another inspection of her own closet. Now that Jo was coming, she suddenly wanted to wear something a bit more festive. Roxanne pushed around her hangers a little longer, and then remembered the batik-turquoise dress she had bought down in Florida when she and Grace had snuck off on their own. She had put it in the basement closet, not expecting to need it any time soon, but now she realized that it was just the right thing for today. The fabric was what had immediately drawn Roxanne to buy the dress in the first place. The bright turquoise was complemented by a light aqua, and silver metallic threads made the dress sparkle. The fabric was a very lightweight knit that showed her figure to its best. The deep vee-neck and the built-in push-up bra actually made it look as if she were better endowed than she really was, and she had the perfect dangling silver and turquoise earrings to go with it. If she borrowed Allison's silver sandals the outfit would be complete.

Allison wasn't quite as asleep as Roxanne had thought, and upon hearing her mother rustling in her closet, she sat up in bed.

"Mom, what do you want?"

"Oh, I'm sorry I woke you. Can I borrow your silver sandals? Do you mind?"

"Why are you all dressed up?"

"I'm not dressed up. This is just a very comfortable dress, and your shoes would match perfectly."

"Well, you look like you're trying to impress someone," Allison muttered.

"What did you say?"

"Nothing. Go ahead, take the sandals. They're under the stuffed purple rhinoceros."

Roxanne put the sandals on quickly. "Yes! A perfect fit. I'll have to shop in your shoe closet more often."

"Don't get used to it Mom, you just caught me in a generous mood."

Roxanne bent down and kissed her daughter on the forehead. "I am sorry I woke you, but you have to get up soon to get ready for your math final, don't you? You remember that Daddy and I will be home late, and you're in charge of the boys?"

"Mom, I have it all under control. Just go to your thing and don't worry about us. I'll take care of everything."

Roxanne felt a pang of mother's guilt. Here she was fussing with her wardrobe so she could look hot at a party and she was leaving the kids home to have pizza delivered. And Allison had to sit through a math final today. *I'll make it up to her this weekend,* she thought.

Another trip back to the mirror to reapply her makeup so that it would last beyond lunchtime and Roxanne was finally ready to go. She arrived at class early and saw her classmates all gathered around the bulletin board. No one noticed her arrive because they were all staring intently at a sheet of paper that was posted. She couldn't get near enough to see what it was, and she was too short to see over the crowd. After another few minutes, Ming walked away from the group and looked as if she was holding back tears. Even after having spent the entire semester in classes with her, Roxanne didn't feel comfortable asking her why she looked so upset. She felt helpless watching the young woman walk quickly towards the restroom.

Eventually, David's long, lean body emerged from the cluster of classmates. When he saw Roxanne he put his arm around her shoulder and started to steer her away from the rest.

Roxanne shrugged off David's arm quickly. *What is he doing? He knows better than that,* she wondered.

"David what is going on here? Who died?" she demanded to know.

"Shh, c'mon let's talk in here," David said, his voice taking on a soothing, rather patronizing tone that could only mean bad news for Roxanne. He moved her into an empty classroom, shut the door, sat them both down in facing chairs, his knees touching hers.

"Everyone is freaking about The List."

"What list? What are you talking about?"

"They posted a list of the students who are invited to audition for the MFA program. It's not even an automatic acceptance, by the way. Not everyone's name was on it."

"Oh, so that's why Ming looked so upset," Roxanne said. She looked at David and he was gazing at her steadily with the most sympathetic eyes she had ever not wanted to see in her life.

"Oh."

"I'm so sorry. I hope this doesn't discourage you from pursuing your dream."

As kind and serious as David was being, as soon as the words left his lips and reached her ears, Roxanne couldn't help but laugh. *Dream*, she thought to herself. *That's all this ever was. It could never be reality.* Even so, the rejection did sting. She hadn't been prepared to wake up yet.

"Who else didn't make the cut?"

"Well, it looks like it was you, Ming, Carla, and Guillermo."

Roxanne let that sink in for a bit. She really couldn't argue with the teacher's choices. She would have also selected those three as the weakest members of the class, but she had never realized that she was a member of that club. All these years she had always believed it wasn't a lack of talent that had prevented her from getting any good parts, she'd always blamed it on her looks. Now what excuse did she have?

"Why didn't I know about this? I didn't know this was

coming. Did I miss an announcement?" she asked petulantly. "I feel like such a fool," she said, starting to get choked up.

"There have been notices on the webpage. But it's also spelled out in the registration materials. You probably just never noticed it."

"Does this mean I can't take any more classes?" Roxanne asked.

"No, they'll always take your money. You're just not on the track for the master's degree next year. You can try again."

"You mean I'm on the loser, no-talent track," Roxanne said.

David stood and pulled her close to him into a bear hug. "My dear friend, you are no loser. You're incredible in so many ways." He leaned in to kiss her, but she pushed him away.

"Thanks David, but this is not the place. You're really very sweet. And you are a dear friend," she said, again starting to choke up.

Now holding her back at arm's length, David said, "And you are one hot lady in that dress, if I may say so."

Roxanne smiled. If she was going to go down in flames, at least she could do it looking great. *They can take away my "dreams of stardom," but my new face is here to stay.* David looked down at her with such concern, she felt herself get warm. She took a deep breath before she spoke.

"Look, I'm just going to do a Scarlett O'Hara on this one, okay?"

"Sure. What?"

"I'll think about it tomorrow! Don't look so sad David. I'm okay. We've got our end of term scenes to get through today, and a party tonight. I now have a wonderful excuse for drinking as much as I can get down."

Roxanne didn't want to spoil the party for Jo or see the look on Ben's face when he heard the news, so she didn't tell either one of them about being left off of The List when they met before the party. However, the secret was out soon enough. She couldn't control the looks and comments she got from her fellow (former) classmates, which scaled the entire range of feelings from the sympathetic ones who kindly told her she'd been treated unfairly to the superior ones, who could barely choke out a hello before hurrying on, not wanting to associate with one of the now "un-persons."

"I'm fine, I'm really not upset," she told her husband and her old roommate. Let's have a good time tonight."

Fortunately, Garrett knew how to throw a party, and the liquor flowed copiously.

Guillermo had also decided that liquor would be the best medicine to assuage his own feelings of rejection, and he had gotten a head start on Roxanne. Clearly drunk, he loudly proclaimed that they had been the victims of bigotry.

"I don't think it's mere coincidence that they left us off that loco list. I mean look who they picked on, the old lady, the quiet Asian, and the hot Latino," he said before taking another shot of tequila.

Old lady? Ouch, thought Roxanne.

"Then where do I fit in?" shrieked Carla.

"Oh. You just suck," laughed Guillermo. The two then hugged tightly and continued their drinking.

Roxanne noticed that Ming had skipped the party. Well, she wasn't going to sneak out with her tail between her legs like that. She gulped down her second vodka tonic and immediately picked up another one from the rows of glasses arranged neatly on the bar in Garrett's apartment. Ben and Jo exchanged looks that told one another it was going to be a long night.

"Hey Roxanne, how are you doing?" Garrett said, with a Grade A sympathetic expression on his countenance.

"Garrett, you throw a faaaaabulous party," Roxanne said. She reached out to him, put her arm around his shoulders and pulled her to him. "Did you meet my friend Jo?"

Garrett looked at Jo, who smiled at him and rolled her

eyes up as if to say, "I'm not responsible for how my friend is acting." Jo was wearing a loosely fitting red silk halter top and palazzo pants that followed the curves of her slim body in the most flattering way.

"It's nice to meet you Garrett," said Jo. "I hope you don't mind my tagging along with Rox to your party."

"Of course he doesn't mind, do you Garrett?" said Roxanne. "I told her that beautiful single women are always welcome at a party, right? Did I tell you that Jo was my college roommate? We used to go to all the parties together. She'd have all the guys falling all over her, and if I got lucky I'd get one of the leftovers."

"Roxanne! Please ignore her Garrett, it's the vodka talking."

"Oh, I know. She's hardly one who would have ever had to take leftovers," he said.

"How are you, Garrett?" said Ben, putting out a hand to shake. "You remember me. I guess I'm the leftover who stayed."

"Oh Benny Ben, you are so silly," said Roxanne. "You weren't a leftover. You were my true soul mate brought to me by the hand of fate."

"Oh yeah, that's right. I forgot. Excuse us please." Ben took Roxanne's hand and led her onto a couch away from the bar. "Let's take a little break Roxanne. I don't want to have to carry you home," he said. "You know you can't tolerate more than two drinks."

"It looks like our friend is reaching her limit," said Garrett to Jo. "I hope she doesn't get sick."

"Oh, don't worry about Roxanne. Believe me, I've seen her in worse shape. She really doesn't drink like that very often—you know, she's the perfect mother and all and doesn't want to set a bad example for her kids--but when she makes up her mind to party, well… But have no fear, Ben is with her and he is her forever loyal protector and keeper."

"So, what have you been doing since your days as a party girl with our friend?" asked Garrett.

Garrett and Jo moved onto a small divan tucked in the corner of the room to continue their conversation. They talked about living in New York, and Jo told him about Tai. At his request, she showed him one of the latest photos she had taken of her daughter. His smile widened as he took in the toddler. "Absolutely beautiful," he said. "Just like her mother."

Jo smiled too. She'd certainly heard lines like that before, but Garrett did seem sincere.

"I hope I get to meet her," said Garrett.

"I think you just might get that wish." Jo was now very glad that Roxanne had brought her to the party. It had been a long time since she'd felt this positive about meeting a new man. She sat back on the divan and Garrett casually managed to drape his arm around her shoulder. They sat quietly together, observing the people and trading little comments about them that were not meant for anyone else to hear.

FORTY-FOUR

BEN MANAGED TO KEEP her from going for a fourth drink, and Roxanne wound up falling asleep on the couch, her head heavy on his shoulder. Ben sat with Roxanne and let the party go on all around him. He didn't know anyone to talk to except Jo and Garrett, and they were keeping each other company. After about an hour, he nudged Roxanne gently awake, then coaxed her to drink some coffee.

Her head beginning to clear, Roxanne remembered she had left Jo to fend for herself. *Where was she?*

After a while she spotted her friend, who was still sitting in the corner with Garrett. She went over to apologize to her.

"Jo, I'm sorry," she started. "I didn't mean to abandon you."

"Oh, I'm fine, Roxanne. Garrett has been a very attentive host."

Roxanne then realized she was actually interrupting what appeared to be a cozy conversation. *This must be the ultimate déjà vu. Here I am back at school, Jo is getting picked up and I'm playing the drunken fool.*

"Great, I'm so glad you two are getting along so well," Roxanne said with forced enthusiasm. "Ben and I are going to take off now. But you don't have to go, Jo."

"She certainly doesn't, I'll take good care of her," said Garrett.

"I do think I'll stay a little longer, Rox. Thanks so much for inviting me."

Garrett grinned and Roxanne felt inexplicably jealous. A vision of Garrett and Jo together in a little boat inside a toilet bowl flashed in her head. Across the room, she saw David busy in conversation with a group of their classmates. He had kept his distance all night.

Roxanne leaned heavily on Ben as she stepped out of the car. She had not gone more than ten feet when the heel broke off of her daughter's silver sandal.

"Aaaaa," she screamed, but Ben was quick and caught her before she fell. "I don't believe it. That's a fitting end to a perfect day. I just broke Allison's sandal."

"Well, I'm sure she'll be delighted with an excuse to get a new pair," said Ben. "Honey, the house is dark, I think the kids are asleep. Let's get you into bed without seeing them."

Roxanne was beginning to sober up, so she listened to Ben, took off the shoes, and tiptoed into the house and up the stairs. She swallowed four aspirin, which in her experience worked well in heading off a hangover, then fell into bed without even hanging up her dress.

"Mom, Dad, is that you?" called Allison.

Ben went down the hall to her room to keep her from talking to Roxanne. "Hi Ally, how was everything? Did the boys give you any trouble?"

"Well, except for not helping me clean up the kitchen. I'm telling Mom…"

"Tell her tomorrow, Allison, she's really tired. Oh, and I'm sorry but the heel snapped off of your sandal."

"She broke my—"

"It broke. It's not cause for a scene. I'm sure Mom will

take you to the mall to get a new pair this weekend. Okay? I'm going to bed now. Good night."

The next morning, Saturday, a spring rain kept the sun from waking the family and no one got out of bed before ten. One by one, first Gabe, then Ben, then Justin, then Allison, and finally Roxanne showered and dressed for a Saturday on which, atypically, no one had anything special planned or anything with a pressing need to accomplish. Ben went out for bagels and by 11:30, they were all sitting around the kitchen table having a late breakfast. Roxanne, feeling she had indulged in too many calories the night before, carefully scooped all the dough out of the bagel and applied the smallest amount of cream cheese to the inside of the remaining outer shell. She didn't skimp on the lox though. It was fish, after all. Roxanne was surprised to see Allison also scooping out her bagel and adding only light Parkay to it. Her daughter certainly didn't have to worry about putting on weight. In fact, she looked a little too thin. *She must have grown a little taller,* Roxanne mused. *I thought she was done growing.*

"This is a nice family breakfast," said Ben. "What is everyone planning on doing today?"

The boys each said they were waiting for word from their friends on what was happening. Allison asked Roxanne if Dad had been right about her taking her to the mall for new shoes. Roxanne agreed to take her at one o'clock, after she had time to straighten up and throw in a laundry.

"You should get some new bathing suits, too. I noticed in Florida that all your suits look sun damaged," Roxanne told Allison. "I think this weekend is a sale, too."

The mall was crowded, as it always is on rainy Saturdays, but Roxanne felt unusually calm and carefree walking with Allison. She hadn't even thought about The List until Allison jolted her memory.

"So Mom, now that your classes are over, what are you going to do? Have you signed up for the next courses? Are you going to take summer classes?"

"I really haven't decided, Ally. I don't think I want to go into the city this summer though, the streets and the subways are just too sticky. I'm just not sure what I want to do about classes in September."

"Maybe you should go to auditions or try to get an agent? That's what Mallory's oldest sister is doing now. She graduated with a BFA in Acting from Boston University last week."

"Oh, I don't think I'm quite ready to go pro," Roxanne said. "But I might check the cast calls for community theaters. I haven't done that in a long time. Now, what do you want to get first, shoes or a bathing suit?"

"Shoes"

Since they were at the mall that Gabe called "The Shoe Store Mall," there was no shortage of windows to browse. "Mom, do you mind if we look in all the windows before I pick which ones to try on?" asked Allison.

"Not at all. Let's just try to remember where we see the shoes we like. In fact, I'll just write down the stores we want to come back to."

For once, Allison and Roxanne were completely in sync. They were both happy to take on the challenge of finding the "best of all possible shoes." Roxanne had agreed that they would get Allison a new pair of silver sandals, plus a pair of black sandals and a slip-on sneaker or moccasin. In the next ninety minutes they covered twenty-three shoe stores, plus the shoe department in Macy's and Nordstroms.

"Okay, time to rest before we go back for the buying," declared Roxanne. "I could go for a frozen yogurt, how about you?"

"That's fine," said Allison. But when they got to the yogurt stand Allison ordered a diet coke.

"Are you sure that's all you want?"

"Yeah, I had a big breakfast. I'm just thirsty, not hungry."

"Since when do you have to be hungry to have frozen yogurt with sprinkles?"

Allison just shrugged and asked to see the list of stores Roxanne had kept. While Roxanne ate her yogurt Allison went over the list, eliminating some of the earlier entries. In the end she had narrowed it down to six stores, and had given them numbers in order of preference. By Allison's calculations, with some good luck in finding the selections in her size, they might be able to get all three pairs without going to more than four of the six. "The last two are just in case," she assured Roxanne.

Allison's shopping acumen proved to be right on target, and after just three stores, they had purchased five pairs of shoes—four for Allison and one for Roxanne.

"I'll tell you what, I'll go put these in the trunk and you go ahead to Macy's and start looking at bathing suits. I'll meet you in the junior department, okay?"

Allison seemed to hesitate at first, but she agreed that was a good plan and they headed off in opposite directions. Roxanne had a little trouble locating the car in the parking lot, and didn't meet up with Allison for about half an hour. When she found her Allison had already decided on three suits and was ready for Roxanne to pay for them.

"Allison, that's really fast. Did you actually try them on?"

"Of course I did."

Roxanne saw the suits were all a size four. "Honey, are you sure? You've never been a four before? Maybe you should try the six. I don't want you wearing the skimpiest suit on the beach."

"Mom, they fit fine. They're making the sizes bigger this season."

Roxanne knew that wasn't true. Although she had been able to keep off most of the weight she had lost after the accident, she still couldn't get into every size eight she tried, and more often than she liked she had to buy a ten. For her own peace of mind she rationalized that the manufacturers were making the sizes smaller, not larger as Allison wanted her to believe.

"Well, would you please humor me and try on just one of them for me before I buy them?"

"Fine. Wait outside the dressing room. I'll come out."

While Roxanne was waiting, she checked her cell phone to see if she had missed any calls. She saw that she had a voice mail from David, but didn't bother listening to it. *He's probably wondering how I am after yesterday. I'll give him a call tomorrow,* she thought. After a few minutes Allison came out wearing one of the bikinis and also had her zippered sweatshirt on over it, but open.

"It's cold in here," said Allison. "See, it fits me."

Roxanne was shocked at how thin Allison looked in the suit. She swallowed the gasp that came involuntarily to her throat and visions of headlines about anorexia flashed in her mind. She knew that Macy's dressing room was no place to start a serious discussion and so she merely nodded.

"It's very pretty. Okay, get dressed and I'll go buy the suits."

Roxanne's mind spun rapidly as they drove home from the mall. Allison put on a new CD, and Roxanne was glad that she didn't have to talk just yet. *What do I do now? Could she really be anorexic? I never noticed before today how little she actually eats. How long has this been going on? What if it's not that but something entirely physical? I've got to get her to the doctor for a check up.*

Just as they pulled into the driveway, Roxanne said, "Oh, I'm going to call Dr. Millner and schedule your annual check up. You just have school in the mornings next week right? So I can make it for an afternoon?"

"I don't need a check up."

"Actually, you do," Roxanne said with the finality that meant she was serious.

"I really don't want to see Dr. Millner. Could I see the woman doctor who started there this year?"

"Sure, that's no problem at all. I completely agree with you," Roxanne said sympathetically.

"I'm afraid she's getting anorexic," said Roxanne to Ben in bed that night.

"Who?"

"Allison, who do you think?"

"Oh, all the girls are thin like that. You were as thin as she was when you were her age."

"No Ben. I saw her in a bathing suit today, or as much of her as she would let me see. Her ribs are showing. I'm worried. I'm going to take her to the doctor's for a check up this week."

"Okay, it sounds like you have this under control then," said Ben, turning over to go to sleep.

Roxanne elbowed him in the back.

"Don't be so complacent! If I'm right this is a very serious condition that is very hard to turn around. And what if it's not even that? What if she has…" Roxanne couldn't even say the word.

Ben sat up. "She does not have cancer. Roxanne, stop being so melodramatic. She probably is just going through a phase. But whatever it is, we'll handle it."

"You mean I'll handle it and you'll watch me."

"No, I don't mean that. Rox, I think Allison is fine, but if God forbid, I'm wrong, I will be there with you to face it. But please, stop imagining the worst, that's all I'm trying to say. It doesn't hurt anything to think positive. Look, you think there is a problem and you are doing the first thing you should do, which is to see a doctor. Let's just wait and see what happens at the check up, okay?"

Roxanne agreed not to panic just yet, but her stomach was in knots as she tried to sleep. She was relieved that her classes had ended and she had no real distractions to keep her from giving Allison her full attention.

FORTY-FIVE

Monday morning after the kids had left for school was the first time Roxanne was alone since Friday. It was also the first time she had nothing scheduled on her calendar. No classes starting, no job, no…nothing. She was so worried about Allison that she had really succeeded in putting off thinking about her acting school future. As soon as the clock struck nine a.m., she called the pediatrician's office and scheduled an appointment for Allison to go in for a check up. The first opening was Wednesday at noon, and she wrote it on the calendar in red.

"Would it be possible to speak to the doctor for just a moment?" she asked.

"What is it in reference to?" the receptionist asked.

None of your God-damned business, Roxanne wanted to shout. She hated when receptionists screened doctors' calls like that. It was bad enough to tell a doctor what was bothering her; she didn't want to repeat it to the receptionist so that she could share it with the other women over their donuts and coffee. *Was there such a thing as receptionist-patient confidentiality? She thought not.*

"I need to tell her about a concern I have for my daughter, and I want her to know about this before she sees Allison.

It will just take a minute," Roxanne said, controlling her temper.

"One moment please."

Roxanne held for about five minutes before the next voice came on the line.

"This is Dr. Merkin, how can I help you Mrs. Thornton?"

"Doctor, I'm bringing my daughter Allison in for a physical on Wednesday. She's sixteen, and I've worried that she is developing anorexia. She's down to a size four."

"Have you noticed any signs of depression or anxiety in Allison?"

Roxanne thought about some of Allison's outbursts that had occurred since her own accident.

"Is there a way to tell with a sixteen-year-old girl? How do you know what's normal angst and what isn't?"

"Let me talk to Allison on Wednesday and see what I can learn, okay? Thanks for letting me know your concerns. We'll find out if there's a problem, I promise you."

Just as she hung up the house phone, her cell phone rang; it was David.

"Hi, how are you, did you get my message?" he asked, sounding overly anxious.

"Actually, I did see that you called, but I never had a chance to listen to the message. I couldn't call you over the weekend, but really David, I'm fine. Thanks for your concern. You're very sweet. You're a good friend, benefits or not."

"So you didn't listen to the message?"

"No, why?"

"Rox, I'm leaving."

"Leaving?"

"My agent called me Friday night. I got a part in a movie. We start shooting Wednesday. I knew about it at the party, but I couldn't say anything to you then."

"Wednesday? As in the day after tomorrow?"

"Yes. I was hoping I could see you to say goodbye."

"How long will you be gone?"

"Well, I really don't plan on coming back."

"At all? What about…" but Roxanne couldn't finish the sentence. *David was young and talented, so why shouldn't he move to LA and try to make it there. He could always be a bike messenger there if things got tough, and at least the weather was warm and sunny.*

"Are you busy today? Could you come in to see me?"

Roxanne sat down hard on the kitchen chair. *What the hell should she do?* She wanted to see David before he left, but was it too risky? She couldn't imagine going in to the city and not mentioning it to Ben. She just knew he would be able to smell the city on her when she got home. *I'll never kiss him again if I don't go.*

"No, I'm sorry David, I can't," she said with a lump growing in her throat.

"But, why? Are you sure you can't move things around? Tomorrow I'll have no time at all."

"I wish I could, David. Believe me. But there's no point," she sighed deeply before continuing. "Go with a completely clear conscience as far as I'm concerned. If an adulterous affair can ever be considered a good thing, then this was one of the best things I've ever done. I'll probably pay in guilt for it for the rest of my life, but the time I spent with you was worth it. Keep in touch. Call me or email me and let me know how everything is going in LA. I'll be cheering for you when you win your first Oscar, I promise."

"Roxanne, I don't know what else to say. I'm sorry if I've caused you pain. I'll miss you."

"I'll miss you too David. I'm going to go now. Goodbye, my friend."

"Goodbye, beautiful," said David. "Hey, and if you're ever in LA…"

Roxanne turned off her cell phone just in case he wanted

to call her back. One goodbye was all that she could manage. She walked into the den and found Clarissa sleeping peacefully on the sofa. She put on a CD and sat next to her. *It was true what they said about pet therapy. Stroking a purring cat was almost as good as a Xanax for calming you down.*

The phone rang again. Roxanne knew David wouldn't call on the house phone, so she picked it up. "Hello?"

"Rox, it's Jo. How are you? You were pretty bombed Friday night."

"Oh, hi Jo. I really did embarrass myself, I guess. But you seemed to be having a good time with Garrett."

"Yeah. Actually, he just left."

"Oh?"

"He spent the weekend here."

"Wow, that was fast!"

"Roxanne, I'm telling you this was not the old Jo acting impulsively. Garrett and I totally clicked. After everyone left, I helped him straighten up and he took me home. He came upstairs and, well, he didn't leave until this morning. He has a job for a voiceover commercial. But he's coming back for dinner tonight. And you should see him with Tai. It's incredible! Roxanne, I'm seriously falling for him. What do you think? You know him. Do you think he's sincere, or am I in for another heartbreak?"

Roxanne thought for a minute and realized that she didn't know enough of Garrett's history to base any predictions on it. All she knew was how he behaved with her, and she had to admit he was a pretty nice guy.

"Jo, I just know that he's divorced with one teenage son. His son lives with Garrett's ex out of state, so they don't see one another as much as Garrett would like to, but he does seem to be a concerned and responsible father. I've never seen him display any questionable behavior. He's been helpful and kind to me, giving me advice on the business. He's funny and smart, and certainly good company; that much I know. I do think he has an eye for the ladies and he seems to enjoy being around the younger girls in classes, but that doesn't make him a perv; he's a pretty normal guy I would guess. I don't know exactly how long he's been divorced or what his relationship record has been like since then. Do you?"

"We talked a lot, actually. He's had one serious girlfriend since his divorce, for about a year, but they broke up—he gave no details. He admits he's dated a lot and you're right about his getting a kick out of being in classes with the young girls, but…"

"But what?"

"He says he feels very different with me. Roxanne, I think you introduced me to Mr. Right. I know it sounds far-fetched, but something here feels so incredible. I feel like my life could be turning around."

And I have a sinking feeling mine is going down the tubes, Roxanne thought.

"Jo, I'm not sure I'm the best one to give you advice. You know my experience with men is extremely limited. But I can't think of any reason for you not to trust Garrett. Just try to take it a little slowly, okay? Don't make any irreversible decisions while you're still on cloud nine from a wonderful weekend. But you know that, you don't really need me to tell you what to do."

"So I have your blessing?"

"What am I, the mother superior?" Roxanne laughed. "Yes, go for it. I will keep my fingers crossed that it works out. Oh, and Jo, I will tell you one thing. I think you've made Ben very happy."

"Ben? Why should he be happy?"

"He's been stupidly jealous of Garrett since I started classes and I told him that we had become friends."

"Well, you know I love Ben, but he does have his stupid moments, doesn't he?" Jo laughed.

"Yeah, he does." Roxanne didn't want to continue taking

the conversation in this direction, but Tai's voice over the other end saved her from making excuses.

"Ahh, someone's up from her nap. I've gotta go. I'll call you soon."

"Do that, be sure and keep me posted."

"So Clarissa, it seems my friends are really doing well," she said stroking the cat. "My little fling has flung himself over to the west coast, and my old roomie sounds like she's falling in love. I, on the other hand, have just bombed out of acting school and my daughter may have a life-threatening eating disorder."

Clarissa stretched out her limbs and mewed softly. Looking up at Roxanne, she moved from the couch to snuggle herself onto Roxanne's lap, essentially trapping her from getting up. "Thanks, fuzzy face. You're the perfect company for me right now." Deciding that she should allow herself the luxury of letting sleeping cats lie, Roxanne reached for the remote control and put Dr. Phil on. Watching other people with completely messed up lives was just the kind of schadenfraude that she needed.

FORTY-SIX

On Wednesday morning, Allison went through a litany of excuses to try to persuade Roxanne to reschedule the doctor's appointment. She had so many things she had to do, and none of them included going to the doctor. Feeling that Allison could not be trusted to come home after school, Roxanne insisted they meet in front of the school so that they could drive directly to the doctor.

Dr. Millner's new partner, Erica Merkin, was just a few years out of medical school. Her long brown hair covered her shoulders in the kind of curls that Roxanne's friends had fought against when they were girls, but were now considered quite lovely. She was, as Sheila, would say, "a big girl, who looked like she had a good appetite." Roxanne wasn't sure she was the right person to tell Allison she needed to gain weight.

Dr. Merkin came out to the waiting room to call Allison in. She greeted Roxanne warmly and asked her if she could see Allison alone for the physical.

"We'll call you in, soon," she said.

Roxanne leafed through the old issues of *People* and *Us* and tried not to jump to any conclusions about what was being discussed in the examining room. After an excruciatingly long twenty minutes, the receptionist told her she could go into the exam room.

Allison was sitting fully clothed on the table, and it looked as if she had been crying.

"Allison and I were discussing her weight loss," Dr. Merkin began. "She knows you are worried about it and she had assumed that you and I had spoken about it before today."

Allison looked up at Roxanne with accusing eyes, and Roxanne responded by squeezing her arm.

"Honey, you can't be mad at me for that. I'm your mother. It's my job to worry about these things, right Doctor?"

Dr. Merkin smiled, but then her expression turned serious. Roxanne felt her mouth turn dry.

"Well, Mrs. Thornton, there are a few things going on that explain why Allison is somewhat underweight right now. She told me that she's been feeling nauseous lately and has been throwing up at school in the mornings."

"You're not saying what I think you're about to say are you?" Roxanne turned white and started to feel woozy.

"Please, Mrs. Thornton, have a seat. Try to be calm. Yes, Allison is pregnant. A urine test confirmed it."

"How? Who? Allison, why?" Roxanne stammered.

"It was just one time. I didn't think it could happen the first time, and the whole thing only lasted a few minutes. I wasn't even sure we'd actually done it. Mom, I'm sorry," Allison started to cry again. "Dr. Merkin, can you just tell her what I told you please, I can't say it," she said through her tears and sobs. "Really Mom, I was as surprised as you are."

No, not quite. Roxanne looked up at the doctor hoping somehow she would tell her this was all a mistake.

"Allison is about six weeks pregnant. It seems that she met a very friendly towel boy at the Florida resort you were staying at. She tells me they got much too friendly."

"I told you I didn't want to go to Florida," Allison said, attempting to put some of the blame on her mother. "I got bored when you and the boys went to Universal. Grandma and Herb stayed in their room all day. Tony was really cute."

"Now what do we do?" said Roxanne more to herself than to the doctor or Allison.

"Allison will have to make a decision, she…"

"I don't want it!" Allison said.

"It's something you need to give some thought to," said Dr. Merkin.

"I don't want it. I want an abortion. Mom, please, I want an abortion."

Roxanne sighed deeply. She was relieved and overwhelmingly sad at the same time. "Doctor, can you help us make the arrangements please?"

"Yes, but you'll have to go for a counseling session first. The facility will not perform an abortion until a social worker has discussed your options. I can schedule that for Allison, you, and her father. If, after that meeting you are still certain you want the abortion, they can make the appointment, usually in two days. Would you all be able to make it tomorrow? I can have my secretary call now."

"Tomorrow?" Suddenly time had lost meaning. Roxanne only wished she could go back in time and prevent this from ever happening. *Why didn't I make her go to Universal? Is this my punishment for cheating on Ben? How is Ben going to take this? Not well. Ben had a very long fuse, but this would definitely ignite it and push him over the edge.*

"Mrs. Thornton? Do you want Katie to call and set up an appointment for tomorrow at the Women's Health Center?"

Roxanne nodded. "Please."

Mother and daughter walked slowly to the car. In her hand, Roxanne held an appointment card for a counseling session at the Women's Health Center for 11:00 the next morning. *Less than 24 hours from now,* she thought.

"Allison, you had to have suspected something, right? You knew you were pregnant didn't you?"

"Mom, I swear I didn't. I really don't keep track of my period, and I was losing weight, not gaining."

"Are you saying you've never heard of morning sickness? Didn't that give you a clue?"

"I don't know. They don't really talk about that in health class all they ever really say is don't have sex, and if you do then be prepared and use a condom."

"So that you knew, but chose to ignore it?" Roxanne said, trying not to raise her voice.

"Well, how could I be prepared for something I wasn't planning? I'm sorry Mom, it just happened."

I need Ben, Roxanne thought. *I don't think I can wait until he gets home. He's got to be a part of this discussion.* "Allison, I'm going to ask Dad to come home now."

"Dad's going to be very mad," Allison said.

Roxanne pulled over and dialed Ben's cell phone number. He answered on the first ring. *That could mean he's either not busy or terribly busy.*

"Can you come home early?"

"How early?"

"Now."

"Rox, what's the matter? Is it Allison? Did you go to the doctor?"

"Yes, we're just leaving. Ben, Allison is going to be okay, but there is a problem and I really wish you would come home and we can talk in person."

"Rox, you're scaring me. What is it?"

"She's pregnant."

"I'm on my way."

Allison didn't speak to Roxanne for the rest of the ride home. "Let's start the family discussion when Daddy gets home," she said. As soon as the car stopped in the driveway, Allison bolted out of the car, ran upstairs, and closed her bedroom door tightly.

Feeling numb from shock, Roxanne headed for the

bathroom. She reached into the cabinet and took the bottle of Xanax out. She popped one of the tiny pills, swallowed a glass of water, and then with a shrug to herself, popped a second pill and swallowed it down.

She lay down on the bed and pointed the remote at the television.

"Today, on Dr. Phil…"

Roxanne's eyelids felt extraordinarily heavy. She pulled herself into a fetal position, hugged the pillow in the sham to her chest and started to nod off. She began to dream about the situation the family was about to confront, but instead of imagining her family sitting in the living room, Roxanne found herself on the set of the Dr. Phil show. Dr. Phil was on her right, and to her left was Ben. To the right of Dr. Phil, in a big overstuffed chair that made her slim daughter look even smaller, was Allison, still crying.

"Are you kidding me?" said Dr. Phil. "You've got to be the worst mother ever!"

"Are you telling me that you've spent the last nine months so absorbed in your own reflection in the mirror, trying to (he made the quote marks with his fingers in the air) make up for your (quote marks again) boo hoo unhappy childhood, that you didn't see what your own daughter was going through?"

"I…I thought she was fine. I…I thought she was just a typical teenager…only she was not like I was, she was…is…so pretty," Roxanne said in a weak attempt at an explanation.

"And where were you, Dad?" Dr. Phil turned on Ben. "Why were you so willing to leave her all alone in a resort full of pool boys and lifeguards?"

"Hey, don't blame me. I'm just the Dad. I was leaving her with her grandmother. How is it my fault if my mother-in-law is a nympho at 75?"

"We have another guest with us who has his own perspective on this family crisis," said Dr. Phil. "Will you please welcome one of Hollywood's newest rising stars, soon to be featured in the next Robert Altman film....David the Bicycle Messenger, or should I say...Roxanne's former Boy Toy."

Roxanne dreamed that Ben stood up and started to take a step toward Dr. Phil, but Phil's producers moved the camera off of him, and gently pushed him back into his seat. "Keep your cool, dude," one of them said.

"Now, Roxanne, I have to ask you again. What were you thinking? Why did you toss aside your faithful husband of 25 years for the thrill of robbing the cradle with this young man?"

"I didn't. And I didn't rob any cradle. He seduced me!"

"Oh? What did he do, give you a ride on his bicycle and ask you to ring his bell?" Dr. Phil said with that smirk on his face.

"Roxanne, are you asleep?" Ben was standing over her. She looked up at the TV and saw that Dr. Phil was over; Jeopardy was just beginning.

"Ben. I'm so sorry," Roxanne started to cry and Ben sat down on the bed with her and held her in her arms.

"Shh, it's not your fault. We'll get through this. Where's Allison, in her room?"

"Yes, she wouldn't really talk about it with me. She's waiting for you. She wants an abortion."

"That makes sense," he said. "I don't see we have any other option here, do you?"

"No, she could never survive going through a pregnancy and giving up a child for adoption. The idea of her raising a child now is beyond absurd. We can't let her ruin her life over this careless act."

"Careless, is that what you're calling her having sex?"

"No, her having sex was outrageous, the careless part was not using any protection."

Ben took a deep breath. He was still processing the reality that his daughter had willingly engaged in sex. He couldn't start arguing with Roxanne now about which was worse, the sex or the pregnancy.

"Are you ready?" asked Roxanne.

"No, but we have to talk to her anyway. Let's go into her room together."

As they walked down the hall, Roxanne felt as if she was wading through quicksand. She couldn't remember ever feeling so miserable. Ben knocked quietly on the door, and then turned the handle without waiting for an answer. Allison was curled up on her bed, clutching her pillow. She was crying. She sat up and cut off her parents before they could speak.

"I don't want to go to that counseling session tomorrow," she said.

"But Allison, I'm sorry, you don't really have a choice," said Roxanne.

"What's this about a counseling session?" Ben asked.

"The clinic requires it. They won't perform an abortion unless she has a counseling session first." To Allison she said, "We'll be there with you, we have to follow their rules like anyone else," she said, thinking that it was too ironic, Allison was obviously not one for following rules.

"I've changed my mind about the abortion. I want to keep the baby. I called Tony. He makes good money at the resort. He wants to take care of me and the baby."

"That…is…not…happening!" Roxanne heard herself shout without being aware that she was forming the words. She looked up at Ben, pleading with her eyes for him to be the voice of reason here.

"Allison, I know this is very hard for you but we are here to help you get through this. Does it really make sense to you to listen to a boy you don't even know over the two people who love you more than anything in the world?" His eyes filled with tears, then slowly trickled down his cheeks.

"You don't know anything about him!" insisted Allison.

"Neither do you," Roxanne said trying hard to keep the anger out of her voice.

"Yes I do. We've been talking on the phone and emailing each other ever since I got back. I only said I wanted an abortion because I didn't think Tony would be so great, but he surprised me with his reaction. He's not like the stupid boys I go to school with. Tony is a man."

"And just how old is this man?" Ben asked.

"He's seventeen, well, he'll be seventeen in three weeks. He's only got one more year of high school left. By the time the baby comes he'll be almost done with school."

"But he's in Florida," Roxanne said, wondering why she was even continuing this line of discussion. The whole thing was absurd.

Ben looked at her, wondering the same thing, he quickly stepped in to move the discussion away from the logistics of how his sixteen-year-old daughter and a seventeen-year-old pool boy could raise a child.

"Allison, this is obviously something we cannot make a fast decision about. I think it would be best for all of us to go to this counseling session tomorrow and talk over the options with an expert."

"Ben, there are no options," moaned Roxanne. "Allison cannot have a baby now. It's impossible!"

"Just because you don't want it to be true doesn't make it impossible," Allison retorted. "It's my life and it's my decision."

"Allison, you are too young to take on this responsibility. Please try to be reasonable," Roxanne said.

"Look it's too soon for anyone to make a decision," Ben said, squeezing Roxanne's hand to signal for her to stop pushing. "Tomorrow we need to meet with the counselor. It doesn't mean a decision is made. Allison, the counseling is for all of us, please will you at least agree to come to the session tomorrow morning."

"Only if you both leave me alone and we don't talk about it until then."

"Fine," they both agreed.

"But you are to stay home tonight…please," said Roxanne.

"You mean I'm grounded?"

"No, I'm just asking you to stay home tonight. Humor me and grant me this request, Allison. I couldn't handle your going out tonight."

Allison started to protest, and then stopped while she was ahead. Instead, she shrugged her shoulders, and said, "I wasn't planning on going out anyway."

Ben put his arm around Roxanne's waist and ushered her out the door.

"What are we going to do?" she asked.

"Rox, I have no idea. I feel like I've been hit by a truck."

"A bus, you mean. Yes, this is just what it felt like."

FORTY-SEVEN

MORNING CAME WAY TOO quickly for Roxanne. She dragged herself out of bed and tried to put on a normal-looking face for the boys. She and Ben had agreed not to say anything to them at this point. After the counseling session they'd decide how to discuss it with them.

"How come Allison is staying home today?" asked Justin.

"She has a doctor's appointment," Roxanne answered.

"She didn't look sick to me," said Justin.

"Unless ugly counts as sick," quipped Gabe.

Roxanne bit her lip to keep from responding.

Ben came into the kitchen in his robe. He looked pasty and somehow older than he did just the day before.

"Hey Dad, are you sick, too?" asked Justin.

"What?" Ben wasn't too quick on the uptake.

"Dad has an appointment near home this morning. Are you guys done? Please get your jackets and go wait for the bus."

"It's not time yet, I want to watch TV for a while," said Gabe.

"Just go to the bus stop. It's good for you to get some fresh air while you wait," Roxanne's voice got louder as she spoke.

"Oh, c'mon kid, something tells me we're better off leaving for the bus stop early," said Justin.

Roxanne and Ben silently watched the boys get their things together and run out the door.

"Is she still sleeping?" Ben asked.

"I'm not sure, but she's not making any noise. Do you want to wake her?"

"Not really. I don't have anything different to say to her than I had last night. I think we should wait to talk until the counseling session," said Ben.

"But what if *she* wants to talk about it?"

"Then we talk. Do we have a choice? It's 8:30 now. Give her another hour and then wake her and tell her to get dressed and have breakfast. We need to leave at 10:30 I'm guessing?"

"Yeah, that's about right. Why don't you go get dressed?"

Ben nodded and pushed himself up from the table. Roxanne knew just how he felt. He just wanted to believe that this wasn't happening.

Roxanne heard the shower go on and started clearing the breakfast dishes. When she closed the dishwasher she turned around to face Allison.

"Oh, hi honey, I didn't hear you get up," Roxanne said. "Um, Dad's in the shower, do you want some breakfast while you're waiting to get in?"

"Mom, do we really have to go to this thing? I told you I don't want an abortion."

"You don't want an abortion but do you really, honestly want to be a mother at sixteen?"

"Well, no, but I didn't plan on this."

"No, you didn't, and neither did Dad and I. But we have to make a plan now. You need to make a decision that will determine how the rest of your life will go from this point on. Dad and I want to help you."

"Why are you being so calm about this?" Allison asked.

"Calm? I feel anything but calm. Sit down please."

They went over to the love seat, curled their legs up under themselves, and Roxanne pulled the afghan throw over them.

"Allison, we're very upset that this happened, but we still love you and we are not willing to give up on you—all the dreams you've had for your future, and yes, the dreams we've had for you, too.

"But what about Tony?"

"What about Tony?"

"He doesn't believe in abortion. He's Catholic."

"Well, I can see how he would want you to keep the baby then, but Allison, I honestly don't believe it's his call to make."

"Of course you say that, you're pro-choice and you don't want me to have a baby."

"I can't argue with either of those statements. They are both true. But even if you weren't my daughter, I absolutely feel that as a sixteen-year-old girl who is not ready to be a wife and mother, you have to follow your own conscience, not his. The reason there is so much controversy about abortion is because different people have different beliefs. It's true; I am pro-choice. I believe that if a pregnancy is still in an early stage, it is not immoral to terminate it if it is not what you want or what you can handle. I can't say that it is not a potential child that is growing within you, it is. But it is not a child *yet*. It can't survive on its own, and at this point I believe it is something that you can ethically choose not to continue. Abortion is not an easy thing to handle either. It's sad and it's scary. But I believe a woman should have a baby because she wants to and that the best situation is if she is married to a man she loves and they are ready to start a family. You are just not there yet, Allison, not anywhere near it. I'm absolutely certain that some day you will be there, but not today. Not at sixteen."

"Plenty of people do it. It's not so terrible anymore."

"I'm not saying it's a terrible thing. But you have a choice; you don't have to change your whole life because you did something without thinking of the consequences. Let's talk to the counselor today, Allison."

"I'm going to take a shower." Allison padded off in her robe and slippers, looking even younger than ever to Roxanne.

The waiting room was quiet. There were women and girls of different ages spread out on the orange vinyl chairs as far from one another as they could get in the space they shared. There was one other young girl with both her parents, and Roxanne felt that looking at them was like looking in the mirror. She knew that she and Ben and Allison looked just as pitiful as they did, their heads bowed, and their stomachs feeling hollow. The mirror mom's eyes were puffy and red, and she clutched her purse across her stomach, just as Roxanne was clutching her own purse, as if it could protect her from the situation she was facing.

When the receptionist called "Thornton," Roxanne, Ben, and Allison rose and walked slowly into the counselor's office. There was a small desk against the wall, and the counselor pushed her chair away from her desk and stood up to shake hands with everyone. She gestured for them to sit, and Roxanne and Ben sat down on the overstuffed couch, while Allison retreated to the side chair. Helene Jeffries pulled her desk chair over to close the circle and began the conversation.

"I understand you've come in to discuss Allison's pregnancy," said Helene.

"Yes," said Ben and Roxanne. Allison looked down at her hands and picked at her cuticles.

Roxanne could hardly breathe. *Could this young woman help them convince Allison that she wasn't ready to be a mother? Would she? Was that why they were here?* She still couldn't believe she was sitting there. The whole thing seemed so surreal.

"Do you want to tell me how you feel about it Allison? Did you plan this pregnancy?"

"No. No I didn't plan it. It just happened."

"Well, you are certainly not the first young woman who has told me that. How do you feel?"

"Terrible. But I don't know if I can go through with an abortion."

"It's a very difficult decision to make."

"We don't think Allison is ready to raise a child," Roxanne spoke up. "We don't want her to ruin her life."

"Nobody wants that. Least of all, I'm sure, does Allison," said Helene.

"Does it hurt the baby?"

"Do you mean, does the fetus feel pain during the abortion?" asked Helene. "Most doctors don't believe so, especially when it is done early."

"Tony will be very upset. He doesn't believe in abortion. He's Catholic."

"Have you and Tony been dating a long time?" asked Helene.

Ahh, perfect question, thought Roxanne. *And it's so much better coming from this woman than from Ben and me.*

Allison's eyes filled with tears. "No. We didn't know each other at all when this happened. We've been in touch since we met, though, and he is willing to take care of the baby and me. He wants me to move to Florida."

Ben's leg began to shake. Roxanne put her hand on his leg to quiet him, but he couldn't contain himself.

"Allison you are sixteen. You are not moving to Florida to be with—him." Ben wouldn't say Tony's name.

Helene put her hand up, signaling Ben to keep calm.

"Do you really want to move away from your family and your friends? Are you in love with Tony?" Helene asked.

"No. I really don't want to move away, and I can't honestly say I'm in love with him. I guess I really don't have a choice, do I?"

"That's not true. But what is true is that whatever you

choose you will live with that decision your whole life. As your counselor, I need to make sure you understand the options. The other choices are to continue the pregnancy and either raise the child yourself or allow the child to be adopted. Not one of them is easy to do, either. How do you two feel about abortion? It seems to be the option you think is right for Allison."

"We do believe that an abortion is the best decision here. I understand how difficult this will be, but I think it would be much harder for Allison if she doesn't have an abortion. I want her to have a normal life. This was not a child conceived out of love between two people who wanted a child. Not to be cold, but it was a mistake, and fortunately it is still perfectly legal to terminate it before it's too late."

"Ben, do you agree with Roxanne?"

"Yes, I honestly do. Allison should not continue this pregnancy for her own sake. I'm sick that she has to go through this ordeal, but we have to do the right thing for our daughter—or rather, she has to do the right thing for herself."

"Allison, your immediate reaction to hearing that you were pregnant was that you wanted an abortion," said Roxanne. "Don't you think you are letting Tony pressure you into doing something you are not ready for?"

"Too late for that discussion," Ben said.

"BEN!" Roxanne gave him a push. "Stop it."

At this point, Allison's tears were flowing down her face. "Okay, okay. I'll do it."

"Before you decide," interjected Helene, "I need to ask you, you said that Tony doesn't believe in abortion. What do you believe?"

"I, I think it's gross, but I don't really believe it's murder either. I just wish I didn't have to do it. I wish it would just go away."

"We all wish that, honey," Ben whispered.

"Have you thought about continuing the pregnancy and giving the baby up for adoption?" Helen asked.

Roxanne and Ben held their breath. They had discussed it with each other, and believed that if Allison decided to do this it would be incredibly heartbreaking, but they didn't have the right to stop her.

"I don't think I could give it up. You always see those movies where the girls are either totally wrecked at giving up the baby, or they decide at the last minute to keep it. I…I just don't think I could do that."

"Do you think you want to schedule the procedure?" Helene asked, very gently.

Allison nodded her head. "Yes," she said. "I do."

Roxanne hadn't even realized that she had been holding her breath up until now. Hearing Allison agree to schedule, she let out her breath, and sunk back into the couch. Ben squeezed her hand.

"We require a two-day waiting period. As you know, there is no going back after the procedure is done. Would you like to come in on Friday at 10 a.m.?"

Allison nodded.

"Friday morning is fine," Roxanne heard herself say. *Fine?* She asked herself. *Fine? Would anything ever be fine again?*

"I have the paperwork and lab results already from Dr. Merkin, so that saves us some work. Allison, you cannot eat or drink after 11:00 Thursday night, okay? I'm going to go to the front desk and make the arrangements now. You can take a few minutes here, if you need to, then meet me in the reception area."

"Thank you," said Roxanne.

Ben stood up and shook Helene's hand. "Thanks very much."

After a few minutes, Roxanne and Ben stood up. They looked down at their daughter, who was still wiping her tears from her face. Ben held out his hand.

"C'mon honey, let's go home."

Allison pushed herself up and out of the chair and motioned for her parents to lead the way out of the room. She followed close behind, matching her pace to theirs so that she would stay out of their sight.

Roxanne stopped at the desk to talk to the receptionist and Ben put his arm around Allison's shoulders and led her to the car.

"We'll meet you outside," he said to Roxanne, who nodded, without saying a word.

They didn't talk at all on the way home. Roxanne and Allison tried to stop crying, but for both mother and daughter, once they started they had a very hard time stopping. The three of them headed straight for their bedrooms. Allison retreated to her bed, turning her music on loud enough to cover any sounds from her parents. Roxanne lay down on their bed, and Ben sat next to her, shaken and sad. He finally let his tears out, and one look at that set Roxanne to crying with renewed anguish.

"It is the right thing," Ben said after a while. "I just don't know how this happened in the first place."

"Yes you do," said Roxanne. "No, I mean, it really could happen to any girl. We should never have left her alone at that resort. We knew my mother wasn't going to pay any attention to her, but we left her because it was easier for us than trying to get her to come along. It's as much our fault as it hers. We thought we could trust her, but we were wrong."

"What about Tony? Isn't it his fault?"

"Who cares about him? Hopefully, we will never see him again. Besides, it doesn't matter anyway," Roxanne pointed out. "The important thing is getting her through the next few days, and then helping her to recover and deal with how she feels about the whole thing."

"What about the boys?" asked Ben. "Do we keep it from them?"

"I hope so. I think we should talk to Allison about how she feels, though."

"Why don't you go talk to her. I think she's had enough of the both of us at once. She probably feels like it's two against one."

"You're right. Give me a few more minutes to pull myself together."

"Mom, I'd die if the boys found out," Allison said when Roxanne posed the question. "If I'm going to do this, I just want to put it behind me. People do it every day, right? We're probably making too much of it."

"*People* are an abstraction. When it's happening to you, it *is* a big deal. But I agree that it would be better not to share this with the boys. When they are older, if you want to talk about it with them, that will be up to you."

"I hope I never have to tell them."

"Allie, speaking of telling, have you told anyone else about this, besides Tony?"

"No," Allison said, a little too softly for Roxanne.

"Not even Mallory?"

"Well, I told her about Tony, but I didn't tell her that I was pregnant."

Roxanne could tell that she wasn't being entirely honest with her.

"You didn't tell her but…"

"She saw me throwing up a few times. She knew about the morning sickness thing. Now what do I do? It's going to be all over school if she knows I'm having an abortion."

"You can't trust your best friend to keep it to herself?" Roxanne asked, trying very hard not to sound judgmental.

But Allison got defensive anyway.

"She wouldn't deliberately tell anyone, but I'm afraid someone will get it out of her. They'll ask her questions about me and she'll break down."

"There's no reason for anyone to ask questions. You can go to school tomorrow, and you'll just miss Friday. You'll stay in over the weekend with a bad cold, and by Monday if you're well enough, you can go back to school. No one is going to question that. That's the one good thing about Tony; I hate to say it. He's in Florida and won't be doing any talking to your friends at school."

"But what do I tell Mallory? She's going to figure it out."

"Do you want to tell her the truth? Or are you afraid you can't trust her?"

"I just don't know for sure."

Roxanne took a deep breath. She was about to give her daughter a lesson in deception, but she felt as if she had no choice.

"You don't have to tell her if you don't want to. Tomorrow, go to school and complain a few times that you're having cramps. You can tell her later that you got your period."

"But what about the throwing up?"

"It happens all the time. It's very common for a woman to get her period after becoming pregnant. Many times women have early miscarriages without ever knowing they were pregnant. You can tell her that you had a scare, but it's over now....Soon that will be the truth," she said, more softly.

"Mom, how come when you're sixteen and pregnant all of a sudden you're a woman. Wasn't I a girl just the other day?"

Roxanne almost smiled. "You *are* a girl, but you've had to make a woman's decision. Getting pregnant and having children is not for young girls. It's very serious business. You'll have time for that when you are really a woman."

Roxanne wanted to hug her daughter, but she stopped herself. She was afraid that if she were *too supportive, too forgiving*, that Allison wouldn't quite understand how serious this had been. I can't make this a Hallmark moment, she told herself. It's hard for all of us, but hardest for her. At least, Roxanne hoped it was.

Somehow, they made it through the afternoon and were able to act normally when the boys got home. Roxanne and Ben were relieved that the boys were busy with one another and that they had enough homework to keep them occupied until bedtime. They got into bed early themselves that night; too emotionally drained to talk, they each escaped into sleep.

FORTY-EIGHT

"I THINK YOU SHOULD go to work tomorrow," Roxanne told Ben on Thursday night. "I can handle it myself."

"Are you sure? But what if something…goes wrong," he said almost inaudibly, not wanting to say it out loud.

"Nothing will happen," Roxanne said, more forcefully than she believed. "Please, let's just get through this without every possible bit of melodrama."

"You're speaking a bit sarcastically about the elimination of our grandchild, aren't you?"

Roxanne couldn't believe he had said that. She had not allowed herself to think of Allison's baby as her grandchild, at least not consciously. She gave him her most wounded look.

"I'm sorry, I didn't mean it the way it sounded. I'll do what you want. If you don't want me to come, I won't."

"It's not a matter of not wanting you," Roxanne insisted. "I just think it will be better for Allison if I go with her alone."

As always, Ben deferred to Roxanne. "Whatever you say. Just please call me the minute it's over."

"Of course I will. Now let's go to sleep so we can get tomorrow's nightmare over with."

The weather of the day matched the mood of the occasion. The sky was a light gray, with no sun in sight, and the air had a damp chill. After the boys were gone, Roxanne threw a fleece blanket in the car for Allison to ride home with, she knew that wrapping herself in it would help. She went into Allison's room to make sure she was getting up, tapping lightly with her fingertips, not really wanting to go in.

Allison was awake and dressed, but she had gone back under the covers and pulled them up over her head to block out what was coming. Roxanne sat down on the bed, and patted her daughter's back through the soft, thick comforter.

"We need to go in about 45 minutes. You want to watch TV?"

"No," came the muffled response. "I'm just going to stay right here. Come back and get me when it's time."

Roxanne had no appetite, but she made herself some tea and picked at the crumbs on top of a streusel coffee cake. She turned the pages of the newspaper, not reading, just glancing at the images without feeling any connection to the world it was describing. She automatically turned to the advice column, but then skipped the page. Too late for advice, she thought. She pushed herself back from the table, feeling like she was swimming in mud, and went back upstairs to get her daughter.

"It's time to go," she said. Roxanne was worried Allison wouldn't cooperate and there would be a struggle. *Please, please just get up*, she prayed silently.

Bravely, Allison kicked off the covers, grabbed her bag and her sweatshirt, and without a word, walked down the stairs and out the door. Roxanne clicked open the door locks and Allison was buckled in and slumped down before she opened the driver's door.

"It's going to be okay," she tried to reassure Allison. She

rubbed her arm and gave it a squeeze, but Allison would not or could not respond.

"Let's just go already," she muttered.

The "procedure" went quickly, with no complications. After only a few hours at the clinic, Roxanne and Allison were back in the car on their way home. Roxanne played some soft music to cover the silence and Allison pulled the blanket around herself, just as Roxanne had known she would. She went straight up to her room to bed, and Roxanne did the same. She had called Ben from the clinic to let him know it was over. Now, not wanting to talk to anyone else, she shut off the phone's ring and allowed herself to sleep away the empty feeling in her gut. *Now what, now what?* she asked herself. *Can this family go back to being normal? Were we ever normal in the first place?*

"Mom, wake up, someone's at the door," Roxanne heard her daughter say. Not wanting to get out of bed, she peeked out of the covers to see Allison standing over her.

"I'm not up to company, let's not answer the door, okay?" said Roxanne.

"It's your college friend, that hot woman, I forget her name."

"Jo?"

"Yes, and she has her baby with her. Please get up and talk to her. I'm going back to bed."

This can't be happening, Roxanne thought to herself. *When did my life get like this? What could Jo be doing here now? It can't be good.*

It wasn't.

Jo started talking a mile a minute before she was halfway through the door.

"I was the last number on his cell phone. The police called to tell me that Garrett was in an accident. A hot dog vendor hit him when he was moving his cart and knocked him into the street. Then one of those damn pedicabs with four Japanese tourists riding on board ran right over him. He's got a broken leg, a concussion, and internal injuries. They don't know if he's going to be all right. I have to go see him, can Tai stay with you?"

Tai looked up at Roxanne and smiled. Roxanne looked at Tai as if she were an alien. *A baby? Now? Really? God, what kind of sense of humor do you have?*

Without waiting for a response, Jo placed Tai in Roxanne's arms. A diaper bag the size of a trunk came out of nowhere and settled at her feet.

"Everything she needs is in here. Just make sure she has her little blanket to sleep with. If you don't have a crib, she can just sleep with you and Ben. I'll be back tomorrow."

What? What is she saying? Roxanne felt as if she were in a dream.

"Jo, wait, this is not really a good time," she said.

"I'm sorry, but I didn't plan this. I have no one else to turn to. My regular babysitter is out of town. You're the only one I know who has a stable, predictable life that I can count on. Please Roxanne, she won't be any trouble, just let her watch some cartoons and she'll be happy."

As Roxanne reflected on the complete irony of the statement Jo had just made, Jo made her move out the door.

"I'll call you from the hospital when I know what's going on," she said. "Goodbye Tai Tai, Mommy loves you. Be good for Aunt Roxanne."

Tai watched her mother leave the room and suddenly realized that she was alone with "Aunt Roxanne."

"Mommmmmmmmmmy," she cried.

"Mommmmmmmmmmmmy."

"I couldn't agree more," Roxanne said as she shifted the squirming child in her arms. "C'mon Tai, let's see if I can find a cookie for you."

Tai's sudden appearance turned out to be a very pleasant distraction for Roxanne. She cuddled her on her lap while Tai happily chewed on graham crackers. When the cookies were finished, Tai looked expectantly at Roxanne.

"Mommm," Allison called from upstairs. "Can you come here?"

Roxanne had no choice but to lift Tai up again and carry her up to Allison. She went into her room to find Allison lying in bed holding her stomach. "I'm still having cramps," she said. "Do you think a heating pad would help?"

"I'll get one. Tai, can you stay here with Allison?"

Allison looked at the toddler and actually smiled. "Hi Tai, are you visiting us today?" she asked.

"Jo had to go see someone in the hospital so Tai is staying with us for tonight," said Roxanne.

"Mommy bye bye?" asked Tai.

"Don't worry, she'll be back soon," said Allison. "Meanwhile my mom and I will take good care of you, okay? Can you put her on the bed with me, mom?"

"I don't want her to hurt you, she might fall on you."

"No, she'll be fine. Won't you Tai? Do you want to see some of my stuffed animals? Mom, give me Babar and Winnie the Pooh."

Roxanne handed over the plush toys and went to get the heating pad. It took her a while to find it, and when she got back about fifteen minutes later Tai and Allison were engrossed in playing Babar visits the Hundred Acre Wood. Allison had managed to get Piglet, Roo, and Eeyore from her shelf and was spinning an imaginative tale about the group for Tai.

"I'll just plug this in for you. Do you want me to take Tai downstairs?"

"No, we're having fun. I'm feeling a little better. We'll just play quietly."

Roxanne hesitated leaving them.

"Mom, I'm going to be okay here with Tai. It's okay; don't

think what you are thinking. She's adorable but I could never do it all now. Just give us a little time here, she makes me feel better."

"Okay, then, I'll just lay down in my room. Call me if you need me. And drink the water."

Ben couldn't stay at his office any longer. At 2 pm he called it a day and headed home. The house was uncharacteristically quiet when he got home. Guessing they were asleep, he slowly climbed the stairs. He was surprised to see Allison and little Tai asleep together in her bed, surrounded by a pile of stuffed animals. In their own room, Roxanne had fallen asleep on top of the covers, clutching a pillow on top of her. He gently closed the door again and went down to the living room to collapse on the couch and wait for the boys to get home. He sent Gabe a text message that the girls were sleeping and to let him know when they were almost home and he would take them for ice cream.

FORTY-NINE

JO LOOKED COMPLETELY WIPED out, but inappropriately happy when she returned the next evening. Garrett was a mess, she said, but he would recover completely, with just a few scars.

"And I discovered something at the hospital," Jo said.

"Oh, what's that?" asked Roxanne.

"I'm in love with him. I'm honestly, really, head over heels in love with Garrett. And would you believe it, he actually loves me too?"

"Well of course I believe it Jo. You are entirely lovable. That's great. Really good news."

"We're getting married."

"What? When?"

"Three days from now. We already had the blood test in the hospital, and I picked up the wedding license at City Hall. We're getting married in the hospital. By then he'll be able to make it down to their chapel in a wheelchair. I want to be his wife and take care of him and I don't want to wait. He wants to adopt Tai, too. You of course, must be my maid of honor. Garrett's son is coming in to be his best man."

"That's really how you want to get married? In the hospital? What about the dream wedding you've planned for your entire life?"

"Oh, that dream ended when I passed thirty. I don't need a dream wedding anymore." She lowered her voice to a whisper, "I think I'm going to have a dream marriage."

"Wait, I almost forgot. You will probably not be the only one to have a change of lifestyle from a lawsuit. Garrett's attorney is quite sure he'll be collecting a huge settlement. Whoever supposed that hot dog vendors carried such good liability insurance?"

"I can't believe it," said Roxanne. "You've really worked all this out in one day?"

"I've waited long enough to find the right man. I'm not going to take it slowly now that I've found him. He's even decided to make a career change, at least for now, so that we can have more time together."

"Is Garrett giving up acting?"

"Not entirely, but he's decided to focus on doing voiceovers. You know, for commercials and films and things. This way he can even work while he recovers. He'll still be acting, even if it's from a wheelchair. Have you ever thought about pursuing that kind of work, Roxanne? Garrett says it's very lucrative, and…"

"And," Roxanne finished the sentence, "it doesn't matter what you look like."

FIFTY

SUMMER WAS UNOFFICIALLY OVER with the start of school. Once the kids were safely on the school bus, Roxanne performed her ritual replacement of her summer shoes and bags with the ones she wore for fall and winter. White shoes and pink sandals out, brown and beige back in for now. She had taken Gabe shopping for new soccer cleats the week before. In fact, both boys had experienced growth spurts over the summer, making back to school shopping more intense than usual. *Ally's growth was definitely more internal,* she thought. Allison had gone for counseling after the abortion, and it had helped her come to terms with the decision she had made. Roxanne and Allison had also had some joint sessions with Roxanne's therapist, Ann.

It had been Ann's suggestion. She had pointed out that Roxanne's own relationship with Sheila was fraught with resentment, and that perhaps talking openly about their feelings could prevent that from happening with her own daughter. Knowing that therapy was something Sheila never would have believed would be beneficial, Roxanne quickly agreed, and was pleasantly surprised that Allison had immediately accepted her invitation.

Allison had a lot to say, and some of it hurt Roxanne deeply. It wasn't that Allison was cruel or overly critical; it was that she made Roxanne realize that she had been repeating some of Sheila's parenting blunders. Because she saw Allison as one of the pretty ones—a second generation Grace—she had not believed that her daughter was as vulnerable and sensitive as she herself had been when she was a child. She saw Allison as she truly was, pretty, smart, and fun to be with. But she hadn't understood that these gifts did not guarantee feelings of security, confidence, and the ability to always make the right decision. Therapy had helped Roxanne put aside her own feelings for once and had helped her to grow too. She was finally able to shed enough of the scars that her own childhood had left on her self-image. She was on her way to coming to terms with who she was now and who she had been before the accident, both inside and out.

Going through her white bag, she found the program for the summer theater production of "Bye Bye Birdie" she had been in two weeks before. Content to be a member of the adult chorus, she had sung "Kids, I don't know what's wrong with these kids today," while disagreeing in her heart with the lyrics. She felt very lucky to have such great kids of her own. Allison had even helped with the scenery and ushered for both performances, which were held at the temple. Best of all, Gabe had been coerced to fill in as a last minute replacement for little brother Randolph in the show. It was his first time on stage, and he was immediately bitten by the acting bug. "He was a natural," everyone had raved. He delivered his lines with great timing and expression, and he sung his solo perfectly.

As was their personal tradition, Ben had taken the day off of work for the first day of school. He had disappeared after the buses left, and now Roxanne heard his footsteps on the stairs.

"Almost done with your shoe exchange?" he asked. "It's a beautiful day and I just cleaned up the bikes and put air in the tires. Are you interested in taking a ride? We could take lunch to the park."

"Sounds great, I'll be with you in a few minutes."

At the park, they found a picnic table and spread out their feast of deli sandwiches, potato chips, and two cans of beer.

"I think the kids were all pretty happy to get back to school," said Ben. "Even Allison."

"Absolutely. They don't know how lucky they are to be able to start life over again each September."

"Yeah, they just have to get on the bus, they don't have to be hit by it," Ben teased.

"True, but here it is September and I've got some decisions to make. I'm not sure what I want to do next, but I think I'm done with acting class. Life is a lot easier to deal with when you have a class schedule to follow, but lately I've been thinking about starting my own business. I'm just not sure what I want to do."

"You'll figure it out. I have a feeling we're in for another exciting year."